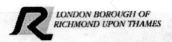

Published in the UK by Scholastic, 2022
1 London Bridge, London, SE1 9BA
Scholastic Ireland, 89E Lagan Road, Dublin Industrial Estate,
Glasnevin, Dublin, D11 HP5F

Text © Luke Gamble, 2022
Illustrations by Jane Pica © Scholastic, 2022

The right of Luke Gamble to be identified
as the author of this work has been asserted by him
under the Copyright, Designs and Patents Act 1988.

ISBN 978 0702 30960 1

A CIP catalogue record for this book is available from the British Library.

Printed by CPI Group (UK) Ltd, Croydon, CR0 4YY
Papers used by Scholastic Children's Books are made
from wood grown in sustainable forests.

1 3 5 7 9 10 8 6 4 2

This is a work of fiction. Names, characters, places, incidents
and dialogues are products of the author's imagination or are used
fictitiously. Any resemblance to actual people, living or dead,
events or locales is entirely coincidental.

www.scholastic.co.uk

THE SECRET ANIMAL SOCIETY

THE FORGOTTEN PHOENIX

LUKE GAMBLE

ILLUSTRATED BY JANE PICA

SCHOLASTIC

To MY MUM
AND ALL THE OTHER
ANIMAL CHAMPIONS
OF THE WORLD

PROLOGUE

The tall trees of the forest speared upwards into the night sky like a row of jagged teeth. Through the mesh of thickly interlocking branches, a sudden flash of golden brilliance blazed out into the darkness. The light began to snake forward, slowly weaving its way between entwined limbs of wood. As it moved, it left an illuminated trail in its wake, before bursting into a clearing and plummeting to the ground.

The little bird was exhausted. The closeness of the trees had made flight virtually impossible, and now it paused to recover whatever strength it had left. Even in the depths of the darkest forest, there could be no shadows heavy enough to engulf its golden flare, and it knew the hunters would be close behind. Craning its head upwards, the bird eyed a glimpse of the night sky above. With a quick darting motion of its beak, the bird plucked one golden feather from its chest and let it drop on to the forest floor. This was a chance to finally get up and away, but if it failed, perhaps others might know of its plight.

The bird flexed its glowing wings. They had lost much of their magnificence during its years of captivity, gaps visible where previously there had been thick layers of golden feathers. Its body was thin and the claws on its once razor-sharp talons were now brittle and cracked. Still, never give up.

A rustle somewhere deep in the forest made the bird start, and a surge of golden light instinctively flared out from its wings in a blinding blaze of defiance. There was no time to waste.

Readying itself for a final push, the bird once again eyed the stars above. There was hardly any wind, especially amongst the still trunks of the dense trees, yet as it tensed its muscles to launch, a sudden chill swept through the clearing.

With a determined lunge upwards, the bird pushed itself towards the sky. Something was wrong. Its left wing couldn't give it the purchase required and the bird floundered, flapping ineffectually as it lurched sideways, before dropping back to the forest floor in a feathery tangle of despair. This had been its best chance yet. For the first time in the history of its existence, the bird knew a new emotion: hopelessness. There could be no escape.

The creature that half hopped on to the track moments later was a monster made of nightmares.

Stumps protruded from the creature's head like vicious spikes, claws sprang from its front paws and, whilst it had furred ears that suggested a softness the rest of its body lacked, its amber eyes were those of a hunting wolf. A fusion of beasts, an abomination of forest creatures, all merged into a single furious being.

The creature bared fang-like teeth as it crept closer to the bird, and the sound that emanated from its throat was a triumphant half howl, half crow. A hideous call that stretched into the night, ending in a long haunting note which hung heavy in the cold air.

Moments stretched as an almost eerie silence once again enveloped the forest. Neither beast moved, the only sound was that of the creature's shallow breath which steamed into the chill of the night.

"Finish it," hissed a voice from the trees. "I wonder if you remember the many times we have done this before. Does a phoenix remember each death? Do you keep count of the deaths you have suffered, little bird? It is getting easier to track you with each rebirth. Your body is almost exhausted, you can no longer fly, but I need more from you yet. There is so much to be done."

There was longing in the voice. A hunger.

"What will you help me create this time I wonder," the figure rasped, stepping out into the clearing to stand behind the mutated creature, watching the cornered phoenix.

"Go!" the command exploded into the night.

The beast, swivelling its big eyes in their sockets, immediately sprang to attack. As it leapt towards the phoenix, it moved with a furious energy and strength that belied its small size.

In two swift bounds it closed on the bird, its fangs ready to bite down and its claws set to grab – but then it froze. The fangs stopped centimetres away from the golden feathers before the creature abruptly stumbled sideways, shaking its head.

The monster seemed conflicted, as if gripped in an internal battle of will. Part of it clearly yearned to strike at the phoenix as commanded, teeth bared in a snarl; yet part of it seemed to be resisting the urge to bite down, pulling it back.

The phoenix remained motionless, watching as the creature staggered. An emotion appeared to flicker across its piercing eyes. Sorrow. But not for itself. The phoenix stretched its head invitingly, as if offering itself up to the monster, understanding which of them was in more danger at that precise moment. It wanted to give the creature a chance. Surely it had suffered enough at the hands of such an evil master.

The bolt from the crossbow thudded into the phoenix with such power that it lifted the little bird from the ground and flung it across the entire width of the clearing, pinning it to the trunk of a tree. Its dying body slumped.

The creature watching cringed and yelped. A noise somewhere between a screech and a howl escaped from its throat.

"You were so close," its master rasped wistfully.

As the body of the phoenix started to glow, the monster backed away, whining. It didn't anticipate the second bolt that shot from the crossbow and pierced its heart. The creature dropped instantly, its body twitching slightly as it lay on the forest floor.

"You weren't perfect, but you will be soon, my little one," the figure said, eyeing the limp form of the monster as it gasped its final breath. Walking over to its still-twitching body, the figure placed a leather-clad foot on its corpse and pulled the crossbow bolt from its chest. The figure gave a little chuckle as the bolt made a sharp sucking noise as it came free. Giving it a quick wipe, the figure slid the bolt back into the quiver.

A flicker of light illuminated the surrounding trees as flames burst up from between the feathers of the pinned phoenix. The brightness of its combusting body was momentarily blinding in the darkness.

The figure shielded its eyes; then, moving quickly forward, dropped the crossbow to the ground. A flaming skull embossed on the weapons stock glared up into the night sky, as the figure dipped its fingers into a pouch that hung from its belt to pull out a small plastic bag.

"Just a pinch." The voice was full of suppressed excitement. Stooping to the combusting body, a hand shot out to take a tiny amount of the ashes left by the flaming bird. Carefully placing them in the bag, fingers then deftly sealed it tightly shut. Then the figure fixed its gaze on the little pile of ashes that remained.

The bolt that had killed the phoenix now protruded from the trunk of the tree; its shaft slightly blackened from the flames but otherwise now bare. The figure tugged it free from the bark and, with a satisfied grunt, returned it to the quiver.

"Now for the rebirth!"

Retrieving the crossbow and slinging it over a bony shoulder, the figure turned to look at the body of the monster which lay amongst the leaves, bathed in moonlight.

"A few more modifications need to be made for you to be a true assassin. The night is but young. I just need to add something that has a bit more of that killer instinct."

The last word hung in the night air as the monster's limp corpse was scooped up from the forest floor. The figure's eyes gleamed in the reflection of the phoenix's flames as they died away, and its face showed a wicked grin.

"Not long now."

There was a sudden sharp high-pitched tweeting that echoed through the clearing. The phoenix, reborn as a tiny chick, tottered backwards a few steps in a pitiful attempt to escape the one who had hunted it.

Too slow. A swift hand clasped the helpless baby bird and thrust it deep into a voluminous pocket.

"Always more to be done," the figure murmured to itself, satisfied with the night's work. Turning, the figure strode off, the darkness swallowing its silent retreat into the trees.

CHAPTER ONE

*In which Christmas is coming and Edith
knows she will be heading back to Forest
Cottage ... but first she must sit a few exams...*

St Montefiore's School for Girls was stricter than any
other boarding school in London. It had standards to
maintain. Whereas many schools would be embracing
a term ending with Christmas plays, carol concerts and
a frenzy of festive cheer, the girls of St Montefiore were
required to sit exams.

The examination hall was predictably stark, cold
and unfriendly. The large fireplace, located in the wall
at the front of the room, cavernously gaped before the
first row of single desks. As usual, it was empty and

unlit. Madam Montefiore had declared that using it was wasteful.

"Children should be active. They should keep themselves warm through industry," she had been heard to say on many an occasion.

The walls of the exam hall were whitewashed, clinically plain and at odds with the dark wooden beams which traced upwards to support the high ceiling. The wood hinted at warmth, and indeed, before St Montefiore's had been a school, this room had been a feast hall. It was hard to imagine that people had danced and laughed in this very place. Had the idea been presented to Edith Wight, who sat alone, nervously sucking the end of her pencil, she would have struggled to believe it.

Not that Edith would have cared. Mathematics without a calculator was her second exam that day. It was multiple choice, so there was always a chance she would get the right answer. But it didn't help much. The questions were impossibly hard, designed to befuddle, outwit and challenge even the most able of children. Despite Edith being in the advanced group for maths, she was stuck.

Angles, fractions and percentages blurred the page as Edith stared helplessly at the sheet, desperately trying to remember formulas she might have come across, but most certainly hadn't been taught. It seemed ridiculous and totally unfair the teachers were making her, and *only* her, sit such an impossible exam. And yet they were. The whole situation reeked of what Anita, Edith's best friend, had declared was "an agenda".

And it was true that the school had an agenda. Edith was now a problem for St Montefiore's. After the holidays, Edith had returned to school a changed girl. Gone was the timid child prone to debilitating headaches. Instead, much to the amazement of both the teachers and her fellow pupils, despite the trauma of her parents being missing somewhere in the Amazon rainforest, despite having been foisted on an uncle she didn't even know existed for the summer holidays, despite leaving as a sickly girl who couldn't go outside without supervision, Edith had somehow come back to school with a new confidence.

She walked with a straighter back, could participate on the occasional school trips to a museum or a lecture, could even go outside at break time – although Edith still preferred to spend it with Anita, sitting in the library studying books about wildlife and the biology of animals. Most dramatic, though, was the fact that Edith had returned with the ability to look her teachers in the eye – a look that belonged to a child who had found "self-belief".

Nothing troubled the teachers at St Montefiore's school for girls more than a child who had found self-belief. Such children were dangerous, difficult and wilful. They were harder to break, more resilient and less prone to tears. The school did its best to expel such children as quickly as possible, yet much to the dismay of Madam Montefiore herself, they were stuck with Edith.

Edith's parents, both renowned scientists and explorers, had gone missing in the Amazon rainforest the previous term. The story had made the national papers. Cambridge scholars lost in the Amazon generated quite some interest. Madam Montefiore had been interviewed, forced to say how brave Edith was and declare the school was fully supporting her through this difficult time. Thanks to a carefully chopped onion, she had even managed to look emotionally distraught for the plight of the young girl in her care.

Expelling Edith whilst the school was still in the public eye would have negative ramifications. The governors would ask questions, especially now the school had publicly stated they were looking after Edith with the utmost care. Madam Margot Montefiore would never risk tarnishing the name of her treasured institution.

No, Edith couldn't be expelled without good reason. She wasn't the sort of child to try to set the school on fire. She was polite and followed the rules. The only solution was to make Edith's life so miserable she wanted to leave the school of her own accord. And so the campaign against Edith had begun in earnest.

Setting a child extra exams just before Christmas was the perfect way to break someone's spirit. They were certain Edith would break. It was a solution that no one would question – dear Edith was simply unable to keep up academically – and the school would still

get to keep all the school fees which had been paid in advance. But to make sure, Edith had been told that if she didn't achieve an A she would be required to repeat the whole year.

"You have fifteen minutes left. When the bell sounds, you will put your pencil down and leave the room in silence." The harsh voice of Miss Bittiful, the joyless maths teacher who sat imperiously behind her desk to the left of the fireplace, echoed across the examination hall.

Everything about Miss Bittiful grated. Her voice, the way she stared down her long nose just over the shoulder of whoever she was talking to, the fact she never dismissed the class when the bell went but always a couple of minutes after – just to make sure the children arrived at the back of the queue for lunch or missed a bit of break.

Edith cast a look at her bag by the door. She could just see the folded-up letter stuffed into the top. A corner of it was poking out slightly. The envelope, having travelled halfway across the world, was dog-eared and battered. More so since Edith had read it several times already, even though Madam Montefiore had only handed it to her at lunchtime.

"Abandoned again, Edith Wight. It's becoming a habit for your parents. Perhaps they are enjoying their cruise on the Amazon without you a little too much?" Madam Montefiore had said, offering Edith a thin, unpleasant smile as she held out the letter.

Edith had been too shocked to reply. She had steeled herself not to gasp and snatch it out of Madam Montefiore's pudgy hand. Instead, she had taken the letter calmly and, with a huge amount of will power, waited until the headmistress got bored and walked off.

The envelope had already been opened, but inside was the news Edith had been waiting for. Her parents were safe. Relief soared through her as she read her father's scribbled words. The floods had subsided, and he and her mother had been rescued by a local tribe.

They had made it to a village and sent this letter via the tribesmen, who had sent a messenger to a city, from whence it had been airmailed to the school.

Apparently, now the water level had gone down, her parents were striking out to find their boat, from which they would retrieve important papers and months of research notes. After that they would return to England. They had made amazing discoveries that the world simply had to know.

That meant they wouldn't be coming home for Christmas, Edith had realized. Tears stung her eyes. What could be so amazing and secretive about bluebottles? she pondered. Why was their research so important that her parents couldn't come home for Christmas? Were *flies* so much more important than her?

She pinched herself for thinking that. Her parents loved her, and she loved them. They would have their reasons. Anyway, back to the boat they were going, and it meant that they would be away for another couple of months. In the closing paragraph, they promised they would be back for Easter.

"Is it from your parents?" Anita had asked, sitting next to her on the bench. She'd leaned over and looked expectantly at the letter.

"Yes." Edith took a deep breath.

"Are they are coming home?"

"They aren't coming back for Christmas, but they are safe, and the floods have subsided. They made it to a village," Edith said in a rush, the words tripping over each other as she looked up at her friend.

Anita smiled.

"That's great! You must be so happy!"

"I am! Of course I am. Only I had hoped… I had hoped they would have been here sooner, to rescue me from this horrible place."

Anita wrapped an arm around her friend's shoulders and gave her a little squeeze.

"But, on the plus side, you'll get to go back to your uncle's for Christmas?"

Edith nodded, brightening. The realization she would be spending Christmas with the Doctor, Betty, Arnold, Francis, Gerry and all the amazing animals at Forest Cottage lifted her spirits enough to return her friend's smile.

"I hope you can come and visit Forest Cottage one day."

"I would love that. And you MUST come to India. My parents are desperate to meet you and I know you would love it. The animals there are incredible."

Edith thought she might just have the edge on meeting incredible animals at Forest Cottage, but she held her tongue. Whilst Anita knew her uncle was a vet, she hadn't told anyone about the *type* of animals he treated. That was all top secret.

"I can't wait. But first I must get through these exams. I've got another extra one after lunch."

Anita's smile dropped.

"I hate it. They told me if I don't get an A in this one, they'll make me resit the year. I'm not sure I can stick it here, Anita," Edith said miserably.

Anita's face took on a horrified expression.

"You can't leave! Don't you dare! I know it's unfair,

but you can do it. You're the smartest person I know. And besides, you can't let them win. Bullies shouldn't get away with it – and I would miss you too much."

Anita gave Edith another squeeze.

"I'll do my best," Edith said resolutely.

In the exam hall, Edith's thoughts were dragged back to the present as Miss Bittiful noisily cleared her throat. She seemed to be taking a sadistic pleasure in watching Edith battle through her awful last day of term. A half smirk was fixed on her pointy face; even her hair seemed to gloat at Edith, piled high on her head in a ridiculous beehive... Edith wondered if Miss Bittiful ever washed it.

As Edith looked at it, the thick mat of hair seemed to take on a life of its own, gyrating crazily with the slightest of movements from Miss Bittiful's pin-like head, upon which it was perched like a tower of grey cobwebs.

A tiny black money spider suddenly flitted across Edith's exam paper, and she jumped slightly in surprise. As she watched, the spider teetered uncertainly.

"Oh, web rot and aphid poo. I'll never find my way back."

The voice reverberated in Edith's head. She quickly stopped sucking her pencil and sat up straighter.

Edith instinctively looked over at the teacher to see if

she had noticed anything and then turned her attention back to the baby spider.

Throughout her life, Edith had suffered from paralysing headaches whenever she went outside or visited somewhere new. Despite seeing some of the best doctors in England, no one had been able to explain why they had occurred. The headaches had resulted in Edith being labelled as a "troubled child" who always had to stay inside, couldn't go on school trips and had "episodes". It was the reason she had been sent to St Montefiore's in the first place – no other school would take her.

Then, soon after going to stay with her uncle in the holidays, Edith had discovered the cause. She wasn't sick at all. In fact, on the contrary: she was gifted. She had a talent, one of the rarest talents on the planet, for she was none other than a telepathic polyglot. She had the ability to communicate with creatures using only the power of her mind. The headaches were the result of an untapped power. Once that power had been realized and unleashed, the headaches had stopped, as if by magic.

Putting her gift to good use now, Edith focused her thoughts.

"Can I help?" she thought softly.

The spider froze, scuttled back a few steps and then seemed to raise its front body in surprise as if just noticing the gigantic presence sitting behind the desk for the first time. Registering Edith looking down at it, the spider stuttered back in shock.

"D... D... Did you just speak to me?"

Edith smiled, casting another furtive glance in Miss Bittiful's direction.

"Yes. I am speaking to you. But I am in the middle of an exam, so I have to pretend I am concentrating on this." Edith gently tapped the exam paper in front of her with the end of the pencil.

"Oh. Right ... well ... fancy that."

Animals were usually shocked when Edith spoke to them and the spider clearly needed a moment to adjust. Edith circled answer B at random on the multiple-choice paper next to a particularly complicated question. She had absolutely no idea how to work out the answer.

"What's the matter? Maybe I can help you," Edith said after a short pause.

"I'm lost. I fell out of the nest and next thing I was on the floor. I climbed up this wooden pole, and here I am. I need to get back to my family and I ... I have no idea where to go."

Edith wasn't sure if spiders could cry, but she thought this little one might be close.

"Let me help you. Where do you live? It must be close

by if you fell out of the nest."

"Well, it's dark and warm … and high. I rarely venture outside; Mother always warns us about the perils of the outside world. But I wanted to see what it was like!"

Edith tried to think. She raised her eyes to the ceiling, scanning it carefully. The room was clinically sterile, without a cobweb or a hint of dust to be seen.

Where on earth would a spider nest in a room like this? The fireplace maybe?

As she cast another fleeting glance towards Miss Bittiful, Edith's eyes widened in surprise. Something small and black seemed to pop out of the towering beehive on top of her head and began to slowly descend towards the teacher's desk. Edith stared. Then another

black speck appeared and started to work its way around the outside of the beehive. And suddenly Edith understood. The spiders lived in Miss Bittiful's hair!

She focused her thoughts, channelling her energy and conjuring images of the tiny spiders in her head.

"Hello there, little spiders. Can you hear me?"

Nothing. Edith squinted in a vain effort to see the spiders more clearly. Maybe they were too far away to hear her. She pushed her mind out further and tried again.

"Hello! Can you hear me?"

Miss Bittiful was staring angrily at the sheet of paper on her desk, tapping her foot impatiently and oblivious to the tiny creatures that were crawling around her head. Or *had* been crawling. As Edith strained to see them better, she could see that both the spiders had frozen still. One was now spinning slowing around in circles, dangling from Miss Bittiful's hair on the end of a silky fine strand of web almost, Edith thought, the same colour as the rest of Miss Bittiful's hair. Perhaps her whole hairdo was in fact a giant mess of spiderwebs. Perhaps the reason it looked like it was made of cobwebs was no coincidence.

"You can hear me, can't you? I'm the girl at the desk with the blonde hair tied in a ponytail."

A tiny voice sounded. *"Bernard – can you hear that?"*

"Bit hard not to. I'm exposed to the elements, risking life and limb here. Are we sure Bert fell out and isn't just hiding from us?"

"That's not the immediate point, my dear. The voice – there is a human girl, speaking to us!"

"Oh," said Bernard.

Edith smiled to herself. Spiders, worms and insects were always the funniest of creatures to talk to.

The spiders, who continued to discuss the situation between themselves, were clearly in a spin and Edith waited for them to calm down.

"Bernard – are you going to talk to her, or shall I?"

"I think you should, darling. Conditions are settling, I should continue the descent."

As Bernard resumed his slow descent to the desk, the other spider spoke to Edith directly.

"Who are you? What do you want? It's terribly rude to just shout at us out of the blue. I've never had a human speak to me like that before."

"Have you ever spoken to any human before, dear?" Bernard's voice drifted up from the desk.

"Focus, Bernard. Find Bert. Of course I haven't, but the point is she shouldn't just blurt out thoughts to us like that."

Edith wondered how else she was supposed to try

to initiate a conversation with a spider other than try to talk to it.

"Sorry. I was just wondering if you were looking for someone? Because I think Bert is on my desk," she said politely.

"I am!" said a tiny voice, and a moment later, *"Mum, Dad! I'm over here!"*

"Bernard – she's got Bert! The human girl has Bert in her web!!!"

"I don't have a web," Edith said. She peered fixedly at the paper on her desk so as not to give any indication she was involved in an intense discussion during an exam. *"I'm a human. Bert fell out of the nest, probably when Miss Bittiful was handing me my exam paper. He's here, on my desk with me."*

"Give him back. You can't keep him!"

Edith rolled her eyes. She looked down at Bert.

"Mum's highly strung. She makes the stickiest webs, though," he said apologetically.

"I think the only way to get you back is when she comes to collect my exam paper. Can you jump up on to her?"

Bert didn't reply. Edith realized he really was just a baby. The jump upwards would be too high.

"You'll have to go over to her." The voice of Bernard reverberated in Edith's head.

"What?" Edith replied, confused.

"The teacher. You'll need to finish the test early. Get up, hand your paper in. Then she'll be sitting down, and you'll be above her – it'll give Bert the height advantage and he can drop down to the nest. You can do that, can't you, son?"

"I think so, Dad," Bert replied timidly.

"Right then, come on. Climb on the human girl and she'll bring you over."

Edith felt a sense of panic wash over her as Bert scampered forward, scuttled on to Edith's hand and began trekking up her arm to her shoulder. If she left now, she'd definitely fail the exam. She had ten minutes left and twenty questions still to answer. It looked like she was going to have to repeat the year at the very least.

Edith spoke up. "I can't come just yet. I have to finish this exam."

"I knew it, she's spidernapping him!" cried the mother.

"Calm down, dear. Look, I can see a paper on the desk." Bernard paused, figuring out a plan. "It's got a load of numbers on it and letters next to each number. I'm pretty sure it's the answer sheet. What about if I call them out to you? You'll finish before time then."

Edith gaped. Did Miss Bittiful actually have the answer sheet on her desk? She scanned her answer sheet for one of the very few questions she was sure she had got right.

"*Let's check. Can you see a C by the number six on the page, by any chance?*"

There was a small pause as the tiny black speck readjusted his position on the desk.

"*Yes,*" said Bernard.

"*Don't be ridiculous, Bernard, you can't read, you've made that up,*" the mother spider chipped in resentfully.

"*I can read,*" protested Bernard. "*I've been living in that hair for a year. All the teacher does is read and when she does, she often reads aloud to herself. You've heard her, dear. At first, I thought she must be talking to someone else, but no, she reads to herself. Especially in the bath. It's a horrifying sight, but anyway, you can't help but pick up a few things. I figured out reading ages ago. I like to relax after a meal of aphid and catch the evening story. She's covered all the classics now. I'm thinking of learning French with her next.*"

"*No, you're not! You're getting Bert home!*"

"*I will, my dear, don't you worry. Now – what other letters do you need to know?*"

Bernard was a practical spider, Edith thought to herself – although he was clearly revelling in showing off his reading skills.

"Well – do you think we could start at the top and..."

"She wants you to CHEAT!" cried the mother. "She wants us to be her accomplices! What do you take us for? Bernard – are you hearing this? Can you believe it? You can't help her."

"We need to get Bert home, darling."

"Bernard, you can't possibly be encouraging this sort of behaviour. Exams are there for a reason!"

"Darling. One good turn deserves another. Now we need to hurry this up. If the teacher stands up again, Bert will never make the jump." Bernard had laced his voice with a bit of steel web and his wife went quiet.

Clearly Bernard could be a formidable spider when pushed, thought Edith.

"One other thing."

His voice suddenly sounded a little further away and Edith could just make out the tiny black speck scurrying over the top of the desk and traversing the answer paper itself. Miss Bittiful seemed oblivious to the small spider darting around in front of her, but she had moved her arm across the desk, forcing Bernard to take emergency action to avoid being crushed or swept off.

"What?" Edith replied, trying to control the smile inadvertently spreading across her face. Bernard was a crafty one.

"There's not a single crumb up here at the moment. Can you get us some food?"

"Bernard, this is not the time! Poor Bert!" his wife wailed.

"Look, darling – needs must. No web mate of mine is going to go hungry if I can help it. I know what can happen if you and the others start getting peckish. There is no way I'm ending up like Uncle Tiberius!"

Edith had never set out to cheat, but desperate times called for desperate measures. She couldn't risk failing these exams – it would give the teachers more ammo to make her time at school as miserable as they could. There was a deal to be made.

"I'll get you food. We'll figure it out. Can you read out the numbers and letters?"

"So, will you give us the food at the same time as you drop off Bert?" Bernard was not to be hurried until the agreement was straight.

Edith contemplated this. It was looking like, in order to get the answers, she would have to launch some sort of spider meal into Miss Bittiful's hair.

"OK. I've got half a sandwich in my bag."

"What sort of sandwich?"

"Cheese."

"Right – a bit of cheese would go down nicely. We

can make this work. Are you ready? I'm going to read the answers now."

There was a moment's silence as Bernard resumed his position. As Edith watched, she could see the black speck start to slowly hoist himself back up the web from where he had descended to the desk.

"1 – C, 2 – A, 3 – D, 4 – B..."

Edith concentrated, carefully checking her answers and filling in the blanks as Bernard rattled them off.

It took moments and, as Edith got to the end of the exam paper, she gave a big sigh of relief. Then, thinking about it, she quickly changed one answer so that it was wrong. She couldn't get one hundred per cent – that would be too suspicious, and the teachers might make her sit the exam again. Ninety-eight per cent would do. It was a solid A. She glanced at the clock. They still had five minutes to go.

"Bert – are you ready?" she said. *"Get on my right shoulder. That should be the closest point to her hair when we get to the desk."*

"Yes, I'm ready."

"Come on, son, I'll be there waiting with your mother," said Bernard encouragingly.

"Oh, Bert, be careful!" wailed the mother.

Edith readied herself and, just before Miss Bittiful

could call out five minutes, she slid her chair back and, without pause, strode over to the teacher's desk.

"I've finished, miss."

Miss Bittiful pulled back slightly, momentarily startled. Edith edged closer and held out her exam paper – and heard a faint yell as Bert made his jump.

"Here I goooooooooooooooooooooooo…"

There was a pause.

"Well done, son. Good jump."

"Thanks, Dad."

"Oh, Bert, thank goodness you're back. Wait until I tell your brothers and sisters about this. You're lucky to be alive! I told you not to go near the outside!"

"Hang on, what about the food?" Bernard asked challengingly.

"I'm going to get it now," Edith replied.

Miss Bittiful was frowning down at the paper.

"You've finished early?" she asked suspiciously.

"Yes, miss. I'll just get my bag."

Miss Bittiful stood up abruptly.

"Did you cheat, Edith Wight? How did you manage to finish this paper before time? No one has ever finished that maths exam early in the twenty years I have been at this school!" Miss Bittiful narrowed her eyes. "There is something suspicious going on here."

Edith took a couple of steps back towards her desk and bent down to pick up her bag.

"Give me that!" Miss Bittiful snapped.

Edith mutely handed over her bag. Miss Bittiful snatched it and began to unload the contents on to her desk. Out came her library book on elephants, her pencil case, her notebook, her half a sandwich wrapped in a creased napkin.

"Ugh," exclaimed Miss Bittiful, casting a disparaging look at Edith as she tipped the bag upside down. Nothing more fell out of it and Miss Bittiful looked disappointed.

Edith gingerly reached forward to collect her things. As she did so, she deliberately knocked the sandwich off the desk and on to the floor.

"Pick that up at once!" snapped Miss Bittiful.

Edith bent down, scooping up the sandwich and pulling out a few bits of cheese as she did so.

"Well, I am surprised to say the least," continued Miss Bittiful. "We will see what score you obtained and, of course, if it is not up to the standards we require from our children at St Margot Montefiore's, you will have to face the consequences. In fact, it is very likely you will have to repeat the year again – and again after that, if necessary. That would be a terrible shame, wouldn't it?"

Miss Bittiful had fixed a sneering smile on her face

and Edith was tempted to protest how unfair it all was, but she stopped herself.

"Yes, Miss Bittiful," she said instead.

Miss Bittiful narrowed her eyes.

"Term ends tomorrow morning. I will ensure Madam Montefiore has your results by then," the teacher said nastily. "Off you go. In the meantime, I would suggest you use the evening to reflect on your appetite for study. You are likely to need a lot of it."

With that, Miss Bittiful turned her back on Edith and bent over her own desk, collecting her things.

It was at that moment that Edith launched the first bit of cheese into the air. It arced gently up before landing softly near the top of Miss Bittiful's beehive.

"*Nice one,*" cried Bernard, and Edith gave a little chuckle as the piece of cheese disappeared into the mass of grey thatch.

"*Have you got any more? We're a big family, you know.*"

"*How many of you live in there?*" Edith asked, aware she only had moments before Miss Bittiful would be ushering her out of the room.

"*This year's hatch was one of the best ever, we had nine hundred and eighty-seven spiderlings. Bert was the last to hatch.*"

Edith's eyes widened in surprise. Nearly a thousand

spiders lived in Miss Bittiful's hair! With reckless daring, she flung out the whole half of the sandwich. It landed heavily on the beehive and Miss Bittiful straightened immediately.

"Did you just ... throw something at me!" she snarled, glaring at Edith, who tried to fix her face with an expression of innocent bewilderment.

"Of course not, miss! Is something wrong?"

Miss Bittiful once again narrowed her eyes and reached her hands up to pat her monstrous tower of hair. The sandwich, though, had disappeared into the thick thatch.

"*Thank you! That will keep us going for a bit!*" said Bernard.

"*And thank you for helping me. If you ever get stuck on a test with this one again, let us know!*" came the little voice of Bert.

Miss Bittiful, seemingly satisfied nothing was untoward with her disgusting hairdo, scowled at Edith.

"Get out and go to your dormitory."

Edith didn't need telling twice. Giving Miss Bittiful a small curtsy, she turned on her heel and bolted for the door.

She couldn't wait to tell her uncle about this when she arrived tomorrow.

CHAPTER TWO

*In which Edith heads to the forest to
meet old friends only to discover that
her help is urgently required...*

"Hello again," Edith said cheerfully as she climbed into the taxi.

The taxi driver's face broke into a wide smile as his eyes crinkled with recognition. He was the same big man with the shaved head who had taken Edith to Forest Cottage the first time she had visited.

"Hello, miss. Nice to see you. Same place again? Middle of nowhere in the spooky wood?"

"Absolutely," Edith replied with a chuckle.

"So I'm guessing it was all OK? I mean – your uncle

does live there?"

"No, actually. Last time, when you dropped me off, I was chased by wolves and spent the summer hiding up a tree. It's a miracle I made it back to school this term."

The man's eyes widened briefly, before catching Edith's grin in the rear-view mirror. Then he burst out laughing.

"I did wonder – and I'm sorry for leaving you in a hurry. I felt bad about that."

"That's OK, you got me to the right place and that was what I needed," Edith replied, smiling at the memory of her first visit to Forest Cottage.

"In fact, when this job came in, I asked to swap shifts. It was supposed to be my day off, but now I know all the short cuts – thought it was the least I could do after last time. Cheaper and faster – mark my words!"

True to his word, the journey passed much quicker than last time, partly because the taxi driver knew the way, but also because they chatted constantly. Before she knew it, they were travelling down the unmade bumpy tracks, winding their way into the heart of the New Forest. By now, Edith knew the driver was called Keith and that he had a daughter the same age as she was who was obsessed with butterflies.

It was early afternoon when Edith climbed out of the

taxi by a huge hedge at the end of a rugged, dusty track. With a shout of thanks, she waved cheerfully to Keith as he drove away, the car moving much more slowly now!

The trees seemed a lot thinner at this time of year, Edith mused, looking at the bare branches all stripped of their leaves and ready for winter. The forest was no longer scary or foreboding. It seemed more like … home. In fact, the trees seemed to welcome her like an old friend.

A sense of tranquillity washed over Edith. Savouring the clean air, she drew in a few deep breaths, relishing its contrast to the smog of the city. She had passed the exam too – the bullies hadn't won. Anita had been overjoyed. Edith's score of ninety-eight per cent had been delivered to her as she left, much to the incredulity of both Miss Bittiful and Madam Margot Montefiore, who had glared at her suspiciously as she walked out the front door.

With a grin and a quick silent thanks to the spider in Miss Bittiful's bountiful beehive, Edith scanned the hedge for the hidden gate, laughing as she spotted it submerged in the undergrowth. Soon, she was barrelling through it, dragging her rucksack with her, before half walking, half running up the winding path towards the cottage, which she now regarded as one of her favourite places in the whole world.

Edith felt a catch in her throat as the house came

into view. Just seeing it made her feel safe and welcome. Smoke trailed from the little red-brick chimney that poked out of the undulating thatch of the roof, the fireplace in the cottage clearly puffing away just as she remembered. She could see the window of the room where she had stayed in the summer, its worn white wooden frame pushed wide open as if welcoming her back.

Despite panting slightly from the trek up the path, Edith broke into a run and sped across the manicured lawn towards the house. On her right was the huge old barn with its cavernous double doors, big enough for a team of carthorses – or a herd of pegasi – to charge through should they wish. Inside was the hospital where the Doctor – her uncle – treated all the animals that came to Forest Cottage needing his help.

She made it about halfway across the lawn before the kitchen door opened and a huge dog bounded out towards her. Part Wolfdog, part Ridgeback, part every other dog you could think of, Arnold was clearly overjoyed to see Edith. His whole body wagged in doggy delight as he launched himself on top of her, knocking her to the ground and dragging his slobbery tongue across her face.

"Errrghhh! Arnold! I'm pleased to see you too, but I don't need a bath!" Edith squealed happily.

"Guess what — we get sausages tonight to celebrate your return! You're going to sneak me some, aren't you, promise me you will? It's been months since I've seen you!"

"I promise! I promise! It's wonderful to see you too — but let me breathe!"

Arnold spun himself in a circle and gave a great big bark of joy. As if summoned, a kindly looking, bespectacled old lady accompanied by a huge mountain of a man appeared on the lawn.

"Edie!" Betty called out. Her wrinkled face was beaming. "How wonderful! Francis and I were just wondering when you'd be arriving. You're much earlier than last time. It's just as well because I don't think Arnold could have contained himself any longer."

"Hello, Edie!" boomed the sonorous voice of Francis.

As Edith struggled to disentangle herself from the big dog, a grinning Francis stepped forward, effortlessly lifting her bag with his finger. The huge muscles on his tattooed arms rippled in the late-afternoon winter sun and a wild mane of blonde hair cascaded over his broad shoulders. He looked every inch the Viking warlord next to the tiny figure of his adopted mother.

"Thanks, Francis," said Edith. Then she wrapped her arms tightly around the old lady and gave her a warm hug.

"Betty, I've missed you all so much."

Edith broke away, turning to hug Francis, coming up to his waist as she did so. The big man's face split into an even broader grin as he wrapped one meaty hand around Edith in return, pulling her tight and almost crushing the breath out of her.

"And we've missed you! Your weekly letters have been a joy, my dear, but there is nothing quite like seeing you again in the flesh. Come inside for a cup of tea and tell me all about your last week at school."

As they moved, a loud caw suddenly echoed around the garden.

"Gerry!" Edith called.

"Hello, Edie! About time we had you back to stay!"

A blur of black feathers topped by a huge orange beak flew out of an upstairs window and careened diagonally down towards the group.

The bird landed heavily on the ground beside Edith – he was somewhat lopsided, having only one leg – and gave another loud caw in greeting.

"Lovely to see you, Gerry. How are you?" Edith said.

"Oh, it's awful, Edie. I'll be so much happier when it's gone. I've had quite enough of it. Now you're here, I am hoping you'll put things back to order."

Edith looked at Gerry, more than a little confused.

"When what's gone?"

"Ever since it arrived, I've been treated like a servant in my own home. I haven't had a moment's peace! It simply will not leave!"

"A visitor?" Edith arched an eyebrow.

Visitors to Forest Cottage were extremely rare, as the Doctor had to keep his work firmly off grid and as secret as possible.

Gerry ruffled his feathers impatiently.

"Not a visitor, a patient – although it would regard itself as an honoured presence, no doubt. No – it's an invader! It's taken us by siege! The most demanding creature ever! I'm run so ragged. I am in desperate need of a nap. It is good to see you again, though, Edie. Make sure you get me a kipper tomorrow, won't you?"

"Of course I will!" Edith laughed as the bird gave a couple of heavy hops before launching himself once again into the air, angling towards the window.

The three of them watched as Gerry missed the opening, thudded into the wrong bedroom window and then readjusted his angle before managing to scramble into the cottage.

"He is out of sorts at the moment," Betty said wryly.

"Aside from wanting a kipper for breakfast, he said something about a particularly demanding patient the Doctor was treating?"

"You are in for a treat," boomed Francis. "We have a rare visitor; it is a special honour! Your uncle will be happy to see you, and you have come at exactly the right time – he needs your help!"

"Yes, a patient who has stayed with us a bit longer than we expected. The Doctor will be anxious for you to determine why, my dear," added Betty.

Edith felt a bubble of excitement rise up inside her. The last time Edith had arrived at Forest Cottage she had been greeted by a pegasus. She could hardly wait to find out what type of animal this rare and special patient was.

"Time for that introduction in a moment. You will need your strength. Tea first and perhaps a slice of my special honey-coated walnut cake – baked this morning!" Betty declared as they entered the sweet-smelling kitchen.

Chairs were pulled up around the kitchen table and Arnold squeezed underneath to press his head firmly down on Edith's lap. Betty poured cups of tea and dished out several slices of warm cake. As she tucked into her first slice, Edith felt a happy glow seep into her soul at being back in the fold of Forest Cottage.

"And how is your friend Anita?" Betty enquired, cutting her another slice.

"She's gone back to India for Christmas. Her main

family holiday was at half-term though, when they celebrate Diwali."

"Oh yes, the festival of lights. That would surely be a spectacle to see."

"She has invited me next year … but I guess it all depends on whether my parents are back."

Betty's face crinkled in sympathy.

"Of course they will be back, dear. They will be missing you as much as you are missing them."

"Did you get a letter as well?" Edith asked.

Betty handed Edith a crumpled piece of paper. It was almost a carbon copy of the note she had received from her parents. It said they were safe; the floods had subsided, and they had made it to a village. The only difference was a line at the end asking if they'd look after Edith for Christmas.

"It's almost word-for-word identical to the one they sent me," Edith said, feeling upset her parents had just written out the same letter twice.

"I imagine sending anything would have been a challenge; short notes are often the simplest," Betty said quietly, a quick frown flashing across her face.

If my parents were missing me so much, then why did they go to the boat to get their notes about flies instead of coming back home to spend Christmas with their daughter?

Edith thought, feeling a tear escape and roll down her cheek. She brushed at it angrily, brushing away the thought too. Then she felt a pang of guilt for thinking badly of her parents. Then she felt angry again. It wasn't her fault. *She* hadn't gone off to the Amazon and not come back.

"I am sorry you couldn't come back here at half-term; the school seems to be making you work extremely hard this academic year." Betty's voice dragged Edith back from her reverie.

Unlike the rest of her class, Edith had spent her half-term at school to make up for having missed the beginning of the autumn term. Her trip to Nepal to save the yetis had spilled over the end of the summer holidays and the school had insisted she make up the time. She had done her best to try and forget the tedious and boring week that was supposed to have been a half-term break.

"Yes, it's not been the best term. They gave me an extra maths test yesterday and told me if I didn't get an A I would have to resit the entire year! The headmistress is horrible, and she hates me. She wants to bully me into leaving, I know she does."

Edith couldn't disguise the anguish in her voice. She had bottled up her feelings for so long, and now, in the comfort of Forest Cottage, they suddenly rushed to the surface.

Betty and Francis exchanged a concerned look.

"I passed the exam in the end because I had a bit of help from some spiders – but how am I going to stay there if they keep doing this to me? I wondered … if I left the school might I be able to come and live here? I'd be so much happier. I'd miss Anita, but not much else."

Betty's eyes, normally so warm and twinkly, took on a more flinty, pragmatic look as she studied Edith.

"We'd love you to live with us, my dear, but what would you do?"

"Why – why, I'd help?" Edith stumbled in reply. "I'd help my uncle look after the animals. I could do that, couldn't I?"

Betty sighed.

"My dear, you will always have sanctuary with us, you know that. But we are not a school. Neither I nor Francis can teach you the things you need to know about the world, and your uncle is far too distracted to be a full-time teacher."

Edith's face fell. She hadn't thought about the practicalities of what she would actually do if she left the school.

"You need qualifications to open doors for you in life. Your parents entrusted you to that school because they felt it was the best option. They didn't intend for you to come and stay with us. They will have had their reasons, even if we don't understand them. As awful as it sounds, the school is a safe place, and there is a lot to be said for that in the world."

"The school hate all the attention I got when my parents went missing. Also, the fact that my headaches have gone … it's changed how they act towards me."

"You have to master your circumstances, Edie, or your circumstances will master you," Francis intoned with a low and serious rumble. There was a pause, then he went on.

"Let's talk to the Doctor. He will help you feel better about things."

Betty brushed her hands together briskly.

"Yes, Edie, now you are recovered after your journey, he will be expecting you for the afternoon rounds in the barn. Are you ready,?"

Edith grinned. She couldn't wait to see her uncle again. They finished clearing the table and then headed across the lawn, the three of them casting totally mismatched shadows on the grass as they approached the huge double doors of the barn.

Francis gave a loud rap on the wood and, without waiting for an answer, heaved them slowly open.

The magic of the barn washed over Edith as soon as

she crossed the threshold. Her eyes adjusted to the light inside the huge building, the interior of which seemed to stretch on for ever. Rows of stalls disappeared into the distance, each containing animals the Doctor was treating. Relaxing her mind, Edith felt a tide of emotion as voices spilled into her subconscious.

"Oh, it's a visitor," tittered a high-pitched voice.

"Who is it?" another creature boomed.

Edith strained to see which animals were speaking through the half-light.

"Have they brought dinner? I'm peckish."

That comment brought a few laughs and Edith saw a load of chipmunks chirruping away to each other in the corner.

"Perhaps they are *dinner,"* echoed a low growl from deeper in the barn, and Edith gave an involuntary gulp, relieved that Francis was close beside her.

"Behave, Horace, you know the rules. You'll get us thrown out and then how will you get your mane back?" another voice, unmistakably belonging to a lion, cut in.

"Just joking, Archie, just joking."

Edith gave a nervous little chuckle and her eyes roved from stall to stall, then up to the ceiling. Sure enough, the white outline of the hibernating baby snow dragon, Yasmin, was still woven between the rafters, stretched out like a silent sentinel above all the animals below.

"Yasmin is still sleeping then?" Edith said.

"She hasn't stirred since your last visit. The Doctor thinks it will be at least another three years before she wakes," Francis replied. "Then she'll need feeding up before being released."

"What do dragons eat?" Edith asked curiously.

"Almost anything they want to," Betty chuckled.

"Yasmin is a nice dragon though, she'll be good," Francis added, sounding as if he was saying it to reassure himself rather than for anyone else's benefit.

"The Doctor is in the treatment room," Betty told Edith. "You go on, dear."

The treatment room was at the back of the barn. Edith began to walk forward, peering at each resident as she did so. Her smile widened as she saw some rabbits jumping over each other and tumbling to the ground, a couple of pigs snuffling in a bucket of apples and a zebra that looked at her with a cool aloofness as if wondering what on earth *she* was doing in a place like this.

Passing the largest stall in the middle of the barn, Edith paused. It was empty now, but it had held a pegasus the last time she had visited. She looked across at Betty, who gave her a cheery wave with one hand.

"We haven't seen the King nor any of the herd since

they brought us home. I am sure they are all fine, though; we would have heard otherwise," Betty said reassuringly.

Edith's eyes lingered on the empty space for a moment as she remembered the adventure that had changed her life; the pegasus king who had carried her down the mountain and helped save the yetis together with his herd. Shaking her head at the memory, she hurried on, following Francis, who led the way towards the back of the barn where the Doctor was busy at work.

Light escaped under the closed door of a partitioned room and Francis strode forward again to rap on it. This time, Edith noted, he didn't pull open the door but waited expectantly as Edith and Betty caught up.

A moment later the door swung inwards, and her uncle stood silhouetted against the light of the room behind him.

"Edie! My dear Edie! How wonderful to see you again! I've been hoping you would show up soon! Delighted you're here! Yes, wonderful!"

The Doctor bounded forward with short rapid steps and flung his arms around Edith, patting her quickly on the back as if she was a favourite dog he had missed but only just realized quite how much.

As he stepped away, Edith looked into her uncle's weather-beaten face, all lined and creased like a broken cobweb. Much to her surprise, she noticed he had tears shining in his eyes. Edith felt as if she had just been wrapped in a warm towel.

"Oh, Edie, I forget myself! It really is so nice to see you again! You had a good journey, I hope? Is school OK? Just as well you've arrived, so much to do! The build up to Christmas is always a busy time. You're where you belong!"

The Doctor paused to draw breath and wiped his brow with his hand, knocking the cap perched on his head askew as he did so. Then he leaned forward conspiratorially and said in an urgent whisper, "The thing is, Edie, I need your help."

Edith couldn't help but grin. Her uncle – dressed in his usual cape and cap – was the most eccentric person she had ever met, but she loved him for it.

"What can I do, Uncle?" she asked.

"It will be easier to show you than explain standing out here! Are you ready, Edie? Be prepared to meet a most extraordinary patient. Quite … temperamental, proving itself to be fairly stubborn in lots of ways, but nevertheless, one of the most remarkable visitors we have ever received. Did you bring your sunglasses by any chance?"

Edith shook her head, wondering why she would need sunglasses inside the already fading light of the barn's interior, let alone during wintertime in England.

"Sunglasses? It's not really the weather…"

"Well, shield your eyes if you must and don't look at our guest for too long. Its brightness can damage the eyes, you see. Especially if it gets startled. Although it's not the type of creature that gets startled too often, if you know what I mean?"

Edith didn't know what her uncle meant at all, but she dutifully nodded, unable to fight back a grin of excitement.

"Excellent!" The Doctor gave a jolly bark of laughter. "I need you to ask it some questions, if you would be so kind?"

Without waiting for an answer, the Doctor spun on his heel and walked back through the door, waving for Edith to follow with two deft flicks of his wrist.

Edith looked at Francis and Betty. They both flashed her a broad smile and gestured for her to go on through the doorway.

The Doctor was already crossing the room and

opening another door by the time Edith had entered.

Jogging forward, she caught up with her uncle and immediately stopped short.

On the table in the middle of the room sat the most beautiful bird Edith had ever seen. It regarded Edith with cool appraisal, clearly unflustered by the appearance of a stranger entering the room.

Edith stared in astonishment, instinctively bringing a hand up to shield her eyes. It wasn't the bird's large size, nor was it the impressively curved beak or long talons that made Edith's jaw drop. It was the fact that its feathers, which cascaded smoothly over its sleek body, shimmered in the purest and richest sheen of gold that Edith had ever seen. Each feather seemed to emanate its own light. Even its beak was gold. The brightness in the room seemed to fluctuate as the bird shifted its position slightly, as if, in turn, it wanted to get a better look at the little girl who was staring at it so rapturously.

"It's a phoenix, Edie. Only a handful in the world, millennia old – no one knows for sure – but the same bird the ancient Egyptians worshipped for immortality and the Roman Empire etched on its coins. Quite possibly..." The Doctor paused for dramatic effect. "... this very bird right here."

"But how..." Edith had so many questions to ask, but she trailed off, awestruck by the bird's magnificence.

"My dear, phoenixes are somewhat unique."

"Are they truly immortal?" Edith asked.

The Doctor pursed his lips. "They have a type of immortality, yes – both a blessing and a curse. Some would say one of the worst kinds."

"They can't be killed?" Edith said.

"Oh, they can be killed. This one will have no doubt been killed many times over the course of its existence. Phoenixes most certainly die – but then they are reborn. They rise from their ashes! It is the fabled cycle of eternal life. No one knows why or how; it is just the way they are."

"I've heard of them, Uncle," Edith said quietly. "But I thought..."

"They were make-believe? A bit like a pegasus or a yeti, you mean?" the Doctor said with a chuckle.

Edith couldn't take her eyes off the phoenix, which continued to gaze calmly back at her. Neither of them seemed to blink as Betty and Francis stepped into the room behind her.

"Can you talk to it, Edie?" the Doctor asked eagerly, a sense of urgency creeping into his tone.

"I'll try, Uncle," Edith replied.

Closing her eyes and calming her senses, Edith concentrated.

"Hello," Edith thought, focusing her mind on the bird in front of her.

It wasn't the best introduction, Edith thought to herself.

The phoenix didn't even twitch in response. Silence hung in the room.

"Hello, my name is Edith. It's nice to meet you," she tried again.

Nothing. Edith's brow furrowed. She screwed her eyes up more tightly than before and tried again.

"Hello, can you hear me?" she asked, a little more desperately.

There was a shuffling sound and Edith opened her eyes. The phoenix had turned to face her.

"Of course I can hear you. I am just waiting for you to say something interesting."

The voice in Edith's head was like an electric shock, as bright and powerful as the golden shimmer on the phoenix's feathers.

"Uncle, it spoke to me!" Edith cried.

The Doctor clapped his hands, making everyone jump.

"Remarkable. Well done, Edie, well done indeed!"

"I thought you said we shouldn't startle our guest, Doctor?" came Betty's voice from the doorway.

"So sorry, so sorry," said the Doctor, waving his hands apologetically.

"It said it was waiting for me to say something interesting," Edith replied.

The phoenix regarded them all with what could only be interpreted as cool disdain.

"Ask it if it needs further treatment? We need to find out why it is ... well ... still here," said the Doctor.

"Still here?"

"Yes. I've given it its vaccination, just like I did the other phoenixes that arrived. They all left afterwards – but not this one! There must be something wrong that I can't pick up on? All it seems to do is sit there and boss poor Gerry about."

Edith turned to the phoenix. *"Is something wrong with you?"*

The phoenix said wearily, *"There is absolutely nothing wrong with me. Although I want the toucan to fetch me another cushion and I'd like the temperature of the room reduced by three degrees."*

Edith repeated what the phoenix said, and the Doctor stared at her, slightly baffled.

"Is that it?" asked the Doctor after a moment's pause, his voice oozing utter defeat.

Edith blinked. *"My uncle, the Doctor, wonders why you are still here?"*

"Finally a sensible question. The Northern Phoenix is missing. We need your assistance to find it."

Edith's mouth must have dropped open a fraction. The phoenix went on, *"I had heard the Doctor had an assistant who was a polyglot, but I never expected you to be so young. I have spoken to several of your kind over the millennia and you are the youngest by far. Perhaps that is why it has taken you all this time to attend to your duties. Do keep pace."*

Edith flushed slightly. Then she turned back to her uncle. "It wants you to find the Northern Phoenix," she said simply. "It's missing."

There was a stunned silence in the room. The Doctor, Betty and Francis all looked grave. "What is it talking about, Uncle?" Edith asked.

"So, the Northern Phoenix is missing," said the Doctor thoughtfully. "Can that be? It's true that it's the only phoenix left that hasn't come for its vaccination yet. But phoenixes never betray their hiding places. Even to those sworn to protect them. They are some of the most secretive and elusive of creatures at the best of times. Ask our guest why the Northern Phoenix would need my ... need *our* help?"

Edith did as the Doctor had asked.

"Because it has been taken. This was all that remained."

The phoenix craned its head, its elegant beak disappearing under one of its magnificent wings for a moment before reappearing clutching a dazzling golden feather.

The phoenix dropped the feather from its beak and it drifted towards Edith as it floated down to the floor. Edith reached forward and slowly picked it up, gently holding the glimmering object between pinched fingers. "It says the phoenix has been taken and this was all that was found," she said.

There was a shuffling in the room as Francis and Betty both edged forward to get a better look.

The Doctor stared at the feather and then back to the phoenix, who in turn watched him carefully, clearly waiting for some sort of response.

"Oh dear," the Doctor murmured.

"A call for help," Francis rumbled.

"It must be desperate indeed," Betty added softly.

"Couldn't it have just lost a feather?" Edith asked.

"Phoenixes don't moult, Edie. The only time a phoenix will ever pluck one of its own feathers is when it is in the most desperate of situations. Even when phoenixes are hunted and killed, they are reborn from their ashes. There is no trace of them left behind. To find a feather like this ... signifies a plight possibly worse than death itself," the Doctor said solemnly.

"It must have been taken, Doctor," said Francis.

"Taken?" asked Edith, still confused.

"Captured," said Betty, nodding her head sadly. "Death holds no fear for a phoenix, but imprisonment..."

"We have a council of our kind every fifty years," the phoenix went on, clearly sensing that Edith was having some trouble making his information understood. *"All phoenixes are required to attend. The Northern Phoenix did not join us last year. It raised some concern."*

"It has been missing since last year? And you didn't send out a search party?" Edith thought the question before she had properly considered what came into her mind. That was the downside of communicating with thought. When in mid-flow, it was impossible not to say what you were thinking.

The phoenix looked coldly at Edith.

Edith swallowed nervously. *"Sorry, it's just that, to me, it seems a long time to be missing someone. My parents were missing, and people were looking for them within days. I didn't mean to be rude."*

The phoenix dipped its head fractionally. They were prickly creatures, Edith considered, thankfully managing to quash the thought immediately.

"When you live for eternity, a year is but a blink of an eye."

Edith repeated what the phoenix had said.

"So this is why our friend hasn't left, Edie. To tell us about the plight of the Northern Phoenix. We would have gone looking eventually, I expect, when it didn't come for its vaccine, but its absence is most concerning," said the Doctor thoughtfully.

"Its vaccine?" Edith asked.

"Oh, it must have its vaccine, Edie. The Northern Phoenix is at great risk without the vaccine. No matter where it is, even if it has been captured and imprisoned, if it is unvaccinated then it is in far greater danger than it realizes."

"But I thought a phoenix could live for ever, Uncle? Why would they even need a vaccination?"

The Doctor sighed and spread his arms wide, shaking his head despairingly.

"I thought the same once, Edie, I really did. But living for ever doesn't mean that phoenixes are immune from infection; it just means they get reborn when they die. They can get sick or injured the same as any normal bird. The problem is that a new strain of avian flu has surfaced. It affects all birds to some small degree, but it seems particularly virulent to the phoenix. If the phoenixes do not receive a vaccination, then the virus can slow their rebirth – no one knows how long for. This could have deadly consequences. If a phoenix doesn't regenerate straight away..."

"Its ashes might get scattered, Edie. And if that happens then it's rebirth will be affected," Betty finished, laying a hand on the Doctor's arm.

"Even a strong gust of wind or someone walking through the pile of ashes and disturbing them could mean the end of one of the most precious creatures to have ever graced the world," the Doctor added. "They can lose a few ashes, that is just the natural order of things, but losing too many can affect how they regenerate. They might come back wingless or lacking a claw, for example."

"This flu slows the process of rebirth, so the ashes remain just that – a pile of ashes – the virus delays the time before they can regenerate into a new baby chick," Betty continued. "The longer the process takes, the more likely the ashes will be disrupted."

"Does our friend have any knowledge on who may

have captured the Northern Phoenix, Edie?" The Doctor was all business now, and there was something in his tone that suggested he might already know the answer.

Edith translated the question to the phoenix.

"There are only a few who could capture one of our kind. It is true we have been caught before, but to ensnare us still takes great skill. The Doctor has battled such evil and won. That is why we require his help."

Edith repeated the words of the phoenix.

"Do you know the type of people who could have done this, Uncle?" Edith asked.

The Doctor nodded slowly. "As do you, Edie, as do you."

Edith felt a coldness grip her tummy. She realized she knew exactly the type of people who could hunt down a phoenix. The same type of people who would kill a yeti in cold blood. Her thoughts flashed back to a hard-looking woman with flame-red hair, holding a dagger with a flaming skull embossed on its handle. Arabella Spearstrike and her team of mercenary killers. After her brush with the Syndicate in the summer, both she and the Doctor had only just escaped with their lives.

"The Syndicate…" She uttered the words as if they were a curse. "We have to find the phoenix."

"Edie, ask our guest where the feather was found. We

must pick up the trail as quickly as possible. There is no time to lose. If it was a year ago, who can say what the Syndicate have done with the Northern Phoenix."

As soon as Edith translated the question, the phoenix lifted its majestic head and said, *"The feather was found in the great forests where the Northern Phoenix has resided for the last four centuries – to the north-east of Augsburg … in Bavaria."*

And with that, the phoenix closed its eyes. The conversation was clearly over.

CHAPTER THREE

In which a new quest takes shape and Edith
wonders what might lie in store for the team
as they depart for the forests of Bavaria...

"There are seven phoenixes in the world. The Green
Phoenix, our current guest in the barn, who lives in the
Green Mountains of Vermont, whereas the Amazonian
Phoenix lives in Iquitos, Peru. The African Phoenix
resides in Blantyre in southern Malawi. The Chinese
Phoenix seems to be the most nomadic of the species,
roaming between China and Russia. There is the Island
Phoenix who rarely leaves the Andaman Islands, the Red
Rock Australian Phoenix, and of course the Northern
Phoenix, who used to live in Greenland but moved south

to the great forests of Bavaria, where it has lived for the last couple of centuries, as far as I understand."

The Doctor rattled off the locations whilst jabbing at points on the world map which Francis had spread out on the kitchen table. Betty calmly placed salt and pepper grinders on each corner to stop it rolling up on itself and Francis stepped back.

"Just seven?" Edith said incredulously. "It seems so few for a whole species."

"Just seven left. No more, no less," the Doctor replied solemnly.

"Don't they breed?" Edith asked, confused.

"No. They are sexless. Most animals reproduce to ensure the survival of their species, but the phoenix have no need. They have evolved so they can't die out. Or I should say, almost. There are some ancient texts suggesting there were at least ten in the time of the pharaohs. But this mutated virus is the biggest threat to their species yet." The Doctor shook his head angrily. "A man-made virus, Edie, like all the worst things in the world."

"And some of the best," Betty chipped in, looking disapproving of the Doctor's sweeping statement against mankind.

"Oh, Betty, dearest. You know what I'm like. I'm just

upset. But it was a virus that man tinkered with, and it seems in this instance to be particularly virulent to phoenixes. There's no stopping it unless we vaccinate."

"How did you find out about it, Uncle?" Edith asked curiously.

"Some flamingos started to get sick in Lake Nakuru and one made it here for treatment. It had all the hallmarks of an avian flu – swollen head, lack of appetite, difficulty breathing, diarrhoea and so on."

"But how did you know it would affect the phoenixes so badly?"

"There is little that can truly impact the regeneration of phoenix, but the last time was during the 1918 influenza. I sequenced the genome and sure enough – the similarities were worrying."

"The 1918 influenza?" Edith was getting confused.

The Doctor cleared his throat and Betty flashed Edith a look as if to say, "You've got him started now." Edith grinned back at her.

"It was an avian flu that made the cross-species jump into humans. In 1918, the flu pandemic killed three per cent of the world's population. Three in every hundred people! Can you imagine the horror! That virus killed more people than all that died in World War One, all that died in World War Two and probably more than those who died in both World Wars put together! But they don't make school children study *that*, do they?"

"Doctor," said Betty, flashing the Doctor a stern look.

"Sorry, Betty, you know how I get carried away! Anyway, the 1918 flu was widely blamed for the demise of the Spanish Phoenix. A tragic event to this day. This virus is a slightly mutated version that only affects certain birds. The good news is the vaccine to protect them is a single injection. One jab can give lifelong immunity."

"What about the flamingos?" Edith asked.

"They get sick, but they rarely die. The phoenixes are much more susceptible."

Edith was reeling. She glanced across at Betty and Francis, who looked solemn as the Doctor started to pace up and down in agitation.

"Vaccinating all the phoenixes should have been straightforward. Word would spread and they would come one after another. Solitary creatures for the most part, but they communicate through the usual channels."

Just as a question formed on Edith's lips – *What on earth are the "usual channels"?* – Francis spoke.

"Owls," he said.

"Owls?" Edith said, surprised.

"Owls," repeated the Doctor. "Strange that owls are the symbol of death in so many cultures, yet they speak a similar language to the bird which is the symbol of eternal life. Owls and flamingos can speak phoenix – and unsurprisingly – to each other. If you ever need the help of a phoenix, Edie, find an owl."

"But the Northern Phoenix hasn't come," Betty said. "And now we know why."

"If the Syndicate – or whoever – has captured it, they won't know how much danger it's in, will they?" Edith said.

"Exactly," said the Doctor, driving his finger into the air to emphasize the point. "The Syndicate, curse them to eternity, have been after a phoenix for decades. There are few things they would prize more. But if they have captured the Northern Phoenix, it is in grave peril. The Syndicate might not be able to end its eternal cycle of life, but the flu can. So we must rescue it quickly and then vaccinate it as soon as we can."

"It might have escaped by now," Betty said calmly. "We just know it hasn't been seen for some time. We can't even be sure it has been captured."

"But the missing feather," Edith whispered. "It has to mean something terrible has happened to it, doesn't it? It must need help. We have to find it to make sure."

"It won't be easy, Edie. The phoenixes are highly secretive creatures," said the Doctor. "Thousands of years ago, they used to roam the earth, glorying in their revered status and imparting wisdom and hope throughout the world. But I fear the species is becoming disillusioned with the world and the creatures within it. The Northern Phoenix is the most solitary and isolated of them all."

"It is a recluse," Francis rumbled. "There have been no sightings for years. Thank goodness the Green Phoenix realized something was wrong."

Edith thought about the bird in the barn. "It was a little bossy," she ventured.

"It is just their way, my dear," Betty said. "They are ancient and somewhat hardened by all they have experienced, and they don't interact with the world much. There was a time they did – the fables of the great phoenix are testament to that – but not these days."

The Doctor nodded his agreement. "They feel pain just like any other creature, Edie," he explained. "The phoenixes now live in hiding because they were hunted so much. Humans again… Man wants what he can't have. The golden feathers of a phoenix are simply too alluring for even some of the most ardent so-called conservationists! The lure of a hunter, seeking a prey that cannot be killed – the endless cycle of living, dying and then living to be hunted again exhausted them."

"All the phoenixes live in secret now," said Francis,

shaking his great head sadly.

There was silence, then the Doctor shook himself. "No matter the challenge, we must find the Northern Phoenix and we must deliver the vaccine. It is unthinkable that a phoenix would die on our watch! We are the custodians of these creatures. We cannot let them down!"

The Doctor pulled back a chair and slumped into it with a sigh.

"Tea, Doctor?" Betty said softly.

"And a warm crumpet with a nub of Cornish melted butter if you have one, dearest Betty, thank you," the Doctor replied almost absent-mindedly.

"So we need to go to Bavaria?" Edith said.

"Yes. Bavaria has been its home for the last few centuries and is where the feather was found. It must be our first port of call," said the Doctor, nodding his thanks to Betty as she handed him a plate of food.

"Surely a phoenix can't be hard to spot – they glow all the time," Francis said.

"If only it was that simple. Sadly, nothing ever is. Especially if the Syndicate is involved." The Doctor took a thoughtful bite of crumpet. "Of course, it might not be the Syndicate – we may be suspecting the worst. The bird may simply be trapped or injured or sick, but out of harm's way. Whatever the reason, we must find it." He turned to Edith. "Edie, we need you more than ever – your ability to speak to the animals in the forest and gather any information will be invaluable. Will you help us?"

"Of course, I'd love to," Edith said without hesitation.

Betty's eyes narrowed in concern.

"Doctor, if the phoenix *is* in the clutches of the Syndicate, it will be incredibly dangerous."

"Betty is right. The forests of Bavaria are not for the faint-hearted, Edie. And you know the people we could be up against. Are you sure you want to come on another adventure?"

"Uncle, last summer I trekked up the Himalayas with you, chased by mercenary killers, rode a pegasus, and met giant yetis – one of whom was having a hormonal mood swing. Surely being in the forests of Bavaria can be no more dangerous than that? At least we'll be doing the chasing this time."

"What do you think, Betty?" asked the Doctor.

Betty remained silent, considering the situation. She eyed Edith, the determined jut of her chin, the hint of steel in her eyes. Recognizing there was nothing she would be able to say to dissuade the girl, she instead fixed the Doctor with a glare.

"You mustn't put Edie in any danger. If you find the Syndicate, you must call the police. You cannot risk her safety again, Doctor."

Both the Doctor and Francis nodded in agreement.

"Of course. We'll leave tomorrow morning. Francis, get the red truck ready, we'll be driving. Arnold must come along – his tracking instincts could be useful. Edie – this will be an exciting adventure!"

Edith smiled at her uncle; she was going on another trip!

A soft whimper emanated from under the table. Edith dipped her head slightly to see Arnold peering up at her.

"I know finding the phoenix is very important – but I hope you haven't forgotten your other priorities."

"What other priorities?" Edith thought anxiously.

"Where's my sausage?"

The morning of departure was a bright winter one. The sort that seemed to lift everyone's spirits before the day had properly begun. There was a light frost on the lawn, a nip in the air but no wind, and the sun blazed in a cloudless sky. Edith smiled as she munched on one of the blueberry muffins that Betty had piled high on the kitchen table.

The Doctor hadn't wasted a moment in packing and had spent the night in his office assembling maps and vaccines and poring over any books he could find that referenced the phoenix and their habits.

Edith and Francis stood patiently next to Arnold, who was slumped against the front left wheel of the Doctor's large red truck. It was a battered old thing with a few dents in the doors and faded sections of paintwork, but Francis had cleaned it so the unfaded bits gleamed in the daylight. As Edith peered through the window, she saw that the inside looked spacious, with comfy seats padded out with cushions and blankets. Francis jammed their bags in the back and Edith waited patiently as the Doctor issued a flurry of last-minute instructions about which animals needed which medication at what time to Betty.

"Doctor, you know I can manage," Betty said calmly. "Just go and find the phoenix and, most importantly, look after Edie."

The Doctor nodded and then circled the truck, inspecting it from every angle. "Francis, have you checked the tyres and oil?"

"Yes, Doctor," Francis replied.

"The plan is to drive through the night so, tell me, do the headlights work?"

"When they're turned on."

Edith couldn't help laughing and the Doctor looked up sharply.

"Don't encourage him, Edie, it's no laughing matter. I had to drive for twelve hours once by the light of a thousand fireflies. You'd think that many would create quite a glow, but it still didn't enable me to see very far ahead. I had more than a few near misses on that trip."

The Doctor gestured with his hand at a large dent behind the front headlight.

"Right, Arnold and Edie, you're both in the back. Hop in and buckle up. Francis, I assume you have all the passports, including Arnold's?"

"All here, Doctor," Francis replied, patting a pocket and nodding amiably.

Francis opened the passenger door for the Doctor as he started to repeat his circuit of the truck, but the Doctor promptly ignored it and walked round to the driver's side.

"Let's get this show on the road!" he said, flinging open the door and sliding into the driver's seat.

After Francis squeezed himself into the passenger seat and the truck had tilted dramatically with his weight, the Doctor turned the key and the vehicle juddered into life.

As they began to pull away, they all waved wildly

to Betty, who stood with a hand raised in farewell, and watched them bump off through the forest. Her little figure slowly shrank into the distance as they trundled through the trees, towards the secret gap in the hedge that Francis had prepared.

The long journey to Bavaria had begun.

CHAPTER FOUR

*In which Edith arrives in a remote part
of the Bavarian Forest. After making new
acquaintances, the search must begin in earnest...*

"The Bavarian Forest is the largest continuous woodland area in Europe," Francis said as he swung the truck into a parking space outside a large, square building.

Aside from a short rest on the train as the car had been loaded on to the Eurostar to cross the Channel, they had driven almost non-stop. They had journeyed through the night, and although it was still early morning, the village in which they had arrived seemed deserted. Edith rubbed at her eyes in defiance of the tiredness that now tugged at the edge of her senses. She had been too excited to sleep, chatting to Francis for most of the journey. Now they had finally arrived, and everything seemed so quiet and sleepy, she suddenly felt a wave of fatigue wash over her.

Edith peered out of the window. A neat wooden sign with the words *Mutig Gasthaus* carved delicately across its front, indicated they had arrived at a guest house. There were no lights on and no sign of anyone moving around.

"It seems very peaceful here," she said, stifling a yawn.

"A sleepy village in remote Bavaria. I doubt there are many tourists trekking in winter. This is almost more out of the way than Forest Cottage!" Francis laughed; the sound seemed almost deafening in the still of their surroundings.

The Doctor, fast asleep in the passenger seat, stirred slightly at the noise, but slept on despite the truck giving a sudden shudder as Francis turned off the engine. The Doctor had passed over his driving duties to the big man once they had crossed the border into Germany, and his soft snoring, in musical synchronicity with that of Arnold's, echoed through the confines of the vehicle.

"Is it a national park?" Edith asked, opening the passenger door and taking a deep, refreshing breath of the cool forest air.

"Yes – a big one by any standards. The forest extends across the German border into the Czech Republic, where it becomes the Bohemian Forest. It is teeming with animals. There are lynx, beavers, wildcat, as well as deer and all sorts of bats. They have even found wolves."

"It's owls we need, though," said Edith, peering at the treetops visible in the distance.

Francis grunted as he unfolded his huge frame and clambered out from the confines of the truck.

"I have no doubt there are many owls in a forest as big as this."

It was as if they had driven into a fairy tale. The guest house was perched on a hill overlooking the tiny village which spread out in front of them. There weren't many houses, but each homestead seemed both sturdy and spacious, with a few wisps of smoke trailing up from individual chimneys, leaving soft smudges of white in the bright blue of the cloudless morning sky. Indeed, it was so quiet and still that the smoke was the only sign the place was inhabited.

A fast-flowing river ran through the centre of the village, in turn spanned by a broad wooden bridge which looked like it had been built centuries ago. The bridge arched gracefully over the water and on to the opposite bank, the top of which was almost level with the guest house. Edith noticed a large white church with an impossibly tall tower, topped by a small dome beneath the spire which jabbed upwards like the point of a needle. The building sat neatly on the other side of the river, as if it was the gatehouse to the forest itself, which lay just beyond.

Tall pine trees coated the walls of the valley behind, thickly covering the ground like the bristles on a hog's back. It seemed beautiful in the sunlight, but Edith could already imagine how daunting a place like this might be at night. She had no time to ponder further, though, as a shuffling noise from the back of the truck made her turn.

"About time! Not a moment to waste. Come on, wake up, Arnold, we haven't got all day!" The Doctor, waking with a start, flung open his door and quickly bounded out of the truck, as if he'd been awake the whole time and it was they who were holding him up.

Giving his cap a little tweak and adjusting his cape, he gestured at Edith and Francis to follow as he made his way in through the unlocked front door of the guest house.

Edith glanced at the still-sleeping form of Arnold, snoring loudly in the back of the truck.

"*Come on, Arnold. Maybe they serve a new type of*

German sausage here?"

Arnold's eyes sprang open.

"I've heard good things about German sausages. They have a bit of spice to them, by all accounts." And the big dog gingerly stretched, then languidly climbed down from the truck. Francis reached down to give him a hearty pat, and the three of them followed the Doctor into the building.

The reception of the guest house was small and cosy. It had a friendly, warm feel and Edith immediately liked the place. Nearly everything seemed to be made of wood. Thick wooden benches were pushed against the lined wooden walls and the wooden floor was clean and polished. Above the reception desk was a large wooden clock framed by a pair of antlers which poked outwards, as if protecting the clock from some unexpected assailant.

The Doctor, ringing a little silver bell on the desk, slowly turned around on the spot, taking in the surroundings and nodding to himself as if reassured by the sturdy construction.

It was a few moments before they heard footsteps and a boy about Edith's age came into the reception and blinked at them in surprise.

"Guten Morgen!" he said.

"Guten Morgen," replied the Doctor, speaking

extremely loudly. "Kannst Englisch?"

"Yes, we can speak English and I can hear you just fine," said the boy in perfect English. A smile creased his lips as he looked at the Doctor in his cape and cap, then his eyes widened at the sight of the huge form of Francis towering over the great big dog that was standing by his side.

"We don't normally allow dogs in here," he said, flicking his eyes to Edith and then grinning. "But we have no other guests, and my mother isn't here, so I suppose we don't need to tell anyone, do we?"

"Aha! A rule breaker! A man after my own heart!" The Doctor beamed. "We need some food, rooms for a few nights, and a map of the area so we can explore! We're not quite sure how long we'll be staying as yet, all depends on how our exploring goes! Can you help us?"

The boy nodded amiably.

"As you may have guessed, the village is in its quiet season. No one is booked to stay all week so you can have the rooms as long as you wish. It's always better when we have visitors! More happens!"

The boy reached down behind the reception desk to lift a large leather-bound ledger on to the counter. Edith noted the red cover embossed with gold writing.

Mutig Gasthaus

"The Plucky Guest House," she said, stepping closer to stand beside her uncle.

"You can read German?" the boy said. "That's good – I still struggle a bit with the reading. The speaking was much easier to pick up."

"I only know very basic German from school," she replied, smiling at him, "but it's an interesting name."

"When we moved here from China, we opened this place and the locals told us we were plucky. The name stuck!"

Edith laughed.

"It could have been worse, I suppose."

"Yes, No Idea What You're Getting Yourself Into Guest House wouldn't have had quite the same ring to it!"

Edith laughed and the boy flashed her a grin.

"I have booked you into our best rooms, and here is a map of the local area," the boy said, pulling out a folded leaflet from a drawer and spreading it out on the flat wooden surface.

"You can see the Tower from here – there are folk tales galore surrounding that place. The main forest trails all start from just in front of it."

The boy circled what looked like an old church on the map and marked one of the trails with his pen.

"This is the best trail, it takes you right into the wood and comes out high up the valley where there is an amazing view. My only warning is that you shouldn't explore after five p.m. – you don't want to be wandering around lost in those trees after the dark."

The Doctor looked up. "Why not? Are there wolves?"

"There used to be wolves in these forests, but they haven't been seen for a couple of years. It is just easy to lose your way as the trees are so thick. You can get lost in an instant – every direction looks the same at night."

The Doctor nodded thoughtfully, watching the boy's face closely. "What is your name?"

"Jian, but my friends call me Zee-Zee." He bobbed his head slightly and flashed another quick smile at all of them.

"And the Tower itself?" the Doctor asked.

"We call it the Tower. It used to be a church which is why it is marked like that on the map. It's now a private home. My mother works for the man who lives there."

"Isn't she busy with the guest house?"

"She's got me to help – and it's not so much work out of season. Tourists come for hikes and walks in the forest when it is summer, and the days are longer, but for several months we see no outsiders at all. So my mother helps out at the Tower. The owner needs help to keep the place clean and tidy, prepare his meals and so on. It's good for us as it means we are busy all year round!"

"It's a shame it's not open to the public," Edith said. "It looks like a beautiful place."

"Well…" Zee-Zee hesitated for a moment. "I'm delivering something there in a bit – maybe you could come with me? You can see the building. The man who lives there, he won't mind, he's, how do you say … quirky?"

"Quirky?" Edith asked.

"He's a bit, well, eccentric." Zee-Zee gave a little laugh and shrugged. "You'll see what I mean if you come with me."

Edith glanced at her uncle, who nodded. "Why not, Edie?" the Doctor said cheerfully. "You go with Zee-Zee while we settle into our rooms. Don't be long, though – we want to set off on a trail this afternoon, so be back for lunch!"

Arnold gave a little whine and Francis patted him with a heavy hand.

"Lunch sounds like a very good idea, but breakfast first! I'm famished!"

Edith gave a little chuckle as she heard Arnold's complaint.

"Always thinking with your stomach!" she replied with a grin.

"It's never let me down yet!"

Zee-Zee glanced over Arnold.

"Your dog can come with us if he wants to stretch his legs. Is he well behaved?"

Edith looked at Arnold and raised an eyebrow.

"That depends on whether you have a sausage to hand…"

***

As the Doctor and Francis unloaded the car and put the bags into the rooms, Edith, Arnold and Zee-Zee set off towards the Tower, a large parcel clasped in Zee-Zee's hands.

The sun was climbing up into the morning sky and Edith relished stretching her legs as they walked down the gentle incline towards the wooden bridge that would take them over the river.

The village had come to life. All the people they passed waved a friendly hello. One smiling lady gave Zee-Zee a huge grin and called out a greeting.

"That's Marie, she does all the laundry for the guest house – she is married to Ernst the baker. It's a small community, everyone knows everyone!" Zee-Zee said, waving back as they strode towards the bridge.

Arnold padded quietly at Edith's side. Before they'd left, Zee-Zee had brought out a tray of cakes for the Doctor, Edith and Francis – and, much to the big dog's delight, a large, cold sausage for Arnold.

"It seems friendly here," Edith said, smiling back as a young man, his cap back to front, walked past and gave them both a big grin.

"It is. Everyone gets on and helps each other out if they need it. The village is peaceful without tourists at this time of year, so there is a real sense of community."

Edith noticed how tightly Zee-Zee was clutching the parcel, as if concerned it might make a jump for it and escape from his grasp.

"What's in the parcel?" she asked, then realized it was a nosy question. "Sorry, it's none of my business, I was just…"

"No problem, but the answer is I honestly don't know. All the deliveries for the Tower come to our guest house. We receive packages like this all the time and I just take them down to leave for the Count. I'm only told they are very important bits of equipment, and I mustn't drop them!"

"The Count?"

"The man who lives there – we call him the Count."

"I don't think I've ever met a Count before," Edith said with a grin.

"He's a friendly one – but I'm not an expert. He's the only one I've met as well! He lives up in the dome part of the Tower, just below the spire, where the head priest and the senior monks used to live when it was a working church."

"How long ago was it an actual church?"

"It was a working church about thirty years ago, then it was abandoned for a bit and then it was finally sold and became the Tower!" Zee-Zee flashed Edith a smile and gave a little shrug. "I'm not too sure on the exact dates. We only moved here two years ago. There's a Chinese festival held every year in Dietfurt. My father was a famous chef and he was asked to prepare the food, but as soon as we arrived we found out the festival had been cancelled. The main sponsor pulled out at the last minute and they couldn't find another. Then ... my father got pneumonia."

"I'm so sorry," Edith said, not quite sure what to say. "It sounds awful."

Zee-Zee nodded. "It was tough. Our tourist visas were about to run out. My father was too sick to move but the only way we could stay was if we had jobs. My mother used to be a vet in China, but she isn't allowed to practise in Germany. So instead, she found the guest house for sale, and we bought it. My mother used all our family savings to buy the business. This meant we could stay in the country on a working visa and then, with the job at the Tower also becoming available, we ended up doing both. The two jobs give us enough money all year round." He swallowed. "But, in the end, my dad died."

"I'm so sorry," Edith said again. "But you stayed in Germany? I mean, after your dad..."

"Yes, with all our money tied up in the Plucky Guest House, we couldn't just walk away and no one seemed interested in buying it back off us."

"Does your mother miss being a vet?" Edith asked. "You might have guessed, but my uncle is one too and I want to be one when I'm older. I don't think my uncle would be able to survive if he couldn't do what he loves."

"She does miss it – but at least she gets to help the Count with all the animals he picks up."

"What animals?" asked Edith, pricking up her ears.

"You'll see," Zee-Zee laughed.

"Do you like animals?" Edith asked.

"I love them. All the books I read are about animals."

"Me too!" she exclaimed happily, glad to have something in common with her new friend.

"I'd love a pet, though – a dog like yours. Hopefully we can get one next year."

"I don't know, dogs can sometimes be a lot of trouble." Edith smiled, reaching down to ruffle Arnold's fur.

"Maybe I'll just stay with Zee-Zee if he feeds me enough sausages," Arnold said to Edith.

Edith laughed and Zee-Zee cast her a confused look, clearly wondering what the joke was.

Edith changed the subject. "Bavaria must be very different to China. Do you miss it?" she said.

Zee-Zee gave a little shrug. "The people are kind and it's also so beautiful here. The villagers were very kind when they knew about my father being so sick. Everyone has been welcoming to us. It's very different to China, but I have made some friends in the village and the local school is good. We used to live in a city, so the scenery is a million times nicer here, especially when the weather is like this. Not so nice when it rains, of course!"

"We know all about rain in England, it can't be worse than that!"

"Ha! So I've heard. I'd love to visit England one day. We also get a lot of snow here. It gets taller than I am! I'd never even seen snow in China. We come from Guangzhou in the south of China where it is mostly warm. Our first winter here was quite an experience! It's not arrived yet, but when it comes everything is covered in a thick blanket for several months. I once even skied down to the bridge from the guest house – it was so much fun!" He glanced at Edith. "It'll be here in a few weeks, if you have a long stay with us!"

"I'm not sure our truck could get through snow, so if it comes early, we might have no choice!" Edith said. She looked around. "It does seem very remote."

"The church used to be a place of pilgrimage. I guess that was part of the appeal; pilgrims wanted to go somewhere off the beaten track."

"Do pilgrims still come?" Edith asked.

Zee-Zee shook his head. "Not any more. Not since it was abandoned."

"Why did it stop being a church?" Edith said.

"Well, it's an interesting one. The story goes that the monks who lived there thought they could see angels in the woods during the winter nights. A bright golden light calling them out to prayer. One night, one of the younger monks saw the light the brightest it had ever been and made all the other monks run outside and into the forest to see if they could find the angel – only he forgot he had left a candle burning. It set fire to the church just after they had all left and a massive section of the building was destroyed."

"That's awful," Edith said. "Was anyone hurt?"

"One monk was burnt – but no one died."

"What happened to the monks after that?"

"They declared it wasn't angels in the forest after all. They thought they had been tempted by a devil. They were ridiculed for burning down their church and chasing what everyone said must have been a glow fly in the forest. People stopped going to the church and there wasn't enough money to rebuild it."

"Then what happened?" Edith asked, fascinated by the story.

"The church was abandoned; it fell into disrepair

until it was bought privately,. The first the village knew of it was when lots of builders arrived one day and began work. The people who owned the guest house before us, they moved here because they helped with the project to restore the building."

"What happened to them? Why did they sell up and leave?" Edith said, intrigued.

Zee-Zee gave a shiver. "It's a nasty story," he said seriously. "Although I don't know how much truth there is to it. Rumour has it, they also saw a golden light in the forest. They went out to see what it was – and that was the last anyone ever saw of them. Their bodies were found next to each other just outside the church. Holding hands. Superstitious people say that ghosts in the forest caused them to die of fright." He lowered his voice. "The strangest thing, though – they were both missing thumbs from each of their hands."

"Thumbs?" Edith exclaimed, horrified.

Zee-Zee shrugged apologetically.

"Yes – their thumbs had been cut off. There was no sign of any other injury on either of the bodies at all. The police couldn't figure out what happened – there are never any robberies here, no motive. It was national news."

"So no one ever found out?"

"No. It is a mystery to this day. No one talks about it, but in the region everyone calls this place the haunted village."

"For a good reason," Arnold grumbled at Edith's side, his voice popping into Edith's head.

"Has anything else like that ever happened here?" As horrible as it was, Edith couldn't help asking more questions.

"Edie, stop! This isn't a good conversation!" Arnold protested.

"It could be useful information. The phoenix was taken. We need to know everything we can about the place!" Edith replied silently.

Zee-Zee shook his head. "Not to people. But occasionally animals are found in the forest..."

Arnold let out a whimper of protest and Edith shushed him.

"Animals?" asked Edith. "But animals live in the forest."

"Well, sometimes animals are also found with body parts missing. An ear or a foot. Maybe it is some sort of lynx that is scavenging."

"Wouldn't a lynx eat the whole animal?"

"Usually, yes – but maybe they were disturbed. Or maybe something else happened. I don't know. No one does. We just don't go out in the forest at night." Zee-Zee frowned suddenly. "You'll be safe here. I am sorry to scare you with these stories, I didn't mean for all that to come out."

Edith smiled back at him. "It's OK. It's a scary story – but, as you say, it's probably just wild animals."

They were midway over the bridge now and Zee-Zee pulled two twigs from his pocket.

"Fancy a game of Poohsticks? I always play this with my mother whenever we go over the bridge. We throw these into the water on this side and see whose twig gets under the bridge first."

"Is there a prize?"

"You get to be the champion at Poohsticks!" Zee-Zee said with a grin.

They both leaned over the side of the bridge and Edith was amazed to see how fast the water was flowing here. It had seemed such a quiet river from a distance. Up close it was more like a raging torrent.

"One, two, three ... drop!"

They dropped the wooden twigs, which bobbed, twisted and turned with the current. They seemed to overlap with each other's and then Zee-Zee's dipped down out of sight while Edith's surged on. The two of them ran to the opposite side of the bridge to see Edith's come out victorious.

Edith gave a little whoop.

"That's a fast-flowing river," Edith said, watching the sticks race off into the distance.

"It's a very strong current – we're all told not to swim in it here in case it carries us away!"

"Honestly, I thought it was dogs who were supposed to get excited about sticks," Arnold said.

"You won because I gave you the good twig," Zee-Zee said good-naturedly.

"You're such a gentleman," Edith said as they started walking again. "What other animals are in the woods?"

"Oh, there were a few wolves years ago apparently, but I have never seen them. I thought I heard one once, but my mother told me it was just the wind in the trees. There are lots of deer, rabbits, wildcats, the odd bear that wanders over from the Alps and all that kind of thing."

"Bears! They sound dangerous!"

"Don't worry – it is very rare. The big animals all seem to have left this area."

"What about birds?" Edie asked, thinking about the owls they needed to find. "We love birdwatching."

Zee-Zee looked at Edith strangely.

"Winter is a strange time to come here to go birdwatching. Many of the birds have migrated and it's not like spring when everything is nesting."

"I love owls," Edith said. "They don't migrate and they come out more when there are less people about. I was hoping we would be able to find some of them."

They were nearing the Tower. Zee-Zee shifted the box in his hands to readjust the weight before answering.

"It's funny you should mention owls. There is a nest of them not far from the main trail. They are noisy at dusk! You can hear them from the village. Once we've dropped off the parcel, we can go back, get your uncle and your giant friend and I'll show you if you like?"

Edith smiled.

"He's called Francis," she said. "But yes, that would be great!"

Just then, Arnold let out a great yowl and stopped stock-still. Edith stopped too. The building seemed to loom over them now they were close, and Edith glanced up towards the domed tower, unable to see the spire that pierced the sky above.

"What is it, Arnold?" she thought, reaching out a hand reassuringly and placing it on the big dog's shoulders.

"I don't like the feel of this place, Edie, we shouldn't go any closer—"

A large arched door swung slowly outwards, and a figure was silhouetted in its frame.

"Edie, stay back." Arnold's voice had taken a darker tone, like a low growl.

Zee-Zee gave Arnold a strange look as the figure stepped forward.

"It's the Count," he said. "Is your dog afraid? He shouldn't be – the Count will be happy to meet you. Don't worry."

As the figure walked slowly towards them, Arnold gave another growl and Edith hesitated, uncertain of what to do.

The Count was dressed in a thick coat with its fluffy hood pulled up over his head. As a result, his face was smothered by shadow.

"Hello, Count," Zee-Zee called cheerfully. "I've got a parcel for you."

Arnold gave another growl, louder this time, and edged himself slightly in front of Edith.

"Stay back, Edie, this Count doesn't smell right. Keep behind me."

"Zee-Zee?" Another voice came from behind the Count and a small, plump woman appeared.

"Mother!" Zee-Zee called. The woman squeezed past the Count, giving him a pat on the shoulder as she passed and came forward to give her son a hug. The Count stopped about three metres from them. Edith could feel his sharp eyes studying her and Arnold intently.

"Zee-Zee, thank you. Who are your friends?" Zee-Zee's mother spoke in a soft, affectionate tone.

"This is Edith, and her dog Arnold. Edith and her friends have just booked into the guest house."

"Lovely to meet you, Edith. My name is Ai Lam. I hope your stay will be very comfortable," Zee-Zee's mother gushed, dipping her head slightly in Edith's direction.

"Thank you, it seems a lovely place to stay. We're glad you had rooms," Edith replied, still eyeing Arnold uncertainly.

The little lady smiled warmly as she took the parcel and stepped back. The Count, standing behind her with his hood up, shuffled almost nervously as he cleared his throat to speak.

"Your dog – he looks like he is part Wolfdog."

Edith felt her jaw drop slightly. The sound of the Count's voice was the last thing she had expected. It was high-pitched and squeaky, and she blinked in surprise.

"Don't let him get any closer, Edie! You can't trust a man who doesn't show his face! Be careful. I'm ready for him if he attacks."

"Arnold! Don't be so silly. We're not going to be attacked."

Even as she thought it, Edith realized she had taken an involuntary step back. Getting a grip of herself, she raised her eyes to investigate the shadow of the Count's hood, determined not to appear afraid. Zee-Zee had said he was a nice man who had helped them, after all.

The Count giggled. He was more awkward than threatening.

"I don't think he likes my hood. The thing is, I don't react well to sunlight, but let's give it a go. He'll probably prefer my face even less."

The Count tittered, reaching up and flicking back his hood as if he could read Arnold's mind.

His face was incredibly pale, his close-shaved head shining in the sunlight, but he smiled shyly down at Edith and continued to shift his balance from foot to foot as if embarrassed to be standing in front of them.

Edith felt herself smile warmly in return and she reached out to pat Arnold, who seemed to relax slightly. He moved forward and gave the Count a cautious sniff.

"That's better!" squeaked the Count happily.

"Yes, I think it was the hood. Thank you for pulling it back," Edith explained. "I'm sorry Arnold was a bit jumpy, he's not normally so easily spooked. As for being part Wolfdog, no one is too sure."

"Oh, but he is. I am quite certain. I study these

things. He is most
magnificent." The
Count reached out a
hand towards Arnold
to pat him.

Arnold tensed.

"Here. Perhaps he
would like some treats?" The
Count tittered again, pulling a small plastic box from the
folds of his coat and opening the lid.

Arnold's whole demeanour changed in an instant.

"Do you think a slice of sausage might win him over?"
the Count laughed.

Arnold wagged his tail.

"OK, maybe I got it wrong. Happens to the best of us,"
the big dog said, nudging his nose up against the Count,
who gingerly tossed him a slice of sausage. *"Now you're
talking! This is my kind of count!"*

"I think you've won him over," Edith laughed, relieved
that Arnold was behaving like normal again.

"Slices of sausage. Before nightfall, the whole village
will know it's Arnold's favourite snack and he won't be
able to move!" Zee-Zee said, a big smile tugging up the
corners of his mouth.

"Ludwig the woodsman always has a packet of

sausage in his pocket. Arnold will find him out later without a doubt," Ai Lam laughed.

"*I can sniff out a sausage anywhere!*" Arnold said contentedly, a bit of drool hanging down from his lips.

"Bavaria's best," said the Count, beaming. "I'm quite partial to it myself. I saw you walk across the bridge and thought he might enjoy a sample. Let me give you the box."

"Just remember they are for the dog, not for you children," said Ai Lam firmly as Zee-Zee took the box. "I'm cooking you a big dinner and I don't want your appetite spoiled!"

"Thank you. I love your Tower by the way," Edith said with a grin as Arnold's eyes fixed on the box as if hypnotized.

"It's a lovely home, but only because of this dear lady." The Count bobbed his head in appreciation towards Zee-Zee's mother, who rolled her eyes back at him.

"Non-stop clearing up after you," she laughed, giving the Count a fond nudge. "Although I've heard it said you're pretty tidy as far as counts go."

"I am about to go out for a walk, but you must come to tea one day, I would love to show you around," said the Count, his face lighting up hopefully. "I don't get many visitors, you know. Perhaps tomorrow?"

"I'd love that," Edith replied warmly. "I'm here with my uncle and Francis. We're here to explore the forest."

"Ah, tourists out of tourist season!" The Count clapped his hands. "Why not! The forest has something to offer all year round! It is just a bit colder at this time of year. Please bring them as well, all are very welcome!"

They said their goodbyes and turned to go.

As Zee-Zee and Edith began to walk away, Arnold spoke.

"Wait, Edie – there is one thing before we go a step further."

Edith stopped and put an arm out to halt Zee-Zee, who stopped with a quizzical expression on his face.

"What is it, Edith?"

"Arnold hasn't moved. Something is on his mind."

They both stared at the dog, who stood rock steady a metre behind them both.

"What's the matter, Arnold – are you OK?"

The big dog gave a single solid beat of his tail.

"Can I have another one of those sausage slices?"

CHAPTER FIVE

In which Edith and the team head off into the forest to meet some owls and start the search for the phoenix – but soon discover that the forest harbours its own secrets...

"What an odd story!" Francis boomed, after Edith finished regaling him and the doctor with the history of the old church and the mysterious deaths of the couple who owned the guesthouse before Zee-Zee and his mother. "Did it seem like a sinister place at all?"

"No! It seemed nice – but Arnold didn't like the Count at first, did he, Zee-Zee?" Edith said as they stood outside the guest house, readying themselves for the expedition into the forest.

"No," Zee-Zee agreed. "Something upset him, but a few slices of sausage soon won him round."

"The quickest way to win Arnold over," Francis laughed. "What was the Count like?"

"He seemed a little ... odd I guess," said Edith. "But in a nice way. I think he's actually quite sweet and maybe a bit lonely – he's invited us all for tea tomorrow. He loved Arnold."

She glanced over at Arnold, who was looking up hopefully at Zee-Zee.

Zee-Zee, seeing the big dog making eyes at him, opened the box containing the sausage slices and hooked one out. With a quick twist, he tossed it to Arnold, who gulped it down in a single swallow.

"Delicious!" said Arnold.

"You'd better do a lot of running in the forest after all that food," Edith thought back, smiling at the big dog.

"Hey! I'm a natural athlete!"

"The Count can seem strange at first, everyone agrees on that, but he's well liked," Zee-Zee added. "He's generous. He gave my mother a job when things were looking pretty bad for her. He's just a bit different."

"Nothing wrong with a being a bit ... different," the Doctor chortled, walking over to join them. "I should know!"

"We're not talking about you, Uncle, we're talking about the Count!" Edith laughed.

"I never thought you could be talking about me for a second, Edie," the Doctor retorted, his eyes twinkling. "It sounds like the Count has a kind heart."

"He does – he loves animals," Zee-Zee went on, "which is always a sign of kindness. Although he's not so keen on some of the guests that have their private functions at the Tower."

"Guests?" the Doctor asked, his jovial attitude suddenly serious.

"Yes, the Count rents out the nave of the church for private functions. When it's the hunting season, big hunting parties come. I sometimes have to be a waiter. They all drink lots of beer and talk about their kills. The Count isn't involved though, he leaves them to it. He loves the forest animals and helps them after the hunts."

"Why does he let the hunters come then?" Edith asked.

"Hunting is part of the Bavarian culture and the Count has to pay for the upkeep of the Tower somehow."

"Do they come often?" Edith asked, remembering with a shudder her past brush with Arabella Spearstrike and her group of killers.

"In the hunting season, it is probably once a month.

Different groups at different times." Zee-Zee shook his head sadly.

"It must be horrible having hunters here," said Edith.

"It is. The hunters must be hosted somewhere though, and we can't stop them coming. At least this way we know where they go in the forest and what they do. When they leave, the Count always goes out into the forest afterwards and searches for any injured animals."

"Ah!" exclaimed the Doctor. "So the Count is an animal rescuer, is he? Well, perhaps that explains why he lives up in the Tower. People who champion animals often prefer animal company to that of people."

"We should know," said Francis.

Zee-Zee laughed.

"He takes them back to nurse in the Tower and my mother helps him to get them better. Sometimes I look after them as well. I have a little room at the back of the guest house with a few cages in there – there are no animals here right now but, if the Count has too many, he'll ask me to take some of the less injured ones. I guess I like both animals *and* people, though!"

The Doctor nodded thoughtfully. "Edie told me your mother is a vet? I'll look forward to having a good chat with her later – maybe she can give me some tips on how to treat an infected ear on particularly grumpy badger I've got staying in the barn right now."

"I'm not sure she has treated many badgers," said Zee-Zee, "but she usually comes up with a way to treat things."

Arnold gave a whine and the group all looked at him.

"Don't suppose there is another sausage going? I'm discovering that Bavaria is the king of sausages, Edie!"

Edith laughed. "I think Arnold wants another piece of sausage."

"Well, he's finished off all the slices the Count gave us. I'll run and see what we have in the kitchen," Zee-Zee said, racing off to check.

"Arnold – you'll need to cut back, or you'll eat poor Zee-Zee out of house and home!" Edith exclaimed, ruffling the big dog's back with her hand.

As he moved out of earshot, the Doctor cast a conspiratorial look at Edith.

"Did you tell him?" he whispered loudly.

"Tell him what?" Edith replied, somewhat awkwardly, wondering what her uncle meant.

"That you can talk to animals using the power of your mind?"

"No!" Edith said. "I'm trying to make a friend here – that's not going to happen if I suddenly tell him I can hear voices in my head!"

"He might be impressed," said Francis.

"He won't be impressed, he'll be freaked out," snapped Edith. "And shh, he's coming back."

Their conversation ended abruptly as Zee-Zee returned, clutching a newly refilled box containing more sausage slices.

"Ha ha – the fastest way to Arnold's heart – through his stomach! Right then, we must be on with our expedition! Let's get going!" the Doctor said, giving his cape a little flourish.

"Where are you heading?" Zee-Zee asked.

"We are heading out into the forest to look for signs of the ph ... owls," Francis said, stumbling over the words.

"Owls?"

"I told you how much I love owls," Edith said, nudging Francis.

"Oh yes," said Zee-Zee. "I could show you where they nest if you like?"

Edith hesitated, but the Doctor nodded enthusiastically. "That would be most helpful," he said. "If it's not too much trouble."

"It's no trouble," said Zee-Zee. "There's a nest not far from here and I can easily come with you. On the off chance someone does show up, I'll leave a note on the front desk asking them to call in and see Mother at the Tower."

The Doctor beamed. "In that case, lead the way, my young friend! The owls await us!"

The five of them walked down the hill, gingerly crossing the bridge as it creaked under Francis's feet.

As they descended the last part of the bridge, the Doctor fell back to walk with Edith. "I want to give you something, Edie," he said quietly, holding out a small tube.

Edith took the tube. "What is it?" she whispered.

"It's a vaccine for the phoenix. Just in case you chance upon the great bird, and for whatever reason I am not to hand. You already know how to inject an animal – I've shown you enough times. Once the phoenix gives you permission, an injection into the muscle on its breast is best – you'll find the syringe and needle in the tube along with the vaccine."

"Do I need to try and keep it in a fridge, Uncle?"

"Not this one. You don't have to worry about keeping it cool – the vaccine is thermostable; it works at all temperatures – well, perhaps not freezing cold or boiling hot but it'll be fine in your pocket." The Doctor chuckled.

Edith bit her lip. The thought of vaccinating a phoenix on her own felt like a huge responsibility. What would happen if she got it wrong and didn't inject it correctly? Would the phoenix die and it be all her fault?

As if sensing her fears, the Doctor gave her a friendly smile.

"Don't worry, you'll be fine, Edie. If it does come to it, just keep your head and imagine it's a normal animal. Forget it's a phoenix. I have plenty of spare vaccines as well."

Edith tucked the vaccine safely into her jacket.

"We aren't going to split up though, are we, Uncle?" she said, still slightly anxious at the prospect of having to do the job herself.

"I hope not, Edie – we need to chat to the owls as the first step. But when we do find the phoenix, there is every chance you will be able to get a lot closer than me or Francis. It might be frightened or wary after its ordeal. You'll be able to explain what the vaccine is and why we're here. Always be prepared, Edie. It's the rule of any good vet – every healer needs their tools!"

The Doctor flashed her a big grin and then skipped ahead, starting a conversation with Zee-Zee about some of the animals that lived in the Bavarian Forest.

It took them about ten minutes before they entered the periphery of the forest. Then, within moments of passing the treeline, they were on a broad track, walking under a thick canopy of green.

The forest was like its own world, separate even from

the tranquil little village. Edith immediately felt a sense of blissful peace wash over her, as if she had crept under a cosy blanket. She felt somehow hidden away from the outside. Sunlight gently filtered through the impossibly tall trees to bathe the forest floor in a rich golden light, and in many ways, it felt as if they had been transported back to the New Forest. The sounds of the birds made the whole place feel alive, yet there was also a sense of calm tranquillity, as if the forest was taking a break during these winter months. It might be a daunting place at night, Edith supposed, but in the daylight it seemed magical.

Edith, Francis, Zee-Zee and Arnold found themselves walking in near silence, savouring the peace, lost in their thoughts. The Doctor, in stark contrast, seemed energized and had started to hum softly, striding excitedly some twenty paces ahead of the rest of them as if impatient to explore the woods like an eager spaniel.

"Now, Zee-Zee, do you know what species of owl nest here, by any chance? They wouldn't happen to be the *Strix uralensis*, would they?" he called back over his shoulder.

"You mean the Ural owls?" said Zee-Zee. "The ones that became extinct here in 1925 and then were reintroduced in the national park in 1975?"

Edith gave Zee-Zee an impressed look and he flashed her a proud grin in return.

"Yes!" cried the Doctor. "Exactly! They are only found in very old trees, if I remember correctly. I once treated one with a bad claw – a fungal infection, could only have picked it up from a decomposing tree trunk, I suspect. In human terms it would be a bit like athlete's foot, but there we are. Anyway, the Ural owl – a large bird with a wingspan that would go from the ground up to your shoulders! They make a *huow-huow-huow* sound. Quite distinctive."

"They don't go *twit-twooo*, Doctor?" said Francis.

"No, Francis, they most certainly do not. *Huow-huow-huow* is the correct sound."

"*Huow-houw-huw?*" Francis tried the sound out, his deep voice sounding more like a foghorn than an owl, which made Edith and Zee-Zee laugh out loud.

"No – more *huow* on the last *huow*. You need to lengthen that *huowww*."

"*Huw-huhuwoooo.*"

"Francis, my dear man, are you deliberately trying to frustrate me? Try it again."

"*Huw-huhuwooo!*"

The Doctor stopped in his tracks and turned once again to look at Francis, who met his eyes and spread his hands helplessly.

"Huow-huow-huow," he said.

Huow-huow-huow.

The Doctor clapped his hands. "That last one was exactly right, Francis! Why, you sound just like a real Ural owl!"

"Er," said Francis, looking up at the trees.

The sound came right back again, this time louder, and the Doctor raised his eyes in surprise.

"Your lips didn't move; how did you do that, Francis?"

"It's not me, that's why, Doctor," the big man replied calmly.

"It's one of the owls!" Edith exclaimed, the penny dropping. "They're answering the call! Uncle, do it again!"

The Doctor's eyes widened.

"*Huow-huow-huow!*" he called, cupping his hand to his mouth to make the sound travel further.

"*Huow-huow-huow,*" answered the call.

The Doctor turned to Edith. "Edie, can you try asking them if they'd meet with us?"

Thinking the Doctor must be making a joke, Zee-Zee looked at Edith, clearly expecting her to try to make the owl call. Instead, he watched her close her eyes in concentration.

"What are you doing?" Zee-Zee whispered.

"I'm thinking of an owl," Edith replied, screwing up her eyes tighter.

Zee-Zee looked at Edith strangely but held his tongue as she waved a hand for him to be silent.

"Hello, owl, can you hear me?" Edith thought.

There was a pause whilst they all stood stock-still, Edith listening intently to see if the owl responded. Zee-Zee looked bewildered. Then a noise sounded softly through the late afternoon air and Edith heard the bird reply in her head.

"It's far too early to be disturbed. What on earth are you doing? Is it humans making that unholy racket? I'm quite relieved; I was worried one of my brethren had the most terrible throat infection for a moment."

"Sorry. I'm afraid it is us making the noise – well, my uncle to be precise. Can you fly over to us so we can meet you?"

"Why on earth would I do that? No – let me sleep and stop making such an awful noise. It's the middle of the day!"

Edith gave a sigh; the owl was clearly going to be a slightly difficult character. *What is it with birds?* she thought. *They're so aloof! This wasn't going to help them find the phoenix...*

"We're not aloof; how dare you! You are disturbing my sleep! But tell me – what did you say about the phoenix?

Who are you to ask about the golden bird?"

Edith blushed, forgetting that when she had a connection going in her mind, all her thoughts were heard by the animal she was talking to. The owl had a point; it was a nocturnal bird and they were disturbing it. She felt her cheeks going red.

"What did the owl say?" she heard the Doctor whisper urgently, and noticed Zee-Zee give her another confused look.

Focusing her mind again, she turned her attention back towards the owl.

"I'm sorry, I shouldn't have called you aloof – I know we have woken you up. But we need to ask you about the Northern Phoenix. We're worried that it has gone missing."

"Gone missing?" the owl said slowly.

"Yes. We're concerned something awful might have happened and it needs our help. Besides, there's a horrible disease – a type of mutated avian flu that can affect phoenixes. We need to find the Northern Phoenix and then vaccinate it."

"The plot thickens," said the owl sarcastically.

"The flu can delay it being reborn – until it's too late. We've vaccinated all the other phoenixes except this one. Can you help us?"

There was a silence. They all waited. Edith had no

idea whether the owl was coming or whether it had gone back to sleep.

Arnold, who had found a patch of sunlight on the forest floor a short distance away, promptly flopped down. *"I'm feeling a bit sleepy, Edie. Wake me up when you've had a chat with the owl."*

Edith smiled, then froze. She could hear a scrabbling noise, somewhere up above them and slightly off to the right.

The scrabbling sound carried on for half a minute or so and then a large shape plummeted through the branches before landing heavily about a metre from Francis.

The bird – which was quite a large owl – gave a shake of its body before spinning its head slowly round to look at them all in turn.

"Amazing how owls can turn their heads like that, isn't it?" said Francis quietly, stepping back slightly so as not to crowd the bird.

The owl fixed him with a momentary glare of disdain, then spun its head nearly one hundred and eighty degrees without turning its body to look directly at Edith.

"You do realize I should be fast asleep right now? Tucked up in my hole, instead of being blinded by

ridiculous sunlight, fighting my way through these blasted branches and then being goggled at by a gaggle of strangers. If you hadn't mentioned the phoenix I wouldn't have come to see you."

"We really appreciate it. Thank you," Edith thought. "As I said, we're worried the phoenix might be in terrible danger."

The owl made a sound that might have been a snort. "Hmmmmph. Terrible danger, you say? I think we all know that. It has escaped a few times, of course. If it had managed to do so in the daytime, perhaps it would have stood a chance, but at night, even a one-eyed wood finch could spot it. Such a magnificent bird – reduced to fleeing for its life! But then none of us are safe nowadays, not with those kinds of creatures prowling the forest."

"You mean there are hunters prowling the forest?" Edith thought with alarm.

"Call them hunters if you will, they are creatures to me." The owl gave Edith a sharp look from its beady eyes. "How do I know you want to rescue and vaccinate it and not capture it for yourselves?"

The owl looked at her with unblinking eyes.

"Well, we don't have any nets and we don't have any guns or arrows with us. We do have a vaccine, though. My uncle, the Doctor, looks after magical creatures like *the phoenix."*

The owl started. Then it gave a little hop and made the Doctor a small bow.

The Doctor, as surprised as everyone else, quickly reached up to his cap, doffed it in the direction of the owl and returned the bow.

"I have of course heard of the great Doctor. I am truly honoured." The owl flicked its gaze back to Edith, exasperation etched on its wizened face. *"Why on earth didn't you say you were with the Healer of the Seven Kingdoms?"*

"Sorry. I should have introduced us all quicker," was all Edith could reply, desperately trying not to think how haughty birds seemed to be, lest she upset the owl again.

"So can you help us find the phoenix?" she thought, before her mind got her into trouble.

"I haven't seen the phoenix for many moons, but it leads a most tortured life. Catching a flu is the least of its worries. It almost got away last time — we saw it reach the clearing — but the creatures were on its trail and then ... well, it's been taken back again."

"Who takes it back?" Edith asked eagerly. *"Where is it taken to?"*

The owl suddenly went silent. It shuffled nervously on the spot.

"How do I know you haven't been followed here?"

"No one has followed us," Edith thought. But the owl still seemed agitated.

"The day is drawing to a close; twilight won't be far away. I advise you to get out of the forest. The phoenix cannot be helped – it is kept beyond your reach."

"What do you mean? Who keeps it?"

"It was captured some time ago – oh yes, like so many other creatures of these woods. But how can you hope to free it? There are only a few of you! You'll need an army – even the giant man and the Doctor won't nearly be a match for the wolpertingers." The owl seemed to shiver. "I must be away. Tell the Doctor he is too late and save yourselves. I must go – there is a chill in the air!"

The owl gave a little bob towards the Doctor and then, with a heave, noisily flapped its body upwards into the trees, leaving the group looking at Edith.

"He said that the phoenix is locked up, but not where or by whom! I think it's somewhere around here though because he said it keeps escaping. And he said there aren't enough of us to save it and something about … wolpertingers? What does that even mean?" Edith said in exasperation.

The Doctor had gone very still and was suddenly looking left and right, peering around them. Francis shifted uneasily on his feet.

"What do you mean 'he' said? I didn't hear anyone say anything?" Zee-Zee asked quietly.

Edith shot him an apologetic look.

"It's hard to explain…" she replied awkwardly, but the Doctor held up a hand.

"The word wolpertinger was mentioned?"

Edith nodded mutely.

The Doctor looked grave. He exchanged a worried look with Francis before speaking in a hushed tone.

"Did the owl say anything else?"

Edith tried to remember every last detail. "He said something about how animals in the forest are hunted and taken away. He referred to the hunters as 'creatures'. The owl said we wouldn't be able to rescue the phoenix, let alone vaccinate it, and that even you and Francis aren't a match for the wolpertingers. It was such a jumble. What *is* a wolpertinger?"

The Doctor reached up and straightened his cap.

"A wolpertinger is not a natural creature, Edie," he said quietly. "It is a beast of nightmares. Even I shudder at the thought that such abominations of the natural world could exist. I have only heard of them through ancient legends – many centuries old. If the owl is telling you there are wolpertingers in this forest, and if that is indeed the case, we have wandered into a situation for which we are wholly unequipped. I would say that we are all quite probably in extremely grave danger. It suggests the presence of dark forces at work."

"Do you mean the Syndicate, Uncle?" Edith said quietly.

The Doctor didn't reply; he was staring off into the trees, his brow creased in consternation.

"We are best to stay close together," Francis agreed.

Zee-Zee looked up at him nervously, utterly confused and bewildered.

"Edie," Zee-Zee broke out. "Were you *talking* to the owl? What is this about a phoenix and wolpertingers? What is a Syndicate? What is going on?"

Edith hesitated, but the Doctor said, "Edie, my heart tells me our young guide here can be let into our little secret. Besides, it is better he knows the truth than tries to make sense of our discussions and comes to the wrong conclusions."

"Secret?" Zee-Zee said, looking utterly bewildered.

"Edith can speak to animals using the power of her mind," the Doctor said slowly.

"What? That's impossible!" Zee-Zee said. He turned to Edith, who gave a slightly embarrassed nod.

"I'm a telepathic polyglot," she said.

"And we've come here to track down a phoenix, rescue it and then give it a vaccine against a deadly disease," the Doctor added. "We thought the owls might have some information for us – and they did. More than we bargained for, in fact."

Zee-Zee's mouth was hanging open. He didn't speak for a moment, scanning each of their expressions and looking for some sign they were making a joke at his expense. They all stared back at him earnestly.

"Oh," he said at last.

"Oh indeed," the Doctor said.

Zee-Zee shook his head. "But a phoenix or a wolpertinger... They don't exist. Phoenixes are from ancient myths and wolpertingers are just part of German folklore. They feature in stories to scare small children. They aren't real. You are all talking as if they might actually exist." Zee-Zee gave an incredulous laugh.

"Zee-Zee, you have just witnessed Edie talk to an owl," said the Doctor. "Believe it or not, we are here to vaccinate a phoenix against a deadly form of avian flu. It may sound unlikely, but we are genuine."

Zee-Zee blinked, his face a picture of utter bewilderment.

"Uncle, what did you mean when you said the wolpertinger is a beast of nightmares?" asked Edith.

"They are a patchwork of creatures fused into one," explained the Doctor gravely. "Each part of a different creature lends the wolpertinger some specific attribute, so the ears of a rabbit would help it hear, the eyes of a hawk could make it see further, the teeth of a wolf would make it a fearsome hunter. No two wolpertingers are the same."

"But that's impossible!" cried Zee-Zee. "You can't put different parts of animals together; it doesn't make any sense."

The Doctor shook his head slowly.

"I wish that were so. It should be impossible, it shouldn't be allowed by the laws of nature and everything by which we and all the other wild and wonderful animals on this planet exist … but you have heard of the centaur – half man, half horse – haven't you? You have heard of the hippogriff – half eagle, half horse – everyone has heard of those magnificent creatures?"

Zee-Zee was still staring at the Doctor, slack-jawed.

"But they are also myths – they aren't real either!"

"Of course they are real! Why, only last year Francis and I treated a hippogriff with a damaged beak! He gave you a nip, didn't he, Francis? Temperamental creatures at the best of times."

Francis nodded solemnly and pulled back his sleeve

to show Zee-Zee and Edith a thin puckered scar along the length of his muscled forearm.

"Just a little beaking, he didn't mean it."

The Doctor smiled. "Oh, they exist as surely as you or I draw breath. But the question you should be asking is – how?"

"I just assumed they evolved, Uncle?" Edith said, mindful of how bizarre this conversation must be sounding to Zee-Zee, who was shaking his head slightly in sheer bewilderment at what he was hearing.

"Mermaids and mermen, they evolved, Edie. Not hippogriffs or centaurs. Nor the Ammit, the 'devourer of the dead' that roamed the land in ancient Egypt, formed by the fusion of a crocodile, a lion and a hippopotamus! It was revered as goddess! Totally uncontrollable, dangerous beyond belief. They were made by human hand – and do you know how?"

Edith shook her head.

"With the help of a phoenix."

Her uncle spoke the words very softly and very carefully, letting the importance of what he was saying sink in.

"The phoenix has the power of rebirth, Edie. If wolpertingers are here, it means they are being made, and the only way that can happen is if freshly killed parts of animals are reborn as one – by using the ashes of a phoenix…"

"So if we discover who is making the wolpertingers, then we discover who has captured the phoenix," Edith said slowly.

"Exactly."

There was a pause as they all took in the information. Zee-Zee shuffled his feet uncomfortably.

"So just so I have got this right – you've really come here to find a phoenix and vaccinate it against a mutated form of avian flu?" he said quietly, looking at Edith and trying to resist the urge to pinch himself.

"Yes, but—" Edith broke off as the Doctor held up a hand, interrupting her. He suddenly froze and then spun around to face back towards the forest path.

"Francis," the Doctor said. "Where is Arnold?"

An indentation amongst the dirt and leaves of the track was just about visible from where they all stood. The sunlight showed through on to the exact spot where the dog had been lying. Edith felt a cold knot of worry ball up in her stomach.

Arnold was gone.

CHAPTER SIX

*In which the group split up, Arnold
must be found, and the Count heads
off with Edith into the forest as its
secrets start to be revealed…*

"Greetings again! Are you enjoying your walk?" a high-pitched voice piped out from amongst the trees. The language was English, but the voice, whilst reedy thin, twanged with a strong German accent.

They all jumped, Francis instinctively took two huge steps in the direction of the voice, protectively shielding the group as a familiar figure emerged on to the path.

The Count, the hood of his coat pulled up over his

face, tugged his hands from his pockets, spreading them outwards, palms upwards, as a sign of peace.

"Sorry!" he said. "I didn't mean to startle you. I walk quietly because I like to see the animals, you know. I usually take my afternoon stroll about now and I saw you walk past the Tower and … well, I thought I might come and say hello," he finished, rather sheepishly.

"And who might you be, sir?" the Doctor said sharply, surprised by the man's sudden appearance.

Zee-Zee came forward. "Doctor, this is the Count who lives in the Tower and who my mother works for. Count, you met Edie earlier, but this is her uncle and their friend Francis."

The Count waved at Zee-Zee and moved closer, pushing back his hood as he did so, exposing his pale face and shaven head.

"Sorry – my hooded appearance can be quite surprising; I wish I could be free of the thing, but I really don't react all that well to sunlight."

"It was more the fact you crept up on us," Francis rumbled.

The Count's head dropped and he spread his hands apologetically. "Again, so sorry."

He looked so miserable at having worried them that Edith jumped in, recalling her manners.

"Doctor, the Count very kindly invited us to tea tomorrow."

"Of course, very kind," said the Doctor. He held out his hand and the Count shook it eagerly.

"Delighted to meet you. I am Count Krampusten."

The Doctor nodded. "May I properly introduce my companion called Francis, and of course you already know Edith and Zee-Zee."

"Nice to meet you," Francis rumbled.

Edith cleared her throat.

"Count, you haven't happened to have seen Arnold, have you?" she asked.

"Your magnificent dog?" the Count said, his eyes lighting up. "What an extraordinary beast. No, I haven't, and I'm sorry to hear he has run off. I am sure he won't be far – probably chasing squirrels. Lots of interesting woodland creatures scurrying about at this time of day."

"Arnold was sleeping," said Edith, frowning. "Besides, it's not like him to run off."

Francis was looking around anxiously, clearly having the same thought as Edith. "Perhaps we should split up and search for him," he said.

The Count flinched. "I hope he comes back soon. It is almost dusk, and it is not advisable to be out in the forest at night."

"Why is that?" the Doctor asked innocently, reaching up to adjust his cap.

The Count cast a furtive look into the trees and leaned closer. "I often find injured animals during my walks. The larger predators come out at night, roaming the forests in search of an easy meal." He shivered. "This forest is … strange. It seems such a lovely place in the day, but at night it really is most foreboding. We should try to find your dog soon, before it becomes too dark and cold and … dangerous."

The Doctor nodded thoughtfully. "Francis – are there any tracks?"

Francis crouched down where Arnold had been lying and examined the soft indentation in the soil. To Edith's eye there seemed to be no sign of disturbance whatsoever, but Francis clearly saw something because he looked up at the Doctor.

"I think he went that way, deeper into the woods. But it's strange; there are many tracks on the forest floor and these signs are very confused."

"Straight on is where the trees get thicker; left leads to a valley and right to the stream," said Zee-Zee, pointing out the different directions.

"It is a large area to cover. Let me help you. Perhaps, as you suggest, if we split up, we will stand more chance of finding him," the Count said.

The Doctor hesitated, clearly reluctant to agree.

"It is a big area, Doctor. I think it's our only chance of covering it if we want to find Arnold before it gets dark," Zee-Zee said.

The Doctor chewed at his lip for a moment.

"Francis, you're the best tracker, so why don't you go straight ahead and see if there are any signs Arnold went that way? The rest of us will do a sweep as a group, loop around and try to cover the valley and the stream. He can't be far. This is most unlike him."

Edith looked into the dark tangle of trees. She hated the idea of Arnold out there, lost and alone. "Uncle, Zee-Zee and the Count know this forest. What about if you go with Zee-Zee to the valley and, if the Count is happy, he could take me to the stream and we can look there? I know it splits us up more, but we can stay in earshot of each other. It is our best chance of covering more ground quickly. Francis can go into the thick trees to see if there is any sign."

"I'd be glad to assist," said the Count, smiling at Edith.

The Doctor hesitated and she added, urgently, "Please, Uncle, we don't have any time to lose."

Reluctantly the Doctor nodded. "Half an hour, no

more. There is no need to panic. I am sure Arnold can take care of himself. Don't forget to call for him, Edie, then shout for us if he comes. Let's all aim to rendezvous back here on the main path, and if for whatever reason we do get separated, head back and meet at the Tower before dark."

The Doctor gave Edith a pointed look and she understood her uncle meant she should project her thoughts as well as her voice.

"We'll all call – hopefully he'll hear some of us," said Zee-Zee, eager to start the search.

The Doctor looked troubled for a moment, lost in some unspoken thought, then his expression cleared and he continued, "Right, let's get to it. Shout loudly for help if required."

A moment later, the group split up. Zee-Zee and the Doctor headed off towards the valley whilst Francis's broad back disappeared into the thick of the trees. Edith turned to look up at the Count.

"Shall we?" the Count said, and Edith gave a firm nod.

It was strange, Edith noted as she followed the Count into the woods; the man seemed to be able to walk in complete silence.

"You make hardly a sound. How do you do it?"

Edith couldn't see the Count's face, but she sensed

his smile as he replied.

"Years of practice. Silence is the only the way to get close to wildlife."

Edith winced as she trod on a twig and it gave a loud snap.

"Sorry," she mumbled.

The Count gave a soft chuckle and carried on gliding quietly forward.

"Injured animals are easily frightened," he explained. "Moving quietly allows me to reach them. The hunters who come here often injure our animals rather than kill. It is nice to rescue those creatures who need it."

"The hunters injure them rather than kill?"

The Count nodded and when he spoke again, his voice was grim. "Not all the hunters are good shots. They miss a lot and they injure plenty. They are only interested in the sport of hunting, not necessarily the result. Wounding is enough for many of them. Blood is all they want. I may have to host them, I don't have much choice there – but I don't have to like what they do, and I do what I can to repair the damage."

"Do you rescue a lot?"

The Count laughed. "Too many! I have quite a collection of animals in the Tower. Zee-Zee's mother is an incredible woman – most gifted. I am sure he has told you she was a vet in China. Zee-Zee has his own little hospital as well. We are quite a team, the three of us. You wouldn't believe the variety of animals we collect after those dreadful hunts." He hesitated and stopped, facing Edith. "I even wonder whether I might help find the bird you are all so desperately looking for?"

The Count let the question hang in the air as the shock of what he had said hit Edith. She involuntarily stopped and took a few steps back. She felt herself push up against the rough bark of a tree trunk.

"What do you mean?" she managed quietly, pushing down a rising sense of panic.

The Count took a deep breath. "I heard you talking in the forest. I heard Zee-Zee say you have come here to rescue a phoenix? The need to administer … what was it … a vaccine? Quite a remarkable thing to overhear – I did assume there was more to your group than met the eye."

Edith didn't know what to say. The Count had overheard them discussing the phoenix – and more strangely, he didn't seem surprised that such a creature existed. Had he heard them talk about the wolpertingers? How much of the conversation had he listened to?

"How do you know about … about…"

"The phoenix? The golden bird that is rumoured to have lived in this forest?"

Edith nodded, unsure if she should shout to her uncle.

"Why, the legend of the phoenix is famous amongst the locals. It's part of the reason I came to live in the Tower – I always wondered, always hoped, such a bird might still exist here. The myth of it is what draws some hunters here this day." His expression clouded. "I am distressed to discover that it too, like your dog, is missing. Are you certain it needs rescuing?"

Edith hesitated. There seemed no point in denying it when the Count had overheard them talking. "It is missing. We think it needs our help," she said cautiously. The conversation was strangely casual – they might be discussing a missing cat, she thought.

"I see. Well, in that case, we must do all we can to find it."

The Count turned as if the matter was decided, and pointed ahead. "If Arnold was chasing something heading in this direction, I think it is most likely he would have run a little closer towards the stream's edge where the going is easier."

With that, the Count began to walk forward again, stealthily crouching down to study the soft sand which coated the shallow bank of the stream.

Edith tentatively followed.

"The phoenix might have been captured – you said that some hunters come here in search of it. Zee-Zee mentioned there are hunting parties who rent out your tower. Have you heard any groups of hunters – anyone talk about hunting the phoenix directly?"

The Count pursed his pale lips in thought.

"There are so many groups that pass through here; but yes, there is one group that somewhat stand out, always talking about the fearsome animals they hunt and the ones they want to capture. They often mention the myth of the phoenix. They are led by a rather arrogant lady with red hair."

Edith stopped walking and the Count turned to look at her, his face an expression of mild surprise.

"You know who I am talking about?" the Count asked curiously.

"Arabella Spearstrike."

"Yes – that's her name. Her and her henchmen. They come here every three months with a hunting party. They hire my old church for their feast events. Once, I heard them mention a quest for a golden bird, but it was several years ago. Their focus is more on killing as much as they can. Those types of big hunts are very common in the state forests of Hohenfels, you know. They have the largest herds of—"

The Count stopped suddenly and Edith craned her head to listen. There was a noise in the undergrowth, twigs snapping. The Count crouched down, and Edith did too, straining to make out the shape of whatever was moving towards them.

They didn't have to wait long. Something large moved into view between the trees.

The Count let out a delighted gasp. "As I was saying, the largest herds of Rotwild – the red deer – in all of Germany."

The deer was magnificent. A huge stag with twelve points on his antlers. As the beast moved forward, parallel with the stream, he too stopped, scenting the air.

"He has smelled us," whispered the Count, his expression one of rapt wonderment as he stared at the creature.

Edith concentrated on reaching her mind out to the deer; this could be a chance to find Arnold.

"Don't be frightened. We're just slightly up the hill from you in the trees."

The stag swung his head sharply in their direction and Edith heard the Count suck in a breath of joyful surprise.

"Sorry to disturb you, but we are looking for my dog. Have you seen him?"

The stag raised his great antlers and stared at them for a moment before responding.

"Stand so I can see you more clearly, girl. And who is that other human with you? Can he too talk to beasts?"

Edith slowly stood.

"Stay down!" hissed the Count, reaching out a hand to clutch at Edith's sleeve. "You'll frighten it away."

"Clearly not," the deer said calmly.

"My dog has gone missing whilst we have been walking in these woods," Edith said, crouching back down to appease the Count.

"I have not seen your dog, but many creatures go missing in this forest, human girl. You should not tarry under these trees when twilight looms."

The stag turned his head again, as if catching a noise that only he could hear.

"There are creatures that abound. Do not dally here; danger approaches. I must go. Good luck in your search. Be gone from here, little one."

The stag suddenly bolted forward, crashing away from them, and the Count rose silently to his feet.

"You startled him," he said accusingly.

"Sorry. I just wanted a better look," Edith replied. She looked anxiously into the trees. *Danger approaches.* How could she warn the Count without explaining her secret?

"He would have made a fine prize for the hunters, a beast as big as him," the Count said bitterly, his eyes lingering on the spot where the stag had disappeared.

"It's hard to imagine there are people who would want to kill an animal like that just for fun."

"They would relish his head as a trophy. Such a waste of exquisite beauty," the Count said quietly.

"We should probably start to head back to the main trail," Edith ventured, her eyes still flicking around the trees.

The Count nodded his assent, and they began to move again.

They had only gone a few more paces when the Count stopped once more.

"There are tracks here, see." The Count spoke in almost a whisper and Edith edged up next to him to see what he was pointing at.

A large paw print was clearly visible in the soft sand by the stream's edge. It looked Arnold-sized and Edith felt a surge of hope in her chest.

"Are there more? Can we track him?"

The Count was lost in thought for a moment, frowning along the edge of the stream.

"It looks like he went into the stream itself," he said at last. "The direction of the paw print suggests he was heading downstream, towards the main river which flows back to the village."

"We should follow him whilst the tracks are still fresh," Edith said, hope surging in her chest.

"We should; we don't

want to risk losing his trail – especially if he has got himself lost. Only we are meant to be meeting your friends back on the main track now," the Count replied.

Edith hesitated. The Doctor would be worrying about her if she missed their rendezvous – but this was too good a lead to pass up. "Following these fresh tracks is our only hope of finding Arnold," she said firmly. "The Doctor will understand and he said that if we don't make the rendezvous, we'd meet back at the Tower. But what sort of creature would Arnold have been chasing that would even go in the water in the first place? It looks very dangerous. I just can't imagine it."

"You are assuming he was the one doing the chasing?" the Count replied levelly. "Not the one being chased?"

Edith's mouth dropped open a little; she hadn't even considered that possibility. Arnold was huge, part Wolfdog. There wasn't much that would be able to chase him – not in Bavaria at any rate. A lion or a tiger might, but they didn't live in Germany.

"Arnold can look after himself. He's bigger than most wolves and Zee-Zee said they haven't been seen here for ages," she said defensively.

"These forests harbour all sorts of creatures, Edith," the Count said softly, shaking his head.

Seeing the expression on Edith's face, the Count

offered her a reassuring smile. "Don't worry, even if he was being chased, he is big and fast. I am sure he is back in the village by now. Shall we continue?"

"Let me just call out," Edith said. "The others might be within earshot." And Edith called out as loudly as she could.

"Doctor, Francis, Zee-Zee!"

Her voice sounded small in the gloom of the forest. She waited, straining to hear some response. Nothing. She was a fool – she had meant to stay within shouting distance of the others. They would be worried. Edith cast a nervous glance towards the Count. The stag had said there was danger approaching—

Just then, there was a crashing noise through the trees. Edith couldn't see what was causing it, but something was clearly moving in their direction.

"We should go," the Count said, alarm his voice.

She cast her eyes around the trees surrounding them.

"Is it more deer, do you think?" Edith asked.

"No, it sounds heavier," the Count replied, tight-lipped, and he reached out a hand to tug at her arm. "It is getting late, and this is no time for us to be out in the forest. Dusk is approaching fast. Let's head downstream, try to find Arnold and meet your uncle back at the Tower."

Without waiting for her response, the Count began

to walk fast, leading Edith along the edge of the stream.

Edith felt a flare of panic. Was the crashing noise caused by the creature that had chased Arnold? She trotted after the Count, consoling herself that if it was, at least it was moving in their direction and not towards any of the others. They were still well ahead of it. It also meant that Arnold had probably got away. They began to follow the water's edge, navigating tree roots and low-hanging branches as they tracked along its edge.

As they progressed, Edith noticed how the stream was getting wider and the water far more turbulent the further they walked. Her feet squelched in the mud at the bank. She imagined Arnold plunging into the cold river and being swept along by its current. She knew he didn't like swimming at the best of times, and what animal would plunge themselves into a freezing-cold torrent of water like that? The big dog must have been running for his life. Had Arnold been leading the creature away from them?

At last, the sound behind faded slightly, and the Count seemed to relax, slowing his pace a fraction.

"What do you think was making that noise?"

"I'm not sure, but I think it was a bear," the Count answered, turning his head to look back into the trees the way they had come.

"A bear? Zee-Zee said they were very rare." Edith was surprised. She hadn't thought of that. A bear would be able to chase Arnold. That would also explain why the stag was so nervous, Edith thought, glancing again at the rushing water.

"Rare doesn't mean they don't roam here, Edith, just that we don't see them very much," the Count replied.

He moved forward again, silent as ever. As she followed, Edith tried to replicate the Count's quiet movement, placing her feet evenly and trying to distribute her weight with each step. If they didn't make any noise, they wouldn't draw the attention of whatever creature was behind them. She sighed in frustration as she slipped on a root, her foot landing on a heavy stick that gave an audible crack as it broke.

"Owwww!" a voice sounded in her head.

Edith looked down. It was hard to see what had made the noise.

"You're so clumsy!"

"Sorry," Edith thought, still unsure of what she was speaking to. She seemed to be apologizing to every animal she met.

"You can understand me? What are the chances of that?! Doesn't excuse you being so clumsy, though. I'm going to need some help here."

Edith strained her eyes, scanning the forest floor and trying to discern where the voice was coming from. The Count, unaware Edith had stopped, had carried on walking.

Edith was about to call out to the Count to ask him to wait, but just as she opened her mouth, she saw a movement under a pile of wet leaves.

Half of the heavy stick lay across a squirming little creature, the weight of it pinning it to the ground. Peering down, she could just about make a small green body, about five centimetres long, with prominent dark spots along its back. Its surface seemed to be bumpy and Edith couldn't help but smile as two high-set eyes peered up at her with heart-shaped black pupils. It looked like a frog.

"Did I hurt you?"

"Well, it's not ideal to be crushed under a stick. Are you going to move it or just gawp?"

Edith quickly bent down and lifted the stick.

"Sorry, little frog," she said.

"Did you just call me a frog? A frog? I am a fire-bellied toad! Look!"

Edith peered as the little creature lifted a front leg to expose some bright orange spots spreading down under its belly.

"*Oooooo, I shouldn't have done that — it hurts!*" he said.

"*Is anything broken?*" Edith asked, concerned.

"*It's a sprain, I think, but I won't be doing much hopping tonight. Nine years I've waited to make this journey and only an hour into my expedition and look what's happened.*"

"*You're nine years old?*"

"*Ten. I only decided I would go exploring after I had turned one. But now I can't move. I think it's a full-body sprain.*"

There was a loud crash somewhere behind her and Edith twisted around in alarm. Turning back towards the stream, she could no longer see any sign of the Count ahead. She cursed herself for getting distracted and not calling out to ask him to wait. She looked back down at the injured toad and made a decision. "*I know people who can help you recuperate and then bring you back here when you are recovered. You'll need to trust me, OK?*"

"*Well…*"

Edith didn't wait for a response but reached out to pluck the little creature from the ground.

"*Are you wearing gloves?*" the toad said.

Edith hesitated. "*No.*"

"*My skin is a bit toxic, not my fault, so don't judge. But use some leaves. Hurry up or that thing crashing towards us will have us for dinner!"*

Edith glanced again over her shoulder. *"Do you think it's a bear?"*

"Let's hope you hurry up and neither of us find out," replied the toad.

The crashing noise sounded again, this time much closer. Edith didn't waste a second more, deftly scooping up the toad and thrusting him, along with a pile of wet leaves, into her pocket.

"Right, run for it!" croaked her new friend, his voice muffled from the depths of her pocket.

There was an almighty cracking of a branch and Edith heard what she thought was a low growl. With a gasp of alarm, she began to run. Whatever was behind her, it didn't sound friendly.

Edith surged forward along the riverbank.

"I think you'll need to go a bit quicker," said the toad unhelpfully.

Edith didn't think the Count could be too far ahead. Surely, he would have realized she had fallen behind and would be waiting for her up ahead...

"It's been very busy in the forest this afternoon — everything dashing about," complained the toad.

"You didn't see a dog, did you?" Edith panted.

"I heard something go past, I was under a leaf at the time, but I saw a stag," the toad replied.

Edith almost lost her footing.

"Both running the same way we're going now, although I imagine the stag would have veered off. They generally don't fare so well around the villagers, if you get my drift. Whatever the first animal was, it sounded like it was more stumbling than running, but the stag was moving like the wind itself."

If it was Arnold, at least he had been heading back towards the village. Edith felt a surge of hope. He must have been chased out of the forest, but why was he stumbling?

It took them a few more minutes before the trees started to thin out and Edith realized they were almost back at the village. She could no longer hear the crashing sound of the creature pursuing her, but she kept jogging just in case. If it hadn't been such a fraught dash, she would have been able to appreciate the amazing beauty of the river, winding its way to the picturesque hamlet, all set in the backdrop of such a stunning forest. Moving out from under the last of the branches, light once again reached the ground and the water sparkled beside them.

Edith felt sweat run down her cheek as she saw the arch of the huge wooden bridge clearly visible ahead of them. This was where Arnold would have climbed up the bank, she thought. Then, to her relief, she saw the outline of the Count at the top of the slope.

"Edith, there you are! I was just about to come back and look for you. What happened, are you all right?" he squeaked as Edith struggled up the bank to meet him.

"I, er, slipped on a tree root," she replied, then dipped her hand into her pocket and pulled out the little toad on his bed of leaves.

"Are you OK after that little run?" she thought to the toad.

"It's not been the best late afternoon so far but I'm hoping it will pick up," said the toad bravely. *"Certainly not hopping, that's for sure."*

"Ahhh," the Count said. He was leaning forward, staring with fascination at the little creature. "A fire-bellied toad!"

"He got crushed by a stick I snapped when I slipped. I haven't learnt about amphibians yet. I was going to ask my uncle to take a look at him. I don't think he is hurt too badly, but it was a nasty squash."

The toad blinked as it was lifted from the pocket amongst his pile of dirty wet leaves and took in the Count, the Tower and the village beyond.

The Count beamed at the little creature. "Why don't

I look after him? He can come to my hospital and then your uncle and Zee-Zee's mother can both help him. Fire-bellied toads have the most amazing skin, you know."

Edith hesitated a moment, but the Count had already reached out to take the toad, using a thin silken handkerchief to scoop it from her hands. Perhaps he would be better able to help the creature than her, Edith thought.

"*What is going on?!*" asked the toad, alarmed at the sudden handover.

"*It's OK, this is the Count, he helps injured wildlife. He said you can stay in his hospital. Get your strength back. It'll be a better place than our hotel room. Listen, what's your name?*"

"*Terry,*" replied the toad.

"*I'm Edie. The Count will look after you, Terry, I promise.*"

"Excuse me, Edith?" ventured the Count. "But are you all right?"

Edith realized she had been staring fixedly at the Count's pocket as she communicated with the toad.

"Yes, just glad I didn't flatten him completely. Thank you for taking him in. He was just by the river, about five hundred metres or so back along the stream. We can hopefully release him in a day or two. I don't think any bones are broken..."

"Oh yes, he'll be fine and, if he is fit to be released, we'll do just that," the Count said, patting his pocket gently.

"*Steady on!*" came Terry's muffled voice from deep inside the cloth, wobbling with the impact.

"Oh, and I almost forgot," said the Count. "I saw a snag of Arnold's hair on the brambles down by the river's edge, and I am sure he has run back to the village. You'll find him there, I'm certain of it." The Count cast a worried look around. "Edith, I know we are out of the forest but I think we should go inside the Tower. We should wait for the others there. It is starting to get dark. Not that *I'm* scared, you understand –" he gave a little shudder – "but I'm worried about you."

"But the Doctor, Francis and Zee-Zee – they can only be minutes away."

"Whatever was following us, we don't want to draw it closer, do we? We're still on the wrong side of the bridge here. I will leave the door light on so your uncle can hurry straight towards it. I am sure any creature would think twice before crossing your giant friend, but us ... well..." The Count spread his hands apologetically. "I don't think I would be much of a deterrent, do you?"

"*You are with me in your pocket,*" came Terry's muffled

voice. *"I'm toxic!"*

Edith grinned at hearing the little toad, despite a creeping feeling of unease. Something didn't feel right. Where on earth could the others be, and where was Arnold? Had he really run all the way back to the guest house?

Edith tried to clear her mind. If she could somehow communicate with Arnold, she would know if he had made it back to the village. She wasn't sure how far her powers extended, but if he was in the village, he might hear her.

"Arnold, can you hear me?"

No response. She screwed her eyes up and tried again.

"Arnold, please answer … can you hear me?"

"Edie … don't…" The faintest thought entered Edith's mind and her eyes snapped open in both relief and shock.

"Arnold – are you here? Where are you? We'll be back at the guest house soon!"

Nothing.

What had Arnold been trying to tell her – not to worry, perhaps? Either way, he was safe. She grinned at the Count. "I think you're right," she said. "We followed the trail here. Arnold must have made it back."

The Count smiled back. "In that case, let's get inside

and wait for the others to catch up."

Moments later, Edith found herself swept along in the Count's silent wake, the door to the old church opening up to welcome them into the building.

CHAPTER SEVEN

*In which the Doctor, Francis and Zee-Zee
make their way back to the Tower, unaware
of a new danger lurking in the trees...*

"Where is she?" The Doctor tutted impatiently.

Having completed a big loop, Zee-Zee and the Doctor had circled round back on to the main path, where they had met Francis. The big man's face had been bleak as he shook his head and shrugged his massive shoulders.

"Edie, where are you?" Francis's shout seemed to be swallowed up by the forest.

There was nothing but silence.

"They were supposed to stay in earshot," the Doctor complained.

"The Count knows the forest almost better than the villagers who were born here," said Zee-Zee. "Edie will be OK."

The Doctor nodded, frustration clearly etched on his face. He lifted his cap and scratched his head.

"Right, let's head back and meet them at the Tower. Perhaps they found some sign of Arnold and have tracked him."

The three of them trudged down the track. There didn't seem to be any point in calling any more; even the birds seemed to have stopped their tweeting.

"When the sun dips below the treeline, it gets dark here very quickly," said Zee-Zee.

"Hmmm," the Doctor said, pausing for a moment to stare off to the left intently.

"Doctor?" rumbled Francis.

The Doctor continued to stare into the trees for a good few more seconds before shaking his head.

"I thought I saw something moving over there."

Francis and Zee-Zee both peered in the direction the Doctor indicated.

"Perhaps it was a fox?" Zee-Zee ventured.

"It looked bigger than that, but whatever it was, it's not there now."

The Doctor gestured ahead and the three of them

resumed walking.

In a few minutes they were approaching the treeline marking the edge of the forest. Beyond, they could see the old church with its big tower, the lights all switched on and welcoming.

"It looks like they are back, Doctor," said Francis, sounding relieved.

"I hope they found Arnold," said Zee-Zee.

The Doctor strode forward eagerly, the others close on his heels. As they came within a few hundred metres, Edith's face appeared at a ground-floor window. She gave them a big wave before disappearing and, a moment later, the door to the old part of the church swung open. Edith ran out on to the path.

"Uncle, Francis, Zee-Zee! I was worried!" Edith called, jogging towards them.

"Edie, there you are, my de—" The Doctor's exclamation cut off in mid-sentence and his eyes widened in shock.

Edith came to a sudden stop as she saw Francis transform. His kind face had become a mask of focused fury and the big man suddenly rushed towards her. As she tried to understand what was going on, Francis barrelled past, and Edith turned to watch him, gasping in horror.

Halfway between the old church entrance and where she now stood, a terrifying creature had appeared on the path behind her. It looked like some sort of giant bear, only it looked more beast than bear, its face somehow distorted. Edith watched as the mountainous form of Francis slammed into it.

The beast was standing up on its hind legs, bear-like, and was easily as tall and bulky as Francis. Both were now locked in a vicious embrace, the massive Viking bellowing a roar of defiant anger as he strained to halt the creature's attack.

"Francis!" Edith called desperately.

"Edie – come to me, quickly," commanded the Doctor, signalling her to get behind him whilst gesturing for Zee-Zee to stay back.

Francis grunted as he reached out a meaty hand to grip at one of the creature's paws. Blocking a downward slash, he just about prevented the beast's razor-sharp claws raking at his chest. His muscles were straining with the effort, and Edith watched as Francis adjusted his stance, spreading his feet wide as he fought to keep balance.

With an audible heave, Francis pushed back against the creature's weight, using the momentary space he had gained to strike into the beast's throat with his free hand. The creature reeled backwards with the impact, stunned for a second, but recovered with phenomenal speed to then hurl itself with renewed anger at poor Francis. The bear-like creature was larger and more fierce than Edith could have imagined – only...

"No!" Edith shouted, realizing with horror what was different about it. It was a creature conjured from the depths of her wildest nightmares. Whilst the beast attacking Francis had the form, size and strength of a bear, it appeared to have the head of a wolf. As she watched, she could see its jaws working ferociously to snap and snarl at Francis, fangs bared centimetres from his face.

Those teeth came perilously close and Francis twisted away – giving the creature the opportunity to strike with its other paw, tearing at the skin on his arm, sharp claws raking through his flesh. A grimace of pain flashed across Francis's expression, and Edith heard him draw a sharp intake of breath.

Ignoring the pain from the now-bleeding wound, Francis closed the distance once more, stepping inside the creature's reach. He wasn't a trained fighter, but his experience of handling wild animals was unparalleled and he was colossally strong. Looping his massive arms around the beast and ensuring he was within the arc of its lacerating claws, Francis gave a mighty shove forward, propelling them both back towards the Tower.

Francis was fighting for his life, Edith thought, feeling utterly helpless. If they could somehow raise the alarm, maybe the villagers could come and help. She looked across at her uncle, who was clearly thinking the same. But before they could do anything, the creature gave a roar of frustration and slammed its head downwards. As Edith watched, the creature opened its jaws and sank its teeth deep into Francis's shoulder. The big man bellowed in shocked response.

The Doctor yelled, throwing caution to the wind, and ran forward to help his friend. The creature, tasting blood, pulled its head back, baring bloodied teeth as if about to bite again, but something seemed to make it pause. Instead of striking down a second time, the creature hesitated. Edith watched the creature tremble slightly. Almost as if it was doing battle with itself.

Francis took full advantage, pulling the beast back towards him, throwing it off balance. Edith saw him grit his teeth, and with a demonstration of Herculean power, he proceeded to heave the creature on to his hip and then hurled both himself and the creature off the path. Together, they hit the incline of the bank beyond.

Entwined as they were, the two combatants promptly began to roll down towards the water's edge. The Doctor, bounding ahead, followed them, his cape flying behind him as he chased after the pair of battling giants. A sudden realization of what her uncle was trying to prevent made Edith gasp. It was clear he was going to be too late.

Edith watched, horrified, as Francis and the creature careered down the bank and, with an almighty splash, rolled straight over its lip and plunged into the river below. Edith's stomach lurched in panic. She dashed after the Doctor and, with Zee-Zee at her heels, ran towards the river.

As Francis and the creature hit the water, the shock of the impact combined with the icy chill forced them apart. Momentarily dropping out of sight beneath the surface, they both fought to thrust themselves upwards. The battle was no longer with each other, it was with the current. Desperate for air, their heads broke the surface.

Then, with a roar of protest, the creature was swept downstream ahead of Francis.

To the observers on the bank, it was clear that getting Francis out of the river was not going to be a simple endeavour. Edith had witnessed the strength of the current when she had played Poohsticks on the bridge with Zee-Zee. Whilst he was nearer the bank than the creature had been, Edith could still see the fast-flowing current had him snagged as he battled to get back to dry land.

"Swim to the side, Francis, avoid the middle of the river!" she shouted desperately.

"Uncle, we need something to throw to him or he'll be taken by the current!"

The Doctor, casting around frantically for something with which to help the big man, seized upon a long branch, which he swung out over the racing water.

"Francis, grab the branch!" the Doctor shouted,

leaning out as far as he could.

With a tremendous effort, fighting against the pull of the relentless current, Francis stretched out one hand. Just as it seemed as if it was beyond his reach, he kicked out. As the the tips of his fingers touched the wood, the Doctor, with a groan of his own, stretched another few centimetres and, suddenly, Francis had grasped the branch.

"Well done, Francis, now hold on and we'll pull you in." The Doctor's voice was heavy with strain. The effort of holding the branch with the weight of Francis on the end of it was immense.

"Edith, Zee-Zee – come over here and help me pull!"

Jolted into action, Edith and Zee-Zee both ran to help. Each grabbing a part of the branch, the three of them started to pull Francis towards the edge of the river.

The current was unyielding, and it tugged at the big man's wet clothes. Francis's face screwed up with the effort of holding on.

"Hold on, Francis, we've got you!" Edith shouted encouragingly, noticing that, whilst Francis had managed to get a proper grip on the branch with one arm, his other hung limp and useless in the water from the damaged shoulder.

They inched backwards, pulling Francis inexorably

towards the bank as the current tugged him in the other direction.

"Kick as hard as you can!" the Doctor called, and Francis's legs moved a little in response, the last of his great strength almost spent.

It seemed to take an age, but finally Francis was half dragged, half levered up on to the bank, and they all sank to the ground exhausted.

Francis lay on his back, his chest heaving and his eyes closed in pain and exhaustion.

"You saved my life," Edith said, looking at the torn tunic and the ruin of Francis's shoulder. Fresh blood oozed out of his wounds and Edith felt a pang of worry. Thanks to Francis, she was unhurt, and now he lay on the ground gravely injured.

"If you hadn't blocked it from getting to Edie, goodness knows what would have happened," the Doctor said, examining Francis's wounds. "You did us proud, Francis, at great personal risk. You saved all of us. Thank you."

"No, Doctor," Francis replied. "The creature, whatever it was, it could have bitten me on my head – it didn't. It didn't want to kill me."

"What do you mean? It wasn't exactly trying to tickle you, was it?"

Francis shook his head, slowly rolling on to his knees and casting a look downstream.

"It bit my shoulder and then hesitated. Almost as if it didn't want to bite me again."

The Doctor glanced at Edith and Zee-Zee.

"Did either of you see that?"

"Yes," replied Zee-Zee. "It *did* seem to hesitate."

"I saw it too, Uncle," said Edith.

"Hmmmmmm," said the Doctor, tapping his chin thoughtfully and then looking up at the Tower, which loomed above them.

"What was that creature?" asked Zee-Zee.

The question hung in the air for a moment. The Doctor's face was ashen, and he shared an anguished look with Francis.

"It was a wolpertinger. A fusion of beasts," the Doctor said quietly.

"One of the creatures that the owl talked about?" Edith said.

"The very same, Edie." The words came out as a whisper. The Doctor turned his gaze on Edith and she couldn't remember his expression ever being so serious and worried.

"It must be the creature that was following us in the woods earlier," Edith said. "It was behind me and the

Count. That's why we had to run back to the Tower. We thought it was a bear that was following us."

"Do you think it got Arnold?" Zee-Zee asked worriedly.

"No. Arnold's alive!" Edith said quickly. "He's somewhere in the village. I heard him – just a few words, but he's alive."

The Doctor nodded.

"At least we have that to hold on to," he said.

"Maybe that creature took the phoenix, though?" Zee-Zee said.

"Wouldn't it just eat the phoenix rather than capture it?" Edith said.

The Doctor shook his head.

"I have no idea, Edie. Whilst it's said they have some free will, wolpertingers are controlled by their creators. It may well…"

Footsteps made them look round. The Count was hurrying towards them.

"Are you all right?" he asked shrilly. "I heard all the shouting. What happened?"

"It came out of nowhere," Edith replied. "Did you see the beast and Francis fighting? Francis saved me."

The Count slid down the last bit of the bank, his hood pulling back to reveal a sheen of sweat on his shaved, pale head.

"I was putting our new toad friend in his cage and feeding the other animals in the hospital when I heard the commotion. I came as soon as I could but all I saw was Francis and the animal fall into the river. Was it a bear?"

"Of sorts," the Doctor said.

The Count crouched down, examining Francis's wounds.

"There was a sighting of a brown bear a couple of months ago. Perhaps it is the same one?" the Count continued.

Edith was about to speak, but she noticed the Doctor give the slightest, almost imperceptible shake of his head. She closed her mouth, pushing what she had been about to say back into her throat.

"It must have been the same bear that was tracking us, Edith. We're lucky it didn't catch us in the forest. Most likely the same one that chased Arnold," the Count said, looking up at Edith.

She nodded, remembering the rustles in the forest. Edith shuddered at the thought of what might have been.

"We must get Francis to safety and tend to those wounds properly," the Doctor said.

Francis raised his hand as if to brush the Doctor's

worry aside, but quickly lowered it again to steady himself. He swayed, unable to get to his feet from a kneeling position, clearly struggling to maintain even that.

"Let's head to the guest house before that beast gets itself out of the water and comes back to find us," the Doctor continued. "Bears are excellent swimmers and it might have washed up a little further downstream. Hopefully, Arnold will have found his way back to the village as well by now. Edie, see if you can call him. He always comes to your voice."

The Count frowned at that, and Edith flushed, understanding what the Doctor meant.

"He won't hear me from down here, Uncle. I'll call him from the bridge," she said hurriedly, with a small nod to show she would try to call Arnold again telepathically.

"I'm sure you'll find he's made his way home," the Count said softly. He smiled at her for a moment as if thinking of something, then turned back to help Francis.

With all four of them lending their strength, they managed to heave Francis to his feet. The big man didn't speak, his lips a thin line as he tried to support himself.

"Hold on to me Francis, you cannot walk unaided," the Doctor said, tucking himself under Francis uninjured arm to take some of his weight. He looked over at the

Count. "I fear it's best if you lock your doors, Count. The beast will come prowling back to the forest once it gets out of the river."

"Do you need help to get back?"

The Doctor shook his head, "Very kind of you, but the three of us can help Francis. Otherwise you will then have to walk back alone."

The Count nodded, he seemed slightly relieved, the same concern clearly having occurred to him as well.

"I am sure the villagers will lead a bear hunt for the beast tomorrow. The forest is no longer safe."

"When word gets out about this attack, everyone will be in uproar. If tourists are frightened to come in the summer, it will be a disaster," Zee-Zee said, looking worried.

"The irony is that tourists like to see bears, no matter what the danger," the Count replied. "It may well have the opposite effect and people will flock here. That said, it was probably just passing through. It is a rare sighting indeed. It will most likely be gone from the area tomorrow."

No one said anything further. Even the Doctor, with his relentless energy, looked exhausted. Bidding the Count goodnight, they huddled around Francis.

It was strange, Edith thought, if anything, Francis

seemed weaker than he had when he had first got out of the river.

"We need to get you inside, Francis, one final effort tonight, my friend," the Doctor said.

Summoning the last of his great strength, the big man gritted his teeth and together they inched back to the Plucky Guest House.

CHAPTER EIGHT

In which Edith and her friends take Francis
back to recover, but Arnold has not returned
and an old adversary arrives at the lodge…

By the time they had got Francis back to the guest house, he was almost unconscious. There had been no sign of Arnold either, despite Edith calling out to him with her mind. She had managed to get a couple of snatches of response from him, but nothing to make much sense of. Zee-Zee had bid them a quick farewell, promising to check around the back of the lodge and keep an eye out for the big dog as he performed his guest house duties, leaving the Doctor and Edith to attend to Francis.

"Will he be all right?" Edith asked, watching Francis

as he lay prone on the bed, the Doctor tucking some pillows under his head.

"I think so," the Doctor said, casting a professional eye over his friend. "Although he's very weak."

Edith nodded. "And Arnold?"

"At least we know he's alive. That creature won't venture into the village itself, so as long as Arnold made it back here, he'll be safe," the Doctor said confidently.

"I can only get a couple of words from him. The connection is too weak to last. I can't get him to tell me where he is," Edith said helplessly.

"He could well be dozing behind someone's thick walls," her uncle said reassuringly. "A friendly villager may have let him in their house for the night. He's probably curled up in front of a warm fire waiting for daybreak so he can come and find us in the morning."

Edith nodded, grateful for the kind words but knowing her uncle would be as worried as she was. It was a vain hope. Arnold would have come straight to find them if he could, she was sure of that. Something wasn't right.

She turned her attention back to Francis, the mattress sagging desperately under his weight. He seemed to be breathing more rapidly than ever and all the colour had drained from his exhausted face.

The Doctor frowned in concern as he studied the injuries, before swiftly cutting away the wet and torn clothing to expose his wounds. He reached for his case of medicines and equipment.

Anticipating what her uncle would need next, Edith ran to the bathroom to fill a bowl with clean water. When she returned, the Doctor quickly began to bathe and clean the torn skin.

"Uncle, there's something I need to tell you," she said as he worked. "The Count said there were a group of hunters that come here. A group that talk about trying to capture the phoenix and are led by a woman with flame-red hair."

The Doctor gave a low hiss.

"We suspected the Syndicate were behind this, Edie. Whether they have been successful in capturing the phoenix and are making the wolpertingers remains to be seen, but that seems proof enough that they are somehow involved."

"Why do they do this, Uncle? What makes them so evil?"

"Money, greed, a thirst for power. Perhaps an obsession with nature. I don't know, my dear; all I do know is that they must be thwarted. If we don't stop them, no one will. Arabella and her killers will continue

to hunt and kill the most precious animals on the planet."
The Doctor gave a little tut. "Pass me that tincture,
please, Edie; we must soothe these lacerations as best
we can."

"The wounds look deep," Edith said, quickly handing
the Doctor the pot he indicated, whilst carefully stepping
around the discarded clumps of blood-soaked swabs that
now adorned the wooden floor.

"Very deep and very savage," the Doctor replied, his
brow furrowed in concentration.

"Are you going to stitch them?"

"Injuries from claws and teeth are often best left
to heal naturally. In many ways the river has helped; it
has washed away much of the filth from the bites and
scratches – but still, these types of wounds are prone
to infection. We dare not trap any bits of dirt or cloth
inside. The wounds will need to drain freely of their
own accord."

The Doctor dabbed at Francis's wounds before
beginning to layer dressings over each laceration. Finally,
he administered several injections to his uninjured upper
arm. Stepping back, the Doctor appraised his work with
a critical eye.

"I have no doubt Betty would have made a neater
job of the bandaging, but that should do. Wolf bites are

notoriously painful, but not as nasty as a nip from a lion or even a pet squirrel, for that matter..." The Doctor's voice tailed off, eyes fixed on Francis's damaged shoulder.

"What's worrying you, Uncle?"

The Doctor bit his lip.

"I don't think this is an ordinary wolf bite."

"But the creature that attacked Francis, it had the head of a wolf and the body of a bear – surely it must be a wolf bite?"

"It's not a typical wolf wound, Edie, and I've seen enough of them. Goodness knows how many lacerated unicorns we've had to treat over the years. Do you remember that outbreak in Mongolia, Francis?"

Francis's eyes fluttered open momentarily and he grimaced in pain, managing a weak nod.

"It was a small herd that was attacked by a pack of wolves in the Mongolian foothills about six years ago," the Doctor continued. "We had to treat a huge number of injuries. Mind you, the unicorns gave a good enough account of themselves, considering the number of wolves we ended up helping as well. Nasty business, being impaled by a unicorn horn. I suspect unicorn foal was off the menu for the wolf pack after that little skirmish." The Doctor leaned forward and pointed to an area of skin just below the bandage. "Do you see here, Edie?"

Edith looked. Instead of the pale whiteness of flesh, a spiderweb of black pigmentation had spread across the underside of Francis's injured arm.

"What does it mean?"

"It means it is poisoned," Francis said simply, his eyes half closed again and his voice weak. "My arm is dying."

Edith gasped and the Doctor nodded solemnly.

"With the way poor Francis must be feeling, I am sure he has already realized. He has been poisoned by something. That wolpertinger was not only a fusion between a bear and a wolf – there must be another creature in the mix."

"But what could it be?"

"If the wolf head had poisonous fangs, that would explain it. This injury has all the hallmarks of venom from a snake bite."

"A snake!" Edith exclaimed.

The Doctor shook his head heavily. "Whoever created that poor creature is an abomination of mankind. A bear and a wolf is bad enough, but to fuse in the fangs of a snake as well … it beggars belief!"

"But you can give Francis an antidote for a snake bite, can't you, Uncle?"

"Oh yes, Edie, absolutely. We must! Without an antivenom, the poison will continue to spread throughout his body unchecked. But the question is, what type of venom is it? The wrong antivenom could make the condition worse."

Francis shifted in the bed and winced. "Does it hurt?" Edith said.

"Not so bad, Edie. Don't worry. The Doctor will find the cure."

Francis tried to give Edith a small, reassuring smile, but Edith could see his eyelids drooping completely shut again and, within moments, he was asleep.

Edith turned to look at her uncle questioningly.

"One of the injections I gave him was a sedative to help him sleep," the Doctor explained. "He needs to rest, and we need to make sure he remains calm – any agitation will only make things worse. Edie, if we don't understand what poison we are dealing with, the only option might be to remove Francis's arm to stop it taking hold and spreading through his body. The worst case…"

The Doctor paused and met Edith's eye.

"What is the worst case, Uncle?" she said.

"The worst case is the unthinkable – so I am not prepared to think it, let alone speak it out loud."

There was a silence in the room for a moment and Edith didn't know what to say. An icy fear gripped her heart. She couldn't bear to contemplate what the Doctor was implying.

The Doctor cleared his throat. "Logic is what we need, my dear. We can but assume the wolpertinger was a fusion of animals found in the forest, that the snake used was a local one. Perhaps the fangs were an afterthought by the creator of the wolpertinger, a poisonous snake that was chanced upon in the forest and added to the mix. As far as I have read from some ancient texts, the animals fuse best when they have been freshly killed, the parts attached within hours of their death and then the ashes from the phoenix mixed before the 'creation' is regenerated as a single creature. If we can determine the type of snake used, I can make the antivenom." The Doctor sighed. "Oh, how I wish Betty was here. Francis needs medical attention – I dare not leave him."

"We don't both need to stay with Francis, Uncle," Edith said softly.

The Doctor looked up sharply.

"You should remain with him to keep him stable, and I can go and find the snake."

Edith said the words before she had thought about it. But as soon as she spoke, she knew it was the right thing to do. It was instinctive – whatever it took, she knew she would do it if she could save Francis.

The Doctor cursed with a sudden vehemence that made Edith jump and paced to the end of the bed, resting his hand on the brass bedstand. It was the only piece of furniture in the room not made of wood and he eyed it in mild surprise for a moment, before drumming his fingers on the smooth polished surface. After he had taken a few deep breaths, he seemed to calm a little.

"It will be dangerous. If Arabella and her killers *are* in the area, it could be more than just avoiding monsters in the forest."

"I know, but you have to stay here to keep Francis alive. There's no other choice."

Francis was in this predicament because he had been saving her. She couldn't just stand by helpless. Edith fixed her uncle with a fierce look. She was going to help.

Her uncle shook his head. "Oh, Edie, I am constantly putting you in peril. I am supposed to be your guardian, yet all I seem to do is put you in dangerous situations!"

Edith offered her uncle a small smile. "Francis only got bitten because he was protecting me. I have to help him, and we have to find Arnold." Edith's voice sounded small, and she felt tears pricking at the corners of her eyes.

The Doctor's face crinkled at the edges as he regarded his niece.

"You are a remarkable girl, Edie. Remember the yetis? Remember when all hope seemed lost?"

Edith nodded, bravely smiling at her uncle.

"You cured the sick one, found the root of the problem, all without me. We found a way to get through that, didn't we?"

Edith remembered the desperate chase on the mountain, how they had been forced to split up, the fact the yeti had come so close to death. And yet, her uncle was right: everything had been OK.

"There is always a way. Light and shadow never stay still! It seems dark now, but we can get through this. You have Wilma's spirit and strength in you. I can see it!"

Edith swallowed at the mention of her dead aunt's name. She had never met her aunt Wilma – she hadn't even known she'd had one until last summer – and yet, they'd had so much in common. Like Edith, Wilma had been a telepathic polyglot.

Edith felt a sense of disquiet and glanced at the slumbering form of Francis. She thought of Arnold, lost somewhere close but out of reach. She had to save them both, she just had to.

A sense of steely resolve washed through her, and her uncle must have sensed it because his face broke into a half-smile.

"That's my girl, Edie."

There was a soft knock at the door. The two of them looked at each other.

The Doctor held up his hand and moved quickly behind the wooden frame.

"We can't be too careful, Edie; we know there is a strangeness in this forest at night."

The soft tapping repeated itself. With a nod from her uncle, Edith cautiously opened the door a crack and peered out.

Zee-Zee stood in the hallway, his face ashen and his hair dishevelled.

"There is no sign of Arnold outside," he said. "But how is Francis?"

Edith ushered him into the room, shutting the door behind them.

"He's in a bad way," she said, gesturing at the prone figure on the bed.

Zee-Zee looked at Edith and the Doctor in alarm.

"The next twelve hours are vital," the Doctor explained, walking around the bed to stand by Francis. "We need to delay the poison spreading through his body and gain ourselves time to make the antivenom."

"Poison?" Zee-Zee asked, confused.

"The creature that fought with Francis wasn't simply

a fused hybrid of a bear and a wolf – it was also part snake. The fangs of the snake injected Francis with a venom which is coursing through his body."

Zee-Zee's mouth dropped open and his eyes flicked to Francis and back again. "Will he survive?"

"He will if we can give him some antivenom," the Doctor replied.

"We think it must be a snake found in the forest – when wolpertingers are created, fresh specimens of animals are needed, so they will have been caught locally... I'm going to find the snake so we can make an antidote," Edith said with a confidence she didn't entirely feel.

"There are only two poisonous snakes in Bavaria," Zee-Zee said. "The European adder and the European aspis viper."

"That's my boy!" exclaimed the Doctor, beaming.

"And it's much more likely to be the *Vipera aspis*," Zee-Zee added.

"How come?" Edith replied.

"Whilst there are only a few of them in this part of the forest, they are more dangerous than the adder. If Francis is really sick, it must be that."

The Doctor nodded approvingly at Zee-Zee's logic. "Adder bites can be extremely serious to the young or very old – but Francis is neither and I doubt an adder bite would pull him down so much. I think it's got to be the viper. Have you ever seen any in the forest?" he asked.

Zee-Zee shook his head. "I know where they live, though. When we moved to the village, the locals warned us to keep away from the place."

"Is it far?" Edith asked.

"Not too far – it's near the bat roost at the bottom of the next valley along. A cave."

As soon as Zee-Zee said it, Edith's mind went back to the caves she had visited on her previous expedition with the Doctor. Somehow, she knew this one would be very different.

"Can you draw me a map?"

"No need," said Zee-Zee, his eyes meeting hers. "I am coming with you."

They looked at each other for a moment, Edith momentarily lost for words.

"It will be safer with two of us," Zee-Zee explained. "But Doctor, can we not take Francis to the hospital? They would have antivenom there."

"It's a good thought, Zee-Zee," the Doctor said. "But we are so remote here. I'm afraid Francis wouldn't survive the journey, any movement is dangerous – and, besides, his wound doesn't look like a snake bite. No hospital would ever give him the antivenom without proof he was bitten by a poisonous snake, and how could we explain what happened? They would never believe us! No, we must make the antivenom ourselves. Once we have obtained some of the venom I will need to dilute it down, make the venom weak enough so that when I inject it into myself—"

"Inject it into yourself?" Edith couldn't help interrupting, shocked by what the Doctor was describing.

The Doctor gave her a grim smile. "It's the only way, Edie. I need a weakened form of the venom to trigger my immune system without making me too sick. It's a delicate business. My body will create antibodies and then, by taking a sample of my blood, I can extract the serum and from that … make the antivenom. It is all we can do."

The Doctor raised his hand to wearily rub his eyes. He once again looked tired beyond words. He cleared his throat.

"Right now, you must both get a few hours' sleep. None of us can venture into the forest at night so you must depart at first light. You'll need all your strength tomorrow – our friends are depending on us."

"But…"

"No buts, Edie; you must sleep. A few hours at least.

You can't go into the forest again now. It is too dangerous by far."

Edith wanted to protest but the Doctor held up a hand. "You'll move faster when you can see where you're going and it will be far safer. In the meantime, I must do some reading on antivenoms, wolpertingers, and give Francis some more medication."

"What if a wolpertinger comes here, to the lodge, whilst Zee-Zee and I are gone?" Edith asked.

"Remember what the Count said. If the public knew they existed, they would be hunted and killed. Therefore, they roam in the darkness. We'll keep the doors locked and we'll be safe at dawn. Wolpertingers are not nature's beasts, Edie. They are man-made. As such, they will have their own limitations. I have read that some cannot go out in daylight, others live but only for a few months, and they all need prolonged periods of rest. They can only be active for short bursts of time. I suspect that the creature that dear Francis fought so bravely will take a significant time to recover after such an intense bout of activity. My suspicion, Edie, and it is just a suspicion, is that the creatures are only active for a few hours each time they are unleashed. Outside of those hours, they will be sleeping."

"So you mean they don't function like normal animals?"

"Exactly, my dear; they are as imperfect as their looks would suggest. It takes many attempts to achieve a perfect fusion of beasts, and judging from the one we saw today, whoever made that wolpertinger is far from perfecting the art. Those creatures, those poor, poor creatures, are unlikely to live long. When do you see a bear, a wolf and a snake together in the wild, Edie? Never! And for good reason. Those animals have been forced into a single being, each of them tormented by being trapped in a body that isn't their own."

"Who made them, Uncle? Do you think it was the Syndicate?" She didn't want it to be the Syndicate, she didn't want to have to face them again, but someone was behind this, and whoever it was had to be stopped.

The Doctor shook his head, a great tide of sorrow washing through him. "I don't know, Edie. I don't know. It is likely our old foe is behind this. We know they come here to hunt; it is the sort of depravity Arabella would stoop to."

With a glance at the huge but softly snoring form of Francis, the Doctor gently pulled open the door of the room. He gestured to Edith and Zee-Zee that they should leave.

"Time for bed. It will be a big day tomorrow. Oh, and Edie?"

"Yes, Uncle?"

"You must be careful talking with snakes. In my experience, they can't always be trusted..."

The Doctor held Edith's gaze for a moment.

"I'll be careful, Uncle."

"Please make sure you are, my dear."

Bidding the Doctor a quick goodnight, Zee-Zee and Edith stepped into the corridor. They stood for a moment in silence. There was so much to take in.

"We'll find the venom tomorrow. We can put all this right. Whatever it takes," Zee-Zee said at last.

"What do *Vipera aspis* eat, by the way?" Edith mused. "I'm guessing it's not children?"

"I hope not!" Zee-Zee gave a laugh. "I'm pretty sure they eat bats."

"Let's hope we don't go batty trying to find the snakes!"

It was a weak joke, but they both laughed, keen to dispel the tension between them and headed to their rooms.

Edith sat silently on the bed. Her mind raced and her stomach churned. There was no way she could sleep. The doubts and fears of what might happen gnawed at her and she stared at the floor, fighting a sudden sense of hopelessness. She thought of Arnold and gave a shiver.

There was a soft knock at her door. Edith stood and opened it. Zee-Zee stood in the corridor, his face serious.

"I can't sleep," he said.

"Me neither." Edith smiled. "Francis needs us, Arnold is trapped, the phoenix must be rescued and vaccinated. We can't waste time sleeping!"

"A bit of fresh air might help?" Zee-Zee said with a grin. "I could do with trying to find some snakes – how about you?"

Edith was turning to pick up a small rucksack before Zee-Zee had finished speaking.

"We'll rescue you, Arnold, I promise, we just need to save Francis first," Edith thought, stepping out of the room and following her friend into the corridor.

It was time to return to the forest.

CHAPTER NINE

In which Edith and Zee-Zee begin
their mission to find a viper ... and
make a new friend along the way...

Edith had felt a pang of guilt at not telling her uncle she was heading back to the forest so soon, but she reasoned he would only try to talk her out of it.

"I've left a note on the reception desk," Zee-Zee said as they stepped out into the cool of the night.

"My uncle would do the same thing in my situation," Edith said, half to convince herself she was doing the right thing. "He only didn't want us to leave straight away because he was worried about us in the dark. If Francis wasn't critical, he would be in the woods himself by now."

"Just remember, if we hear anything that could be a wolpertinger, we'll have to run fast," Zee-Zee said. "We can't wait to see what it is."

"My uncle said they are only active in short bursts. That big, bear-like creature won't be looking for us. No one will expect us to be searching for vipers at this time of night. As long as we're quiet and careful, we'll be fine … and then all we need to worry about is how we catch a poisonous snake." Edith laughed, trying not to think what a madcap plan this was.

"Who are the Syndicate?" Zee-Zee asked after a moment's pause.

Edith swallowed, unsure how to explain.

"They are a group of killers who hunt down rare animals like the phoenix. The Count described their leader, a lady with flame-red hair, as part of a regular hunting party that go to the Tower. Only there is nothing regular about them." She thought for a moment. "We know whoever has the phoenix must also be making the wolpertingers," she said. "The ashes are the only way to bring the wolpertingers to life. Arabella Spearstrike must have a base here."

Zee-Zee was silent for a moment. Then he said, "I know who you're talking about, I've seen them at the Tower. She is a fearsome woman. I don't think that group have the phoenix, though – if they did, why would they keep coming back?"

"I don't know, perhaps to collect forest animals they want to fuse. If they are in the region, who else can it be? What if they have now captured Arnold and have him trapped in a lair?"

"Then we'll just have to find it and rescue him as well," Zee-Zee replied.

The night sky showcased a half-moon, and its light made the going easy until they entered the great forest itself. As they walked under the trees, the shadows darkened and Zee-Zee flicked on a pocket torch, its thin light illuminating the trail in front of them.

"Will you be able to recognize the way in the dark? Everything looks different."

"I think so," Zee-Zee answered. "It's not that complicated a place to get to, it's just a long walk. By the time we get there it'll be almost dawn."

They walked in near silence, both too tired and too nervous to make small talk. Instead, they each focused on following the trail and not tripping over any roots that jutted out into the path. Shadows seemed to swirl around the edges of the torch beam and Edith's ears strained to hear if any creatures were moving amongst the trees. But the only sounds they heard were their own feet tramping onwards, the soft crunch of their footsteps swallowed by the darkness.

It wasn't cold, but it was tiring, and after an hour or so, the two of them paused to catch their breath. Edith pulled off her small rucksack, handed Zee-Zee a biscuit and offered him a sip of water from her water bottle.

"It's supposed to be me providing the guests with food, not the other way around," Zee-Zee said, grinning as he took a long sip of water before handing the bottle back.

"Always be prepared – at least, that's what my uncle says."

"What else have you got in there?"

"A plastic box with some holes punched in it."

"What for?" Zee-Zee said, perplexed.

"We'll need something to transport our snake in when we find one." Edith said. "And it was all I could find when I got back to my room."

"Good thinking!" Zee-Zee grinned. "I didn't even bring water."

"But you did bring a torch, so you win on being prepared! That said, I think it's starting to get a bit lighter…"

"I forgot my watch, but dawn can't be that far away," Zee-Zee agreed, flicking off the torch and giving his eyes a moment to adjust to the gloom. "I'll be able to work out where we are in a minute – and how much further we have to go."

As they resumed walking, it quickly became apparent that the forest was waking up. Instead of the nervous fear of the dark, a sense of peace and calm slowly wrapped around them. The whole forest soon felt like a completely different place to the one they had been so frightened of last night. If Edith hadn't had a tight ball of worry gnawing at her in the pit of her stomach, it would have been almost magical. A faint chirping of a bird sounded from high above in the canopy of trees, signalling the day was about to begin.

"It's a spotted nutcracker," Zee-Zee remarked.

"It's great you know so much about the local wildlife; we'd be really stuck if it wasn't for you. Finding the owls was amazing," Edith said as she trudged on.

"I love animals. As soon as we got here, I wanted to learn about the forest creatures on my doorstep."

"You'd get on well with my friend Anita," Edith said. "She studies every book about wildlife that she can find."

"She sounds great," Zee-Zee replied. "Is she back in England?"

"Right now, she'll be in India – that's where she's from – but we go to school together in England."

"That's a long drive to school!" Zee-Zee said with a smile.

"She boards, silly. We both do. But we're trapped in a city. We don't have anywhere like this to escape to at the weekend."

"I know, I am very lucky. In a few minutes, all the birds will start to sing."

"Ah, the dawn chorus!" Edith said, excited to hear it.

"Exactly, it starts half an hour before full sunrise and lasts until about half an hour after the sun has come up. All the birds will start calling in their flocks, defining their territories, calling out to try to attract a mate. Listen, it's starting now!"

Edith craned her head up to look at the trees above. At first she only heard a couple of birds' voices, but soon more and more began to join in.

"Morning, morning, morning ... another day is dawning!" shouted one exuberant voice.

"Not this again," said another.

"Morning, morning, morning ... another day is dawning!" shouted the voice again.

"We need to move tree. How this idiot keeps it up for an hour, I have no idea."

"Morning, morning, morning ... another day is dawning!" shouted the voice.

Edith giggled as she opened her mind to the other birds calling out.

"*Morning, Ruby!*"

"*Morning, Klaus.*"

"*What's up, Charlie!*"

"*Sunrise, same every day. We could easily have another hour's kip. What is wrong with you people?*"

"*Anyone seen that white-backed woodpecker?*"

"*Why?*"

"*He was hammering my tree yesterday.*"

"*So?*"

"*It's my tree!*"

"*Beautiful day alert! Wake up! Wake up! Wake up!*"

The voices were spilling over each other and, as Edith arched her head further up, she could now make out their shapes: birds in almost every treetop, perched on their uppermost branches.

"*Look at those two wingless wonders. Up early, aren't they?*"

"*Watch your eggs, people.*"

"*It's winter, you fool, we don't have any eggs.*"

"*Someone always has an egg in this forest, never doubt it.*"

"*I wonder what they're doing out at this time of day?*"

"*Anyone know where the snakes live?*" Edith thought,

almost shouting the words with her mind.

The silence that suddenly descended on the forest was absolute. It was as if a tap had been turned off. Zee-Zee shot Edith a baffled glance and stopped in his tracks, craning his head up as well.

"The birds have all stopped," he said, a slight tremor in his voice.

Edith cleared her throat sheepishly.

"I'm sure they'll start up again in a minute," she said. "Come on, let's keep going."

"Something's unnerved them."

"Erm … I may have caused a bit of a stir." Edith started to walk again just as the birds started up an almighty chatter.

"DID YOU ALL HEAR THAT????? A GIRL WHO CAN TALK TO US!!"

Edith shook her head. The racket the birds were making now was sure to be noticed by anyone in a five-mile radius. What had she been thinking, advertising their presence like that? There was no sneaking along now.

A heavy beat of wings descended from the treetops, rapidly followed by another and another after that. Birds of all different species were flocking down to examine the two of them.

"Edie, what on earth's going on? We are about to be mobbed by birds!" Zee-Zee said, looking around in alarm.

"I called out to them with my mind, and it's given them a surprise. They're just keeping an eye on where we're going and what we're up to. Let's keep walking, I'm sure they'll soon get bored."

They walked on, Edith inwardly cursing herself for being so reckless.

"How far do we have to go?" she shouted over the din.

"Just around the bend," Zee-Zee replied, quickening his pace, his eyes nervously darting around as different birds jostled each other for the best view of the pair of them.

Edith eyed the bend of the track in the distance.

"Shall we run a bit?" she said.

Zee-Zee needed no encouragement and, within a moment, they were both running along the track. Birds of every description called and hollered a greeting at them, whilst swooping down to get a look at the girl "who could talk to birds".

Panting, Edith rounded the bend and pulled up short with a sharp intake of breath.

Ahead of them, the path straightened out and continued down a slight incline, before forking. Edith looked in the direction of the left-hand track, which descended steeply down a high bank, winding its way

towards a giant pile of stones. There, amid huge boulders of rock, each half covered with moss and in the shadow of the forest floor, was a cavernous black hole. Beyond was an eerie, empty stillness.

Zee-Zee skidded to a stop behind her. "Edie! Are you OK?"

"I think I can see the entrance to your cave," she replied.

Zee-Zee offered her a huge grin. "It's a bit of a

surprise, isn't it!"

"You should have brought a bigger torch," Edith said. The cave entrance, framed by its colossal slabs of stone, looked more foreboding than she could ever have imagined. It looked like it would swallow the sun.

Slowly, they made their way down the near-vertical bank and began to walk towards the cave entrance. The forest birds, realizing the show was over, and for some reason not keen to go anywhere near the cave entrance, had made their way back up to the treetops. Edith overheard several birds complaining as they arrived late and wondered what all the fuss was about. She grinned.

"The birds seem to have got bored," Zee-Zee said, his voice now clearly audible over the receding racket.

"The sooner they go back up to the treetops and start singing normally again, the better," Edith said, casting her eyes upwards as feathered wings fluttered above them.

"If any of those wolpertinger creatures were watching, we couldn't have made more of a disturbance." Zee-Zee sighed. "We've got to hope they do only come out at night."

"I know. I'm sorry. I sometimes forget it's not normal that I can talk to animals. It was silly to shout out to so many like that."

"It's OK. If I had a superpower, I'd want to use it!" Zee-Zee smiled. "Look, we're here, and no wolpertingers got us!"

Edith flashed him a grin of thanks. She gestured ahead.

"This place doesn't look too welcoming," she said, trepidation creeping over her as she edged warily towards the cave mouth.

Zee-Zee stepped up beside her to walk by her side. His presence was reassuring, even though he was clearly as nervous as she was.

"Are the snakes in the cave itself, do you think?"

"I don't know," replied Zee-Zee. "All I know is that they're in this area."

Edith quietly moved on, her eyes scanning the rocks. This was ideal snake territory: lots of cracks and crevices in which to hide. If they were going to be anywhere in this forest, this would be the spot. Her foot slipped on a stone, and she dropped down to one knee.

"Be careful, Edie. We don't want you to get bitten, that wouldn't help the cause at all."

"I'm being careful," she replied. "But we need to find a snake, not hide from them. They've got to know we're here."

A sudden fluttering made Edith look up. A small black shape, moving impossibly fast, darted between her and Zee-Zee, weaving through the air before crashing into the stone wall at the entrance to the cave.

"*Uggggghhhhhhhhh!*" the shape groaned.

Both Edith and Zee-Zee exchanged a glance of surprise and ran over towards the shape, which now lay in a tiny heap on the forest floor.

"It's a bat!" exclaimed Zee-Zee.

"It's hurt," Edith said, crouching down to look.

"Be careful. Bats carry disease."

"*I don't have a disease!*" said a voice in Edith's head.

Edith needed no further encouragement. She bent down and scooped the bat into her hand. Only it wasn't a bat.

"Oh!" Edith exclaimed, almost dropping the little creature.

"*Of course, if I did have a disease, say rabies for example, I'd now bite you and that would be that.*"

Edith held the creature gingerly and studied its features. It was the size and shape of a bat. It had bat wings. But its face was covered with fur and its toes were furred claws, not bat like in the slightest. To cap it all, it also sported a small but very fluffy tail that twitched as Edith turned to show Zee-Zee.

"What is that?" Zee-Zee said, as shocked as Edith.

"It's got the body of a bat but the tail of a…"

"*Squirrel,*" the little creature finished.

Edith gasped. *"You're a wolpertinger!"*

The creature's head dipped.

"It's OK. Are you hurt?"

The creature didn't answer.

"So have you got rabies?" Edith thought with a smile.

"Luckily for both of us – no," said the creature, regarding her with wide eyes.

The wolpertinger weighed almost nothing. Edith marvelled at its delicate body as it flexed out tiny claws to straighten itself in her palm. She had never held a bat before, and whilst she had heard them in the rafters of Forest Cottage, she'd never seen one up close. She peered at an outstretched wing, studying it carefully. Something wasn't quite right.

"Shall we aay a prayer. I'm feeling very holy today," said the little voice.

"Holy?"

In reply, the bat stretched the wing out a little further. Edith looked and, sure enough, she could see what wasn't quite right. There was a large hole and tear in the middle of the wing.

"*Does that hurt?*" she thought.

"*No, but it does make a whistle when I flap it.*"

Edith shook her head, smiling. The wolpertinger was a joker.

"*Is that why you crashed?*"

"*More of a partially uncontrolled descent, if you don't mind. I admit my flying is not what it was, but that's what happens when you have been fused with a squirrel. You aren't quite yourself, if you know what I mean.*"

"*I thought wolpertingers were nocturnal, that you sleep in the day. What are you doing flying around? Have you been … sent by someone?*"

"*You mean my creator?*" the creature said testily.

Edith hesitated. The creature didn't seem like it was under anyone's control and she didn't want to offend it.

"*Well, yes. I thought whoever made you could command you?*"

The little creature looked totally dejected.

"*Nope. I'm still me,*" it said, shaking its little head.

"*What do you mean?*"

"*It didn't work. I was fused with a squirrel, as you can see, but only the body parts. It wasn't a proper meld. After the process, I was still me, a bat. Just a bat with squirrel features. I was of no use, just a discarded experiment. She thought I couldn't fly, but I can! I escaped!"*

Edith's heart raced. *"She?"*

The little creature tilted its head. *"The one who made me."*

"What is it saying, Edie?"

Zee-Zee had walked over and was gazing at the little creature in fascination.

Edith quickly explained. "He said it was a 'she' that made him. They thought he couldn't fly, but then he escaped."

"I was trying to get back to the cloud."

"The cloud?" Edith asked, confused.

"The cloud. Don't you know what the cloud is?"

Edith shook her head.

"We bats fly in a cloud, live in a colony, hang out in cauldrons. That kind of thing. For all your powers of communication, you don't know much bat lingo, do you?"

"Sorry – I'm learning all the time," Edith said, shaking her head as she tried to remember all the terms.

"Well, you're doing well to talk to me. You're the first human who I've ever heard speak in my mind – although your voice is a little gruff, if I'm honest."

Edith smiled. She'd never been described as gruff before.

"Will it heal?" Zee-Zee said, pointing at the

creature's torn wing.

"*I doubt it. People are born with one kind of voice, and it generally sticks with them for life.*"

"*He meant your wing!*" Edith laughed.

"*My pride after crashing so close to home is as important as my wing.*"

"*I know, sorry, I was just wondering if you will be able to fly again?*"

The creature seemed to consider this for a moment. "*I think the rip is getting smaller day by day. I should be soaring the night skies with my friends before the next full moon ... if they'll have me back.*"

The bat spoke confidently, but Edith caught the note of uncertainty in his voice.

"*It's not healing, is it? How long have you had that tear?*"

The creature was quiet and seemed to shrink a little in her hand.

Edith looked again at the hole. It wasn't just a clean punch through the wing membrane; it had a long tear lancing vertically beneath it.

"*Maybe I can help you. My uncle, he's a vet and he has all sorts of medicines and equipment. I'm sure he'll have some glue and we can...*"

"*Your uncle? I've got uncles, thousands of them. Did*"

any of them come and try to rescue me? No, not one. Why would your uncle help me if my own won't?"

"I'll help you," Edith said.

"You'd go to the trouble of taking me, whatever I am now, some creature you've only just met, back to wherever it is you've come from and fix my wing?"

"Yes!" Edith replied, rather defensively.

The creature gave her a cool look. It was quite a thing to be appraised by a wolpertinger and Edith found herself under careful scrutiny.

"Why are you at the entrance to our cave anyway? You know, there are a lot of snakes around here, you should be careful."

Almost on cue, a rustle at their feet made both children jump. Edith heard Zee-Zee take in a sharp breath. "Edie!" he said, pointing.

Edith looked at where Zee-Zee indicated and immediately took a step back. A snake, about a metre long, was sliding towards them along the edge of the entrance to the cave. It stopped and pulled its head back in a threatening pose, its eyes fixed on Edith.

Edith stared back at the snake, wondering what it was looking at, before it dawned on her that its broad, triangular head with slightly upturned nose was fixated not on her but on the creature she held.

"Give meeee the battttt," the snake hissed.

"Oh dear. They always hang about here when the sun comes up, waiting for stragglers. Vicious horrible things. You have got me tight, haven't you?"

Edith took another step backwards and the snake slithered forward to maintain the distance between them.

"Edie, I think it wants the creature," Zee-Zee said in alarm.

"It's not getting it."

"Give meeee the battttt," the snake hissed again.

The snake moved closer, its muscular body seeming to tense. Edith looked at the triangular black markings that zigzagged down its back.

"Ifff I bite you, you'll soon drop it, then I'll get a nice tasty mealllllll."

"No! Wait," Edith said, quickly retreating, still clutching the creature tightly in her hands. *"Can't you go off and find some other food?"*

If the snake had been surprised that Edith could talk to it, it gave no sign. Instead, it slithered forwards relentlessly – eyes riveted on the creature in her hands.

"I wannnnttttt thatttt battttt."

"You can't have it!"

"Yesssssss I cannnn. Ittttt was our kind of snake that killed Queen Cleopatra, little girl. You'll die quickerrrrrr

than her. Talk all you wantttt, it makes no difference, I want that batttt!"

The snake suddenly surged towards Edith, who stumbled backwards, her foot catching on a rock. She fell heavily on to the ground.

"Look, let me go and save yourself," cried the wolpertinger. *"The snake wants me, it can't eat you. I'm done for anyway, I won't last the week limping around like this. Everyone has written me off, I'm a fusion of confusion. I've had a good run, now is my time."*

"I'm not letting you go!" Edith said, shuffling backwards and trying to regain her feet.

The snake gave a hiss of triumph and lunged towards Edith.

"No!" The shout was both desperate and defiant. With a loud crack, Zee-Zee leapt forward and brought a large stick down, slamming the ground hard between Edith and the snake.

The snake, shocked by the sudden movement, skidded sideways to avoid the stick and furiously pulled its head back in a striking pose. It flicked its unnerving gaze between Zee-Zee and Edith.

"There's enough poison in me for the two of you little people. I'll deal with you firsttttt!"

The snake lunged again, but this time at Zee-Zee,

who raised his stick and somehow managed to block the lightning-fast strike. The snake pulled back, hate seeming to radiate from the depths of its black eyes.

"I won't be the only snake around here for long. Just you stay where you are, little onesssss…"

Edith, scrabbling to her feet, shouted a warning to Zee-Zee.

"There are more snakes here, Zee-Zee, be careful!"

"I hope not! One is bad enough! They're far more aggressive than it says in books!" he shouted, keeping his eyes fixed on the coiled malevolence between them.

"I had no idea snakes would be so horrible," Edith exclaimed. "How are we going to get them to help us if all they do is attack!"

"I've been told some species of snake are nice," said the wolpertinger. *"It's just this lot, they're awful. They hunt together so if they find one of us injured or alone, they can corner us and sneak up behind. They don't come into the cave, though. If you can get inside, you'll be safe. There are too many bats in there for the snakes to risk it. We may be small, but together we can swarm them, you see."*

"How can we get to the entrance?" Edith thought frantically, casting her eyes back and forth. The snake was blocking their path.

"You need to be quick. Grab a stick like your friend

had, use it to keep the snake away and edge towards the cave. When you're close enough – make a run for it!"

"Behind you!" Zee-Zee suddenly shouted, pointing with his free hand.

Edith spun round. Too late, she saw another snake slithering towards them. It moved so fast, Edith knew she didn't have time to get to the cave entrance.

"*Oh no!*" the creature said, catching a glimpse of the second snake approaching. "*Nothing for it. Thanks for trying to help me, I think I need to return the favour.*"

Before Edith had time to register what was happening, the wolpertinger wriggled out of her hand and launched itself directly towards the snake blocking the cave entrance.

The snake, its eyes watching the stick in Zee-Zee's hand, didn't notice the creature hurtling towards it until it was already too late. In the blink of an eye, the wolpertinger had closed the distance and, flinging itself at the snake, jumped on to its neck.

"*Whattttttt!!!!!*" the snake hissed in surprise, its taut body reflexively twisting and curling around on itself, trying to throw off the furry creature.

"*Run now!*" the brave little beast squeaked as it gripped at the snake, sinking its own teeth into the snake's scales.

Edith and Zee-Zee exchanged a surprised look before seizing the opportunity the little creature had given them and made a dash for the cave. In seconds, they found themselves in the sanctuary of the huge entrance.

From there, they turned to watch the fracas. The other snake was now darting ahead. It paused mid-slither, before hissing in triumph.

"I'll getttttt the battttt."

It surged towards the two animals that flailed on the forest floor.

"Watch out! The other snake is coming!" Edith shouted at the wolpertinger, who was somehow still lodged firmly behind the snake's head, out of reach of its fangs.

Time seemed to freeze as Edith and Zee-Zee saw the spectacle in front of them unfold.

Just as the second snake prepared to strike, the wolpertinger let go and shot high into the air, in the direction of the mouth of the cave. As the creature was catapulted upwards, so the strike of the second snake descended, right on to the back of the first snake where the creature had been lodged until mere moments before.

"*Owwwwwwwwwwwwwwwww!!!!!!!!!!*" The hiss of the snake was more like a roar as the second snake struck it. It whipped round and, in the blink of an eye, had sunk its fangs into the body of the second snake.

"*Youuuuuuuu bittttt meeeeeee!*" the second snake cried in both shock and pain.

"*You bittttt meeeee firsttttttt,*" the first snake replied, its voice already a little quieter.

Then the pair of them slumped to the ground and lay still.

Edith and Zee-Zee stared back in disbelief at what they had just witnessed.

"Snakes have natural immunity to their own venom – they've evolved to become immune because they often bite each other when fighting or mating. Those two will recover soon enough," Zee-Zee said anxiously. "And there could be more snakes coming."

"You've done a lot of reading!"

"I spend a lot of time sitting behind that reception desk!" Zee-Zee replied with a bark of laughter.

Edith nodded. "Before we go anywhere, I need to help our new friend."

Quickly stepping back out of the cave entrance, Edith

bent to scoop up the furry beast which lay a few steps in front of them.

"Are you all right?" she said.

"Fused with a squirrel, a torn wing, stuck outside all day and now a battle with a deadly snake. Fair to say I've had better days," the wolpertinger replied.

"You saved us! Thank you!" Edith said, giving the creature a gentle stroke.

"I'm not a pet, stop that."

Edith immediately removed her hand from its head.

"I owed you one, that's all. One good turn deserves another."

"But you could have died!" Edith exclaimed.

"I don't like those snakes," the creature said. *"They've bitten a few of us, killed three of my cousins, you know, I couldn't let them get their way. Besides, if they'd got you, we'd both have been done for. They would have nailed me the moment you went down. Surprise was the only way."*

"You're amazing!" Edith said.

"I really am," the creature answered, without a shred of modesty.

Edith couldn't help herself giggling at the brave little beast.

"What's so funny?" Zee-Zee asked.

"The creature, he's very confident," she replied

with a smile.

"*What's your name?*" she thought.

"*Blaze,*" the creature replied.

"*Blaze the bat?*" Edith said, unable to hide the smile in her thought.

"*Well, I was. Now I am 'Blaze the whatever I am'.*"

"*I think you're amazing just as you are, and when we fix your wing up, you'll be back with the colony in no time.*"

"*I'm disgusting. Bree won't ever love me again,*" he said quietly.

"*Bree? Is she your … girlfriend?*"

Blaze gave a little sorrowful shake of his body. "*She was. Before I was … taken. I was scooped up in a net and some sort of cloth was thrown in with me. It smelt horrible. The next thing I remember was waking up and finding myself turned into … this. She won't want me now. I'm ruined.*"

"*That's not true! You're still you!*" Edith protested. "*Do you have any idea who is doing this to the animals in the forest?*"

"*The only person I saw when I woke up was a hooded figure. I think it was a woman, though; I heard them muttering to themselves and it sounded like a woman's voice.*"

Edith's thoughts immediately went to Arabella

Spearstrike. She shuddered.

"*What was the place like, where they did this to you?*"

"*It was a room full of cages, full of animals from the forest. A place of nightmares. All of us were locked up, blankets over our cages. They took one look at me, saw my damaged wing and threw me away. I was of no interest.*"

"*How did you escape?*"

"*In the rubbish. I crawled out of the bag and made my way back to the forest.*"

Edith pondered this. How many places in the village could house animals undetected?

"What's it saying?" Zee-Zee asked.

"That whoever made him threw him away in the rubbish. He escaped from a bin bag. Which might be a clue..."

"All the rubbish is taken to a communal area on the outskirts of the village. There's no way of knowing where the individual rubbish bags come from," Zee-Zee replied with a helpless shrug.

"But at least we know the wolpertingers are made in the village – or very near."

Zee-Zee pursed his lips. "No one in the village would do this kind of thing. They are all nice, honest people."

"It must be somewhere close. Are there any other places where someone could be doing this?"

Zee-Zee looked dumbfounded. He shook his head slowly. "Nowhere I can think of. Perhaps the Count will know more – he's explored the whole area right around the village."

"First we need to get our new friend to my uncle. Then if we can find where they try to create the wolpertingers, perhaps we can start to unravel what on earth's going on and find the phoenix."

"You see. Your superpower again! It's so great you can talk to animals," Zee-Zee said suddenly.

Zee-Zee was the only person her age who had witnessed Edith's powers in action. The fact he didn't think she was a freak made her feel a warm glow at the words.

"It was pretty cool how Blaze saved us," Edith replied with a grin.

"Blaze? That's a cool name! I've never seen heroics like it. To take on two poisonous snakes! Incredible!"

The little creature wriggled in Edith's hand, and she glanced down to see Blaze bristling with pride. His spirits seemed somewhat restored.

"What shall we do now?" Zee-Zee asked.

Edith snapped her fingers. "We need to get some venom out of those snakes. There's no point taking them back. They'll never help us conscious. All they want to do is eat our new friend. Now's our only chance to get whatever posion they have left."

"I can do it. Pass me the box, I'll squeeze out what I can into it."

Hanging the box to Zee-Zee, Edith watched as he cautiously approached the unconscious snakes. He carefully opened their mouths in turn by grasping behind their heads and pushing their fangs over the lip of the container. The tiniest amount of fluid rolled down the inside of it from each snake.

"I'll make sure to keep this upright but there's virtually nothing left. They've used up all their venom on each other," he said with an exasperated sigh, quickly releasing the snakes and hurriedly stepping back into the cave entrance with Edith.

Zee-Zee held the box up and the two of them stared at the minuscule amount of venom in the bottom of it.

"I doubt that will be enough to make an injection from," Edith said wearily.

"Why do you want venom?" Blaze chirped up.

"Our friend has been bitten … by a … well, he's got snake venom in his system. We need to make an antidote to save him." Not wanting to upset Blaze, Edith decided against explaining that a different sort of wolpertinger had attacked Francis.

"We came to see if the snakes would give us some venom we could use – only, this won't be enough. It's hopeless. We need to find another snake."

"Hmmm," said Blaze thoughtfully. "My friend Bucky was bitten by a snake twice. He was very ill the first time but survived. The second time he was absolutely fine. No ill effects at all! The snakes were mad about that – you should have heard them hissing as he swaggered around."

Edith thought about that for a moment, and then her eyes widened and she looked at Zee-Zee.

"What?" he said, wondering what had come over Edith.

"Blaze has just been telling me about a bat that survived being bitten by a snake. He then got bitten again and the snake bite had no effect on him at all. He was immune."

"Lucky bat," Zee-Zee replied.

"Don't you see? That first snake bite gave him the antibodies his body needed to fight off the second. What if we could get the blood of an animal that already has the antibodies in it? We could use that blood to make the antivenom. It would save so much time – we wouldn't need the snake, my uncle wouldn't have to inject himself – we could save Francis right away!"

Gradually Zee-Zee's mouth twitched upwards. "You're

a genius, Edie. Where are you going to find this animal, though?"

"I know a good place to start," Edith said with a grin.

She turned back to the bat in her hand.

"Do you think Bucky would help us? We need some of his blood to help our friend."

"His blood?!" Blaze exclaimed, clearly shocked by the suggestion. *"I don't think Bucky would like that!"*

"Well, we need the blood from any creature who has survived a viper's snake bite. We can use that to make the antivenom."

Blaze was silent for a moment. *"How long ago would the animal have to have been bitten to still have the antibodies?"*

"I don't know," confessed Edith rather sheepishly, *"but I think the more recently the better. The number of circulating antibodies are what we're after, and they will be highest when an animal is just recovering."*

"OK," said Blaze thoughtfully, pausing as if working out whether to say anything more.

"Do you know any other creatures that have been bitten by those snakes and are still alive?"

Blaze let the question hang in the air for a moment. *"I believe I do. How much blood do you need?"* he asked.

Edith gave a shrug. *"I'm not sure. It's my uncle who is*

the vet. I'm just his assistant."

"Well, it had better not be too much," Blaze replied sharply.

"Why not?" Edith asked, confused.

"Because I'm not very big…"

CHAPTER TEN

*In which Edith and Zee-Zee return
to the guest house to find out that the
Doctor has made a new discovery...*

The Doctor's stomach rumbled. Giving his tummy a rub, he cast his eye around the room for something to eat.

Francis stirred on the bed. "You're still here, Doctor."

"More important is that you are too," replied the Doctor with a chuckle.

Francis gave a weak smile. "I feel like I have been trampled by a herd of elephants."

"You look a bit like it as well, my friend. But you're stable, the medications I have given you are doing their job. The crucial thing is that you remain still."

"Where is Arnold?"

The Doctor shook his head. "He hasn't returned yet."

Francis closed his eyes momentarily and made as if to sit up. The Doctor rushed forward and placed his hands on the giant man's shoulders.

"You must remain in bed, Francis. You are no good to us unconscious, or worse."

The Doctor fixed Francis with a steely gaze and Francis gave an exhausted sigh. A sheen of sweat glistened on his forehead.

"What about Edie? Is she OK?" Francis asked, sinking his head back once more on to the pillow.

"She has gone into the forest to find some snake venom so we can make you an antidote and get you back on your feet. She's with Zee-Zee – they snuck off in the early hours of the morning."

"They went back into the forest at night?" Francis said, horrified. He made as if to try to sit up again. The Doctor placed a hand on his undamaged shoulder and pushed him down.

Too weak to resist, Francis slumped back.

"Against my instruction, I might add, but she is brave and determined. I found a note left on the reception desk. My sincere hope is they will arrive back here shortly." The Doctor grimaced as he stared out of the window towards the forest and the trees beyond.

"What's the plan?" Francis mumbled, fighting to keep his eyes open as a wave of fatigue swept over him.

The Doctor turned his attention back to Francis.

"To get you healed, find Arnold, track down the phoenix and achieve what we set out to do! Since the ashes of the phoenix are required to make a wolpertinger, it is safe to assume that if we can discover where the wolpertingers are created, then that is where the phoenix will be captive."

"Do you think Arnold was captured by the hunters who are making these monsters?"

The Doctor bit his lip. "It is quite possible. I cannot think as to why he hasn't returned otherwise. Edith cannot make the communication hold when she reaches out to him, so we don't know where he is – only that he is alive and somewhere near."

"Perhaps they want Arnold to be part of a wolpertinger and that is why they have captured him," Francis said.

The Doctor grimaced. "If we rescue the phoenix, whoever is doing this won't be able to create any more wolpertingers."

Francis's face twisted momentarily as a spasm of pain rippled through him. "The creature I fought … it wasn't evil."

"Indeed," the Doctor replied.

"Could you treat the ones that have been created – reverse the process?"

The Doctor sighed. "They are beyond my skills to help, my friend. They are merged animals, fused into a single entity. How could I extract the head of a wolf – without a wolf's body to attach it to? No, they are far beyond my help now. All we can do is free them."

"Free them?" Francis said, unable to hide his shock.

"Free them, Francis. As you said, they are victims of this evil, not evil themselves. Those creatures must find peace somehow. They won't live long, but what life they have left must be a free one." He clapped his hands. "Now, we both need something to eat. I will go to the kitchen and see what I can rustle up. You need your strength to keep fighting the poison."

"Let me guess, marshmallows and cheesy chips, Doctor?" Francis gave a weak smile.

"Can you manage a few, if they have any?"

"I'll do my best."

As the Doctor spoke, the sound of a powerful engine reverberated from outside. The Doctor arched his eyebrow and turned back to the window, peering out.

"What is it?" Francis murmured.

"I can't see – it must be coming from around the

front of the building. Strange to hear such a deep engine. Sounds like a truck, wouldn't you say?"

On receiving no response, the Doctor turned and gave a small sigh. Francis was fast asleep again. Ensuring his breathing was nice and steady, the Doctor slipped out of the door.

Softly closing it behind him so as not to disturb Francis, the Doctor hadn't gone more than five paces when a small lady, carrying a huge bundle of towels, burst around the corner and crashed straight into him.

As they bumped together, each of them immediately rocked backwards. The lady gave a small gasp of surprise

and the piles of towels she had been carrying flew up in into the air and fluttered down on to the floor.

"So sorry, so sorry, let me help," said the Doctor, hurriedly straightening his cap and his cape, before bending down to start picking up the towels which now lay scattered all over the corridor.

"My fault, don't worry," the lady said cheerfully.

Together they gathered up the towels. As the Doctor rose, he paused. "Excuse me, are you Zee-Zee's mother?"

The lady gave a broad smile and a nod. "My name is Ai Lam. I trust my son has been looking after you well during your stay?"

"Absolutely," the Doctor replied. "Zee-Zee told me you are a vet?"

"*Was* a vet," Ai Lam said, a flash of bitterness passing over her face. "Now I spend a lot of time cleaning – although I help the injured animals the Count collects at the Tower. You are a vet also?"

"Yes, in England."

"We could do with your help over the next few days," said Ai Lam. "Another group of hunters are due to arrive at any moment and there are always injured animals after their visit."

"I'd gladly help. Hunting for sport is both barbaric and inhumane. What people do to animals is often a reflection on how they treat humans. We met the Count last night, a very pleasant man."

"He is a good man and he dislikes these hunters. I wish he didn't host them at the Tower for their hunting feasts — but we all must do what we must to make ends meet, I suppose," Ai Lam said, taking an armful of towels from the Doctor.

"How is the little fire-bellied toad that Edie saved yesterday doing?" the Doctor asked.

Ai Lam looked at him blankly. "I didn't see one at the hospital. Did you take it to the Tower?"

"Edie and the Count did," said the Doctor. "Perhaps it was released first thing."

"It is possible. The Count often goes out very early. I will go and look later."

"Zee-Zee mentioned he has a hospital at the guest house. I look forward to seeing it."

"It is empty now, but often quite full after one of the hunts!" Ai Lam replied. "He takes in all the overflow animals when the Count has no more space at the Tower."

The Doctor nodded, his expression pensive. "What about our dog Arnold? Have you seen him? He went missing in the forest yesterday afternoon and we think he came back to the village, but we've been unable to find him."

"I'm so sorry, Zee-Zee told me. No, I haven't seen him. He said you were chased by something that looked like a bear? Quite terrifying. It attacked your friend. Is he recovering well? Is there anything I can get you?"

The Doctor shook his head wearily. "Very kind, but we are treating him as best we are able. I came to find some food if it might be possible, some cheesy chips, perhaps? And you wouldn't happen to have any marshmallows, by any chance?"

Ai Lam laughed. "I think I can help on both fronts. Please, follow me and let's see what I can find."

As Ai Lam began to walk down the corridor, carefully carrying the towels in front of her, the Doctor followed.

"The hunters today will no doubt be excited to know there is a bear in the vicinity," she said. "I suppose that is the only good they do, they scare away the dangerous predators. At least this group are only coming for a couple of days. They will arrive today to do their scouting. Then they will feast in the Tower tonight and discuss what they hope to shoot. In the morning they will go off hunting. A bear's head would surely delight them as a trophy. They would put it on the table at their final feast night before they leave the day after tomorrow. They used to come twice a year but now it is every three months."

She turned her head and noticed the tense expression

on the Doctor's face.

"Don't worry. If your dog has come to the village, he cannot be in any danger. They go deep into the forest – to areas the Count identifies for them."

"He identifies areas for the hunters?" the Doctor asked, surprised. "I didn't realize he was so involved."

"He says it is the only way he can think of to limit their presence. If they get what they want, they leave quicker, rather than tramp through the forest over days, killing indiscriminately."

Suddenly a bell rang out and Ai Lam's eyes widened in surprise. She glanced down at her watch.

"That must be the hunters, they have arrived early. The Count asked me to give them some maps. Give me a few minutes to see to them, and then I will get your food. I can bring it up to your room?"

"Of course, absolutely no rush. You must deal with them first," the Doctor replied.

Ai Lam gave a grateful nod and then, pausing to place the towels in a large cupboard, she quickly strode off towards the reception.

The Doctor waited a moment, then followed Ai Lam down the corridor. He watched as she disappeared through the doorway and into the small lobby area of the guest house. Voices spoke sharply beyond the door.

"Where have you been? I am on a tight schedule."

The woman's voice was heavily muffled through the wood, yet it sounded horribly familiar to the Doctor. He felt a chill grip his chest and his brow creased in consternation.

"So sorry, I will get your maps now, madam," came Ai Lam's voice.

"I also wish to speak to the Count," the other woman demanded angrily.

"He is not available this morning, madam. He has his ... rest at this time of day."

The lady gave an explosive and unpleasant laugh.

"Rest?! He can rest when we are gone. Last time he was sick, the time before that he was away. I will speak to him *now*, before we begin to scout the area for the hunt tomorrow."

"But madam—"

A deeper male voice with a thick Eastern European accent cut across Ai Lam before she could finish her reply.

"Wake him up. Tell him that if Miss Arabella wishes to speak with him then he will come down from his Tower or we will go up and get him."

Arabella Spearstrike! The Doctor's sharp intake of breath was as instinctive as if he had been plunged into a bucket of icy-cold water. Then the anger took hold. His fingertips went white as they dug into the door frame and it was all he could do to refrain from charging into the reception. His nemesis, his most bitter enemy, was here. A lady who represented one of the most ruthless and vicious organizations on the planet: the Syndicate. A group dedicated to profiteering from the destruction of mythical creatures.

"Now, now, Ivan," Arabella said. "There is no need for threats. I think our point has been understood. I think our friend here realizes that the Syndicate has specific requirements and if the Count is unavailable to discuss these."

The Doctor could hear the menace in Arabella's voice as she tailed off, her meaning clear.

There was a long pause and the Doctor strained to hear what was going on. Something slammed, then he heard footsteps outside. Tentatively, the Doctor opened the door to the reception and peered through a crack. Looking through the window of the reception beyond, he could make out three figures walking away from the guest house: the small, diminutive form of Zee-Zee's mother dwarfed by the giant shape of Arabella's bodyguard Ivan and, of course, the lean angular figure of Arabella Spearstrike herself, her flame-red hair streaming behind her.

The Doctor gritted his teeth. The Syndicate were behind all of this; he had been right from the start. Somehow, they were linked to the wolpertingers, the missing phoenix and now poor Arnold. The coincidence of their arrival was too great to ignore. The moment Arabella found out he and Edith were in the vicinity, she would know they were there to track down the phoenix. They would be in even more peril. Arabella had tried to kill them before. This time would be no different.

The Doctor cursed. He had no doubt now that Arnold had been caught for them to hunt or even to make into a wolpertinger. He wondered what the Syndicate were doing with the wolpertingers. Hunting them no doubt.

The more extreme the better. He could imagine what their requirements would be – one that roars as it flies, a creature that can both dig into hiding yet will pounce on prey. Trophy hunting for the deranged elite. The very thought of it made his blood boil. And Arnold, his dear Arnold, kept in a cage and waiting to become part of their next "creation".

The Doctor didn't hesitate; he knew what he had to do. He crept outside to follow the trio. Keeping his distance and darting from the cover of one building to another, he watched their procession to the Tower. Ducking behind a wall and peering over its top, he looked on as Arabella, Ivan and Ai Lam crossed the bridge.

Staring past them, the Doctor could see a huge black truck reversing outside the entrance to the old church. It must have been the vehicle he'd heard earlier, the roar of its engine drowning out the sound of the river. More men were suddenly visible as they disembarked from the truck and swiftly opened up its back.

Balling his fists with distaste, the Doctor watched from his hiding place as the doors to the old part of the church swung open and cages were quickly loaded into the back of the vehicle. *They must be for the animals they kill or capture on the hunt*, the Doctor thought. It took but moments before the men were once again climbing back inside the truck and the engine roared into life, its deafening sound echoing through the peaceful village. Craning his head, the Doctor peered towards the other side of the building, trying to work out where Arabella, Ai Lam and Ivan were.

It took him a second to spot them – they were clustered together in front of the Tower, standing together on the bank above the river, out of earshot of the rest of Arabella's men. As the Doctor watched, he saw a door open and the hooded figure of the Count emerge from the building. Even though the Doctor couldn't hear what was being said, it was clear the Count was uncomfortable. He began gesticulating wildly and pointing at something up in the Tower. Ai Lam moved away and began to walk back to the guest house.

The Doctor shrank back so he couldn't be seen. It would look most odd if she realized he had followed her to the Tower.

He eyed the riverbank. If he could edge his way down this side of it, he might be able to get closer and hear what they were saying. It was worth a try.

Pulling his cape tight around him, the Doctor crouched and made a dash for it. He was over the edge of the bank in a heartbeat and slid down to the water's edge. The noise of the water muffled any sounds he made, but down here, the wrong side of the water, he couldn't hear the voices of Arabella and the Count. He had to get nearer.

His eyes swivelled to the bridge. He couldn't just walk over it – there was no chance of him approaching unseen by that route – but he grinned as an idea formulated in his mind. He could maybe go under it.

Scampering along the riverbank, the Doctor carefully studied the wooden frame that supported the bridge. There was a ledge, not wider than the width of his hand – but it was all he needed. He could get across the river and drop down on to the opposite bank, where he should be able to hear the conversation.

The Doctor moved nimbly, belying his portly physique; he slipped once and almost ended up having an early bath, but with somewhat remarkable agility, he quickly recovered his footing and was on the opposite side in moments. Swiftly adjusting his cap, he stole down the far side of the bank, then crept closer to the group.

Tilting his head, endeavouring to tune out the sound of the rushing water below him, the Doctor strained to hear the voices.

"Will they provide good sport?" Arabella said harshly, her tone demanding and fierce.

"It is such a waste," the Count said defensively.

"You may find what we do distasteful, but they are there to be hunted." Arabella laughed. "Can you guarantee good sport, that is the question."

"You do not deserve to hunt them," the Count replied, his thin voice strained. "The creatures are … wonderful."

The Doctor caught the fear in the Count's voice. He admired the man, standing up to Arabella and her killers.

"Wonderful with their heads on the end of a spear, perhaps," Ivan declared.

The Count drew in a sharp breath.

"You have no appreciation for the magnificence of what they represent!" he said angrily.

"I think it is time we discussed our specific requirements with you inside," said Arabella sharply.

"There is no need to go inside," the Count said uneasily.

"On the contrary, there is every need." Each word dripped with sneering menace. "It is important that you clearly understand what I demand, and that is best explained within your lair."

The Doctor couldn't see what was happening, but he heard footsteps moving away. The voices became muffled. There was the sound of a door closing.

"Blast," the Doctor said to himself. Did the Count know the danger he was in? He had been standing up to the Syndicate, and that took real courage, but at what personal cost? The Count probably had no idea what a ruthless killer Arabella was, and now she was inside his Tower. He had to help him.

Pushing himself off the bank, the Doctor stole forward and crept over to the door. The moment he touched the handle, it swung open on well-greased hinges.

Crouching, he edged inside, keeping low against the wall.

The room was a vast open space. Pews were pushed against the sides of the hall. It was clearly the main part of the old church. Down the central aisle, long trestle tables were set up. Bare now, the Doctor realized they would be where the hunters would have their feast.

Seeing a passageway behind where the altar would have once been, the Doctor moved forward. This would surely lead to the Tower above and must be where Arabella and Ivan had taken the Count to outline their demands.

The Doctor eased his way noiselessly into the passage. Stairs ascended from here, and he slowly began to climb, placing each foot in front of the other as lightly as possible.

The Doctor reached the first landing – clearly the Count's living quarters – and, straining to listen for any muted conversation, paused, holding his breath. There was only silence. In one corner of the landing, a large tapestry hung down against the wall. There was something curious about the way it was hanging, and the Doctor moved towards it. Creeping over, he gently lifted the tapestry up. Behind it, he could just make out a hidden entrance, with another narrow walkway and more narrow stairs at the end.

The Doctor didn't hesitate, and pushing behind the tapestry, he hurried towards the stairs. At the top stood a thick iron door. Faint voices could just be heard coming from the other side. The Doctor pressed his ear against it and listened.

"… that last one looked like a squashed snake with crow wings. I've seen better-looking corpses." Ivan's voice sounded harsh.

"They represent years of…" the Count protested.

"They represent money," Arabella cut in. "Money that enables you to engage in your little … 'hobby' without anyone asking you difficult questions. Is it true that you can control them?"

"They do my bidding, as I am their creator."

The Doctor jerked back, his heart in his mouth. There was no mistaking it. That was the Count speaking.

"How do you communicate?"

"I direct them."

"How?"

"As one would train a dog," the Count replied. "They come into existence and I am all they know. They obey me without question."

"I want dominion," Arabella said quite simply. There was a hunger in her voice that made the Doctor shiver.

"Dominion?" the Count gasped.

"I have dedicated my life to hunting creatures such as these, mythical beasts that still roam the earth. But I want more, I want to control them – and I will in time. There are humans who have a power even greater than your own. A natural power. We are aware there is one who may lead us down that road. But for now – your creatures are in demand for the sport they bring."

"A human who can speak to animals?" the Count's voice sounded incredulous.

"You are not the only one with a gift, Count. There are others, and their abilities would have extraordinary uses for an organization such as ours. But for the moment, that is not your concern. You must focus on improving your skills and providing me with wolpertingers for our mutual benefit."

The Doctor felt his legs almost buckle. Did Arabella know it was Edith who had that power? There was no way. They had all been so careful.

"What do you do with my creations after they have been hunted?" the Count demanded.

Arabella laughed cruelly.

"You mean after they have been killed?" said Ivan. "None survive – you can be sure of that. We sell what parts we can; the rest we either serve to the guests as dinner or we burn."

Arabella's voice cut in sharply. The Doctor could imagine her hard, flat stare.

"You are being well paid, but the next specimen I collect must prove to be a unique challenge."

"Perhaps I am ready to create a new species rather than the creatures you just slaughter?" the Count said. He spoke with a relish that made the Doctor's skin crawl.

"I have the perfect fusion in mind. Why, only yesterday, I obtained a magnificent creature, a huge dog, that will enable my new creation to scent out both prey and predators. We can continue to improve upon the existing experiments."

Arnold! The Doctor grimaced and squeezed his eyes

shut for a moment. It was all he could do to stop himself barging into the room and trying to throttle both Arabella and the Count. He made himself breathe out slowly. He wouldn't get within two metres of them before Ivan was on him, and all Arabella's killers were outside. No, he had to be smart.

Arabella barked a loud laugh. "No. You are getting above yourself. I am not yet interested in your hybrid deviances other than the immediate challenge they provide for people paying to kill them. This next one must surpass any to date. The hunt we have planned will need to be exquisite. The parties involved have promised considerable investment in our organization. Investment we need to fund our own extensive organization. Then in time, we can allow your vision to develop."

"But I can already create..." the Count began.

"I need your best yet within the month. If it is not ready for this hunt, I may well tire of your arrogance and put an end to your 'experiments' once and for all," Arabella cut the Count off, her voice like steel, the threat in her tone unmistakable.

"A month?" The Count's voice now sounded panicked.

"Do you have a problem with that?" Ivan snarled.

The Doctor edged himself even closer against the door, desperate not to miss a word of the conversation.

"B-b-b-but a month is too soon!" cried the Count. "You must understand, the phoenix is only just reborn, it will not survive yet another short life cycle. To have a wolpertinger ready within a month would mean I'd need to make it in the next couple of days. They need nurturing and feeding to be strong before they can be handed over. I don't yet have all the animals I require. The demand on the phoenix – to remove more of its ashes … it may not survive—"

The Doctor heard a sudden sharp smacking noise, then a cry of shock and pain.

"Now, now, Ivan," Arabella said silkily. "Don't damage him. He must remain in one piece – that is, whilst he is still of use to us. You *are* still of use to us, aren't you, Count?"

"Yes," the Count hissed.

"It is good you have spirit," Ivan snarled. "It will make things more interesting if you are unable to deliver what has been asked."

"There is no one else who can create these masterpieces. You need me," the Count cried, managing to sound both fearful and furious.

"We need you about as much as we need one of your wolpertinger's turds," Ivan retorted.

The Count gasped in outrage.

"Let us not get too worked up. The Count knows how much we value his skills. His creations are of tremendous benefit to us, and we appreciate his work."

There was a pause. The Doctor waited, barely daring to breathe.

"I need the ultimate wolpertinger," Arabella continued. "Your best work yet. It must challenge some very demanding and ... bloodthirsty individuals. If you don't yet have all the creatures you require, then you need to rapidly acquire them. As for the phoenix, if it can't regenerate this time, take all the ashes you can, and we will capture another of the birds. The Syndicate will assist. We intend to round them up anyway. Wolpertingers have immeasurable value and their production is an important source of income. Soon we will facilitate wolpertingers of people's choosing, create them to order. The possibilities are limitless. An elephant crossed with a crocodile! Think on your wildest ambitions, Count. Do you see? The trade in them could be limitless. Your time will come!"

There was a silence. Then, "I understand," he said slowly.

"Good. Well, that concludes our meeting. Ivan and I will bid you farewell. We will be back later after we have scouted the area ready for tomorrow."

"Of course, madam."

The Doctor had heard enough. He had to leave undiscovered. The Count was working with the Syndicate! His mind reeling, he turned and begun hurrying back down the steps, pushing the tapestry aside. Then he ran full tilt down the next staircase. Faintly, he heard what could only have been the heavy iron door being dragged open.

Breathlessly, he slipped out of the front door and began skidding back down the bank of the river.

He had learned that it was the Count who was behind the whole debacle. He was the root of all evil in this place. Worse was that he had learned why. Arabella Spearstrike and the blasted Syndicate were paying him to create wolpertingers for their sick hunting. He thought of Arabella's words: *There are humans who have a power even greater than your own.* Was Edith the human who Arabella had spoken of, with gifts that could prove useful to the Syndicate? Could it be his niece that she was talking about? The power to talk to animals, to control them, to make them do their bidding – whether to be killed or, he supposed, to kill was a power that the Syndicate would do anything to get their hands on, and with the Count and his ability to create wolpertingers, could they take it from her? The

Doctor shuddered.

He shook his head in disbelief as he ran. Once again, the Syndicate were enmeshed in a wickedness of unparalleled magnitude.

He had just days to try to stop this evil once and for all.

CHAPTER ELEVEN

*In which Edith and the Doctor make
a plan and the clock is ticking...*

The Doctor paced up and down Francis's room, pausing only to cast a quick glance at the slumbering form on the bed. Occasionally Francis would twitch, his body battling the venom as it seeped into his circulation.

There was a light tap at the door and the Doctor spun, darting over to peer through a crack in the door before opening it wide.

"Edie, Zee-Zee, you're back!" he said with a broad smile of relief.

"Uncle, look at this," Edith began, holding out her hand. Blaze sat calmly in her palm.

"A bat? With a fluffy tail and a squashed-up face?"

"A wolpertinger. He saved us."

The Doctor's gaze flicked from Edith to the creature and back again.

"A wolpertinger that didn't work," Zee-Zee added.

"Hey – I'm right here, you know. I work!"

The Doctor's eyes gleamed as he studied Blaze and then deftly reached out a hand to scoop the little creature from Edith's palm and raised him up to his eyeline.

"You are unique, my little friend. That is always a blessing, never a curse. Don't forget that."

"I'm beginning to like your uncle already," Blaze said, sitting up a little straighter.

The Doctor cleared his throat, handing Blaze back to Edith. "Francis is holding on, but time is against us. Tell me your news and what we need to do with this little one. Then I'll update you on developments here."

Edith and Zee-Zee wasted no time in explaining their adventures in the forest.

"Good thinking with the stick, Zee-Zee," the Doctor commented as Edith told him about the fight with the snakes.

"It was Blaze who saved us, Doctor. He jumped on to the snake, and we made it to safety," Zee-Zee said.

"Still, your action protected Edie and it was brave to

take on an aggressive snake."

"Edie was the brave one; she wouldn't let the snake eat Blaze."

The Doctor nodded and smiled at his niece.

"Blaze has the antivenom, Uncle," Edith said. "He has antibodies in his body."

"I'm mostly still bat," Blaze added.

The Doctor pursed his lips. "It's a clever idea to try to take it from Blaze. There's no denying that it would be faster than trying to make the antivenom ourselves, but…"

"But what, Uncle?" Edith asked.

"But is Blaze's blood compatible? If not, we would be putting Francis in even more peril! There are several different blood types amongst humans, let alone amongst animals. My blood type is O, for example; my red blood cells have no antigens so they are safe for anyone. That's why I could have made the antivenom. We have no idea if Blaze's blood would be a safe match."

"What would happen if they don't match?" Zee-Zee said.

"Francis would suffer a major internal reaction and his body would shut down. He would die."

"I didn't think about the need to match blood types. I never even thought of it. I'm so silly," Edith said quietly.

She felt helpless; after all that effort, Francis still might not survive.

"*But my blood is already a fusion,*" Blaze said to Edith, avidly following the conversation.

"*What do you mean?*" Edith said.

"*I've got squirrel blood in me already, haven't I? Whatever they did to me, they must have changed my blood so it can be mixed.*"

Edith repeated what Blaze had said to her and the Doctor nodded thoughtfully.

"It is called xenotransfusion – the transfer of blood from one species to the veins of another. Blaze could be right. His blood must have been modified along with the rest of him. His bat body has been melded with that of a squirrel. He has not suffered any adverse reaction. Perhaps wolpertinger blood can be mixed with any species."

"What other choices do we have?" Zee-Zee added. "The snakes will never give us venom willingly – we know that now. I only got the tiniest amount; it's not enough."

There was a long pause. "You're right," said the Doctor heavily. "We don't have many other options." He glanced at Blaze. "Is your friend certain he wants to help us? He'll be very weak after we take his blood."

"I'm ready! But don't forget – you promised to help fix my wing!" Blaze piped up in Edith's head.

"He wants to help, Uncle, but he has a big tear in his wing and he can't fly. Can we fix that for him?"

The Doctor immediately walked over to a bag in the corner. "Edie, we can do something about that right away."

The Doctor started rummaging around, pulling out a small bottle from the bag. "Hold him still, Edie," the Doctor went on. "And Zee-Zee, if you don't mind, this is a job for all of us. Could you please come over here and spread his wing out whilst Edie holds him? I'm going to glue the hole."

"Glue it?" Zee-Zee asked.

"Regeneration of a bat's wing material can be miraculous," said the Doctor, examining the wing, "and often it can happen on its own. But sometimes, with large tears like this, a helping hand is required to get the process off to a strong start."

"They can heal by themselves?" Zee-Zee said, fascinated.

"Small tears heal quickly. The wing is living tissue, so it has all the components necessary to heal over time. The problem is large rents like this don't really have the chance. They need to be glued together so the tissue can then knit itself. Blaze will need to fly gently, give his wing time to strengthen, or the tear will open right up again."

"Will the glue cause any issues?" Edith asked.

"Not if we're careful. Edie, you must also tell Blaze not to lick the seam."

"*Got it*," said Blaze cheerfully.

The Doctor worked fast. Pulling a small roll of tape from his pocket, he tore off a strip and placed it behind the bat's outstretched wing. Next, he gently pulled the two edges of the tear together, so that they were held by the tape. Then he opened his bottle of glue.

"A small amount like this will do the job perfectly, Edie, but we need to be careful not to crease the wing." The Doctor's face was screwed up in concentration as he deftly brought the two edges together until they aligned perfectly.

"There," he said, stepping back and regarding Blaze's outstretched wing. "We'll remove that tape in a moment, as soon as the glue has dried. As I said, Edie, please tell our new friend to take it easy for a bit. Normal tears take about eight weeks to heal, so no flying in strong winds. In fact, he's to glide as much as possible."

Edith relayed the instruction to Blaze, who gave his

wing an experimental flap.

"*Amazing! Now, take my blood!*" he declared.

"He's ready for us to do the transfusion, Uncle," Edith said.

The Doctor tapped his chin. "We can either take this from the cephalic vein, which is located along the leading edge of the patagium, or we can use the saphenous vein. That's found in the uropatagium and runs parallel to the femur…"

He glanced up to see both Edith and Zee-Zee looking at him blankly.

"I think go for the wing, Edie," the Doctor said, handing Edith a small needle and tube.

"Me?" she exclaimed.

"You're my apprentice, aren't you?" the Doctor said with a grin.

Casting a nervous look at Zee-Zee, who gave her an encouraging nod, Edith very carefully studied the small vein that ran over Blaze's wing.

"*Don't miss!*" Blaze said.

Edith began to insert the needle.

"*Does it hurt?*" she thought.

"*Not in the slightest,*" replied the brave little creature.

As the blood began to drip, the Doctor carefully manoeuvred the tube to collect a few drops.

"Excellent job, Edie. I have a feeling Blaze's blood will be more potent than a creature many times his size. Bat blood has always been used in ancient folklore as a cure for all sorts of things – for good luck; as a cure for baldness, rheumatism, consumption. The link with bats and witchcraft goes back into the mists of history. But Blaze has something even more special – the power of the phoenix is within him. We should only need a few drops."

"Phoenix-infused bat blood! Now that sounds like a potent mix!" Blaze declared happily.

The Doctor studied the blood in the tube and nodded to himself in satisfaction.

Carefully mixing the blood sample into a fluid infusion, the Doctor rigged it up on a drip so it could trickle into Francis. Francis lay still and didn't stir or flinch throughout.

"Well," said the Doctor, checking the drip, "all seems to be fine. We will have to observe Francis carefully for the next few hours. Now listen carefully, I'm afraid I have something rather shocking to tell you."

His face took on a deadly serious expression. A knot of worry solidified in Edith's stomach.

"Is everything OK, Uncle?"

"The Syndicate are here. We knew they would somehow be involved with all this misery, so that is not surprising. However, the person who is making all the wolpertingers, the one who has the phoenix, who has captured Arnold … is the Count."

Edith took a step towards the bed and slumped down on the edge of it. Zee-Zee just stared at the Doctor, his face uncomprehending.

"No, it can't be," he said.

"I'm afraid so," the Doctor sighed. "I overheard them talking. He is working for Arabella Spearstrike. Supplying her with creatures for the Syndicate to hunt."

He quickly explained all he had seen and heard in the Tower.

"And he has captured Arnold as well?" Edith whispered.

"Yes, to use him in his terrible experiments. He fooled us all," the Doctor replied, his lips a thin line of suppressed anger.

"We must find a way back into the Tower, a way to free Arnold," Zee-Zee said, looking just as shocked as Edith.

Edith didn't speak for a moment. Then she said, "The Count must have drugged the sausages! That's why Arnold fell asleep. He wasn't chased – he was taken!" She turned her gaze on Zee-Zee. "He gave the sausages to you!"

The statement sounded like an accusation. The words were bitter on Edith's lips but she had to know. She stared into Zee-Zee's eyes, watching for his response.

"No!" Zee-Zee's voice raised itself in an earnest, vehement denial. He looked crushed and spread his hands helplessly. "I had no idea about any of this. I don't understand. I mean, I knew the Count was strange, but he has been so kind to us. So generous. I had no idea he would do something like this."

"I'm sure it was a woman's voice I heard in the place where they made me. A room full of cages," Blaze said, his voice still a little sleepy after the transfusion.

Edith's head spun. Did the Count have an accomplice? Aside from Arabella, there was only one woman she could think of. She couldn't bring herself to voice her thoughts.

Zee-Zee swallowed, tears springing into his eyes.

"I never thought he would drug and kidnap Arnold. I would have thrown the sausages in the river had I even suspected it. Please believe me!"

Edith looked at him, fighting back tears of her own.

"You do believe me, don't you?" Zee-Zee said again, desperately looking from Edith to the Doctor.

Edith nodded, her body sagging slightly, not trusting herself to speak. She realized she had been holding her breath for what felt like an age. She exhaled heavily. It would have been almost unbearable to think Zee-Zee was also involved in all of this somehow.

"Yes, of course we believe you, Zee-Zee," said the Doctor, taking a step closer. "But what about your mother? Do you think she suspects what sort of man the Count really is?"

Edith realized that her uncle had had the same thought she had.

Zee-Zee bit his lower lip and shook his head.

"I asked her about the wolpertinger," he said. "It's the first thing I did when we got back."

"What did she say?" the Doctor asked gently.

"She asked if you were all safe. She is sure we were attacked by a bear and what I described was my imagination." But Zee-Zee sounded uncertain.

"What are you not saying, Zee-Zee?" the Doctor persisted.

"Do you remember she warned us not to eat the sausages, Edie? She might have thought something might happen if we did."

Edith nodded, replaying the moment that Zee-Zee's mother had handed over the box of sausages.

"She wouldn't ever want to hurt you or anyone, especially not Arnold, but ... she knows he loves animals, that he would always have an animal's best interests at heart. He sedates the ones he finds injured in the forest to bring them back to the Tower. My mother may have been worried he got them muddled up with normal sausage slices."

Edith gasped. "How can he love animals after what we know he has done?" She couldn't help her voice rising in outrage.

"Oh, Edie," the Doctor cut in. "He is animal obsessed. How he could he not be? In order to create a wolpertinger, you must understand the creatures you want to combine, know them intimately. It is a dangerous and strange love for animals, but a love nevertheless."

"My mother will not defend what he has done, but without him, we have nothing – no money, no food. We would be lost and my mother … she would do anything to protect me. The Count gave us a chance…" Zee-Zee's tone was one of abject anguish.

"How can your mother not know about the wolpertingers? She's there every day!"

Zee-Zee gave a firm shake of denial with his head.

"No. She would never get caught up this type of horror. As I said, she knows that the Count gives the animals drugged food sometimes if they're frightened, but only to make them go to sleep so they can be helped.

My mother is a good person, Edie, you must believe me."

Blaze had heard a female voice in the background of wherever he had been taken. But perhaps he hadn't. Perhaps it had just been the Count's high-pitched voice.

Edith gave Zee-Zee the best smile of reassurance she could muster. If Arnold was sedated at least it would explain why he had felt so sleepy in the forest and why she hadn't been able to properly communicate with him. He was still drugged!

"But why did the Count pretend to help us search for Arnold?" Edith asked.

"Simple," the Doctor replied. "Firstly, to throw us off the scent. If he was seen to be helping us look, we wouldn't be looking for him. Secondly, and more importantly, he overheard us talking about the virus. He doesn't want his captive bird at risk. That's why he lured you away – to get the vaccine. That wolpertinger that was following you both through the forest – it wasn't chasing you, Edie; it was protecting him. It had taken Arnold and come back to its master."

The three of them looked at each other in silence for a moment, contemplating the horror of all that was unfolding.

"How can we rescue Arnold and the phoenix?" Edith asked helplessly. "They outnumber us!"

"*I can help!*" Blaze broke in, his expression one of fierce determination. "*That Count can't be allowed to do this. We are at war! I must take this news back to the colony. They can help us even the odds!*"

Edith turned to the Doctor. "Uncle, Blaze wants to go back to the forest – he thinks the colony might help us break into the Tower."

"He shouldn't be flying just yet, Edie; the glue is still binding. Give it a few hours."

"*There's no time,*" squeaked Blaze. "*I must go now. If the colony leave for the night's hunt, it'll be too late to help rescue your dog and the phoenix.*"

"He says if he doesn't go now, he won't be able to talk to the colony."

The Doctor walked over to study Blaze's wing.

"All right," he said reluctantly. "But tell him he must fly slowly and very carefully. If he pushes it, the tear will reopen."

Edith didn't waste a moment, repeating the Doctor's instructions to Blaze. Then, gently scooping him up, she took him to the window and opened it enough for him to launch himself off into the afternoon air.

"*Be back soon!*" he cried. "*Keep the window open!*"

"He is a good friend," the Doctor said.

But Edith noticed that his expression was grim.

"What is it, Uncle? I am sure Blaze will come through for us."

"It's not just that, my dear. Our window to save Arnold and the phoenix is small. To stand any chance, we must act now. Arabella and her hunters will be out in the forest this afternoon, scouting the area for their hunt tomorrow. That evil man will be alone. It's our one chance to overpower him and rescue those creatures. But we cannot leave Francis until the transfusion has finished."

"You must go now," croaked a deep voice.

All three of them jumped at the sound of Francis speaking behind them. The big man had his eyes open and he had clearly been listening to the conversation.

"You must go now," he repeated. "Save Arnold and the phoenix."

"Francis, we cannot leave you…"

"No. Please, Doctor, please go and rescue Arnold. I am already feeling stronger. If you wait for me to be back on my feet, it will be too late for him. If I was going to have a reaction, I would have had it by now." And his voice tailed off to a whisper.

Edith couldn't help herself. She rushed to his bedside. "But what if the antivenom doesn't work properly? What if you suddenly get worse again? I can go back and try to find more of those evil snakes."

Francis shook his head, a smile tugging at the edges of his exhausted mouth.

"If that needs to be done, then you can save me after you have rescued Arnold. I'm strong enough to hold on for a little longer yet and feeling stronger by the minute. You must go now, in the daylight."

Edith looked at her uncle. The Doctor chewed his lower lip, his eyes flicked to the window and he stared out towards the Tower, lost in thought.

"Uncle?"

The Doctor gave a great sigh.

"Francis is right, Edie. Time is very much against us. Arabella and her killers are distracted whilst the Count will be planning to make his wolpertinger. Our best chance to rescue Arnold and the phoenix is probably now, in daylight, when nothing is prowling around the Tower itself."

The Doctor turned to face Zee-Zee.

"Your mother may be able to help us. Do you think she will?"

"I think so," Zee-Zee said. "Once she hears the full extent of what the Count has done, the harm he has caused, my mother will go to the ends of the earth to stop him." Zee-Zee looked up at the clock on the wall. "She is between shifts at the Tower so she should be back here, somewhere in the guest house."

"Would you mind asking her to meet us in the reception?" the Doctor asked, arching an eyebrow.

Zee-Zee nodded.

"Thank you, Zee-Zee. We'll meet you down there in ten minutes."

Having made the decision, the Doctor seemed galvanized with energy. As Zee-Zee left to find his mother, he strode across the room and began flinging things into his bag, talking to Francis all the while.

"Francis, you must not move. Do you understand how important that is, my friend? Let the antivenom do it's job. We have enough to contend with without you succumbing whilst we are gone."

Francis nodded and closed his eyes. Within seconds he was back in an exhausted slumber.

"Come on, Edie, now is our chance. I want you to take these and stuff them into your pockets." He handed Edith some vials and a couple of needles and syringes.

"They might come in handy. After all, we don't know what we'll find when we get into that tower – and it's best you're equipped. I'll explain what they are as we walk."

With that, the Doctor

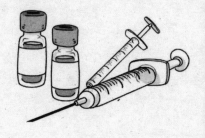

pulled open the door and strode out into the hallway. With a final glance at Francis, Edith followed. She felt sick with worry – but what choice did they have? Both of her dear friends were in the gravest danger and time was against them.

CHAPTER TWELVE

In which Edith, Zee-Zee and the Doctor attempt to raid the Tower, but an unexpected twist puts all their hopes in jeopardy…

Edith, the Doctor, Zee-Zee and Ai Lam huddled in the shadow of the vast Tower. It loomed ominously over them.

They had all met in the reception of the guest house and Ai Lam had listened to the Doctor carefully. Initially, she had been in denial, the scale of what had been going on right under her nose beggared belief. Finally, as the pieces of the puzzle had started to make sense, she had shaken her head with wearied acceptance, her face etched with a deep-seated sense of fear and trepidation.

Horrified by the web of deceit the Count had spun around her and Zee-Zee, she had agreed to help.

Having just come back from her shift, she knew the Count was heading out for a "walk" before the hunting feast tonight; there was something he had said he wanted to try to find in the forest. She said they had the best chance of rescuing Arnold and the phoenix if they left immediately. The problem, she had told them, was that she had no keys to the top part of the Tower and they would have to somehow get through the heavy iron door that the Doctor had encountered on his last visit.

"Any windows?" the Doctor asked now, as they stood looking up at the Tower.

"There is a small one, very high up on the side," Ai Lam replied, pointing. "You can just make it out. That's the window into the hidden rooms right at the top. The ones that overlook the river."

The Doctor nodded and said nothing. Edith wondered what her uncle was planning. The door to the level of the secret room sounded impossibly heavy and thick and, without a key, she couldn't imagine how they would get through it; but she trusted him implicitly.

"I will let you in the side entrance before walking round to the front. The Count will be expecting me to have opened the front door and I can keep watch from there," Ai Lam said, her eyes darted around the building to make sure they were unobserved.

"How long before the Count comes back, do you think?" the Doctor asked.

Ai Lam shrugged. "He could be back in two minutes or two hours. I think it depends whether he finds what he's looking for. But if he thinks you have been in the Tower, he will suspect I let you in. The risk –" Ai Lam's eyes locked on to Zee-Zee's – "is very great. If he even thinks I am untrustworthy, I am certain he will fire me. Without his support we'll be penniless here … and if he catches you…"

Edith swallowed, a lump forming in her throat as tears brimmed in Ai Lam's eyes.

"Mother, we must do this. We have to stop him," Zee-Zee said softly.

"I'm sorry I didn't believe you about the bear creature…" she said to Zee-Zee.

"He can't be allowed to do these things, Mother," Zee-Zee replied, placing his hand gently on her shoulder.

Ai Lam dipped her head as the Doctor nodded.

"Zee-Zee, this is as far as you go as well. Edie and I must do this alone. Your mother is right, if the Count sees you with us, he will know Ai Lam let us in the Tower. If just Edie and I are discovered, there is every chance he will believe we broke in or stole a key. As things stand, the Count has no suspicion that we know he is behind all this. He won't be looking for intruders."

Zee-Zee made to protest but the Doctor held up his hand.

"You will be of immense use to us keeping watch from outside. You need to be out of sight, but if the Count returns early, you must signal so we know to hide. Perhaps you can even distract the Count if needs be. Understand? It will buy us a little more time to hide or hopefully escape before he even reaches the front door." The Doctor held Zee-Zee's eye until he gave him a single nod of acceptance.

The Doctor cleared his throat before continuing.

"Ai Lam, you must act as if nothing is out of the ordinary. If we are discovered, you must be surprised. If we fail, we will need your help to tend to Francis and alert the authorities to where we are. There is slim chance they will respond in any timely manner, but it is the only chance we will have."

Ai Lam nodded.

"But Doctor, I really could help," Zee-Zee pleaded.

The Doctor held up his hand. "Zee-Zee – you know the owl sound?"

Zee-Zee also gave a quick nod.

"That's the signal. Your help out here is as valuable to us – if not more so – as it would be inside the Tower itself. Giving us the vital warning to hide could make all the difference. If we can avoid detection, we may still succeed if we are in the Tower itself – whether the Count is there or not."

Edith gave Zee-Zee a warm smile.

"I'll see you soon," she said.

Zee-Zee looked at her, the reluctance of being left behind etched across his smooth features. He glanced at his mother who reached out to squeeze his hand.

"Good luck," he said quietly. "I'll be right outside if you need me."

"Then let's go," said the Doctor.

Stepping nimbly aside to let Ai Lam lead the way, the Doctor gave his cap a quick readjustment and, with a glance of farewell at Zee-Zee, tucked in beside Edith. They followed the small lady as she led them to a side door midway down the old church building.

Zee-Zee stood back and watched them go with a look of pained regret. Then he too darted off the path, racing to find a hiding place from where he could keep a lookout and call the warning signal if the Count returned.

Upon reaching the door, Ai Lam hurriedly unlocked and opened it for the Doctor and Edith to slip inside.

"The lower door at the end of the church leads up to the Tower section," she whispered. "It will be open but, as I mentioned, once you go up the stairs, the doors at the upper levels are always locked. The secret passageway to the Count's private section is hidden behind the tapestry. You will need to get through the heavy door at the top somehow and I have no idea where a key might be. I've never been in there myself. I think he keeps it on a chain around his neck... If he returns to find you trying to break in, you could be trapped in the narrow stairway... There won't be many places to hide."

"Will the Count use this door when he comes back?" the Doctor asked as he and Edith stepped into the gloomy interior of the old church.

Ai Lam pointed. "The Count always returns through the main entrance. That's where I will go now. When he comes into the church, he walks through the building and goes straight up to the Tower. If Zee-Zee hasn't managed to alert you, I will also drop something as a signal."

"Thank you, Ai Lam."

"Good luck," she said softly, and, with that, she quickly pulled the door shut behind them, leaving Edith and the Doctor standing in the dark, listening as the sound of Ai Lam's footsteps receded from outside.

"Right, Edie, I've been up to that secret passageway before. It's where I heard Arabella and the Count discussing their hideous plans. Follow me."

Edith nodded, her eyes darting nervously around the gloom. The old church seemed far more eerie than the time she had been in it before. With no lights on, it took her a moment to get her bearings.

"This way," her uncle whispered. He gave her a reassuring smile. "Don't worry, my dear. There will be no wolpertingers hiding here. The Count will not have expected us to have broken in."

"How will we get through the door on the upper level, Uncle?" Edith asked.

"Leave that to me. I haven't yet found a lock I can't get through. Remember, with all the lights off, look for a glow – a phoenix can vary the strength of its light but it can never totally hide it."

Edith couldn't help but grin at the twinkle in her uncle's eye. *He's almost enjoying this*, she thought to herself.

"Come on," the Doctor said. "Let's go and find our friends, shall we?"

The Doctor swiftly led Edith to the doorway behind the old altar. In moments, they were both entering the tower section of the building. The stairs were narrow and dark. Edith began to climb upwards, her breath coming in short sharp gasps as her legs burned with the climb.

"This is as bad as the mountains!" she heard her uncle exclaim.

They paused momentarily on the landing to catch their breath, then pushed past the tapestry and began to climb up the secret passageway until they stopped outside the huge, heavy door. Edith heard something that made her heart almost stop.

"Uncle!" she said suddenly, cocking her head.

"*Whooo-hoooo-hooooo*," came the faint noise.

"It's Zee-Zee! The Count's coming back – and we've only just got to the door! Shall we run back down and hide in the church?"

The Doctor gave a firm shake of his head. "Step aside, my dear, and let me look at this door. A little skill I picked up in Mexico a few years back. There was a report of a chupacabra with an infected tooth, terrifying creatures by all accounts, but we must do what we can in such circumstances. We never found it, but our guide was a most resourceful character. Taught me and Francis a few handy tricks."

Rummaging in his pockets, the Doctor produced a small leather pouch, bending down to unroll it on the floor.

"Edie, whilst I'm doing this, can you try to reach out to Arnold and the phoenix? Prepare them for our visit. This will all be quite rushed, I suspect."

Edith tried to focus her mind as her uncle began plucking out various pointed instruments, inserting two of them into the keyhole of the big door and grimacing with concentration.

"The trick is to shift these driver pins until they reach their shear line, and the lock should open..." the Doctor muttered to himself.

"Arnold, can you hear me?"

Edith waited, willing Arnold to answer.

"Arnold?" Edith gritted her teeth as she pushed the thought out.

"Edie ... Edie ... is that you?"

"Arnold, we're coming, we're going to be with you in a moment. Where are you in the room?"

"I don't know. There's a blanket over the cage. I'm all headachy... Is the Doctor with you?"

"Yes, we're trying to pick the lock. The Count is coming so we'll have to find somewhere to hide when we get in the room. Are you OK?"

"I'll tell you something, Edie," Arnold said.

"What?"

"I'm really hungry…"

Suddenly there was an almighty crash below and the Doctor and Edith looked at each other in alarm.

"Ai Lam has dropped something. It's the signal the Count is inside. He's coming through the church," Edith said, fighting to keep the panic from her voice.

"Did you manage to speak to Arnold?" the Doctor grunted, twisting his hands this way and that as he poked at the lock.

"Arnold said he's in a cage but it has a blanket on it. He doesn't know much more."

The Doctor didn't say anything, just nodded. Then there was a loud click. The lock had sprung.

Withdrawing his lock picks, the Doctor stood and put his shoulder against the door.

"Quick, Edie," he said. "Help me push."

As Edith leaned her weight against the heavy metal door, it slowly began to open. They could hear footsteps below them and then a voice rang out.

"Count?"

The footsteps halted. It was Ai Lam's voice – she was speaking loudly.

"Do you want me to bring you anything?"

"No, I must get this injured creature upstairs where

I can tend to him. You know I like to be left in peace up here, Ai Lam. I will come down later," the Count replied.

With a final heave, the Doctor and Edith squeezed through the doorway, and together they pushed the door shut again as quickly as they could.

"Can you lock it?" Edith said as they gave it a final heave and it shut with a click.

"There is no time, Edie. We have but moments to find a hiding place in this room."

Turning, Edith gasped. She hadn't noticed immediately, but there was a glass partition spanning the width of the whole room. It was a double entry/exit system, she thought, like in a laboratory. The glass door leading through it also seemed locked, but she couldn't see a keyhole.

Spotting a button on the wall, Edith pushed it hard, and the glass door clicked open in release. Together they dashed through the partition. Aside from a faint glow towards the very back of the room, the darkness made it nearly impossible to see where they were going.

"Can you see anywhere to hide?" the Doctor asked.

Edith looked around at the impossibly high walls. There had once been another set of windows up there, but now they were blocked up. Instead of pictures, there were rows upon rows of hooks. Each one was adorned

with either a bleached white animal skull, a stuffed animal head or a set of horns and antlers. All of them were angled towards the middle of the room, as if waiting for a speech to begin. It was horrifying, Edith thought, as her eyes flashed around each in turn.

"There are so many heads…" she whispered. "Why?"

"He is a troubled man," her uncle replied sadly, "living behind that mask of benign civility."

Despite the gloom, Edith slowly began to make out many large objects, each covered by a thick blanket.

"They must be the cages, Edie," said the Doctor, noticing them as well. "Don't disturb anything for the moment, but I am certain that Arnold will be in one."

Edith's heart skipped a beat with the thought that Arnold was close.

"Uncle, I can see a faint glow at the back of the room," she said urgently.

"Yes, well spotted, let's head towards it," the Doctor said quite calmly.

Edith followed her uncle as they darted between the covered cages. As the glow at the far end of the room grew stronger, her uncle slowed, and Edith craned her head around him so she could see the bird beyond.

The phoenix was motionless at the bottom of a large domed cage. There was no blanket over it and she stared at the bird in concern. Something about the phoenix immediately struck Edith as odd. Whilst it was noticeably smaller than the one she had met before, it was also less radiant, its glow dull and flat. Edith threw a worried look at her uncle.

"It's sick," she said softly.

The phoenix sat quietly. As diminutive a figure as it was, it still radiated a power that drew Edith closer. As she studied it, Edith realized something else was wrong. The phoenix wasn't … whole. Its tail feathers appeared somewhat stunted and one wing was lower than the other. As her eyes began to take in more details, she saw with a shock that it was also missing a toe on one of its feet.

"What's happened?" Edith spoke the thought aloud, unable to stop the question escaping her lips.

The Doctor shook his head in anger. "The Count has taken too many of its ashes. The phoenix has been damaged irreparably. It can no longer be reborn complete. It is a disgrace, an outrage."

Edith cleared her mind, doing her best to keep calm. *"Can you hear me? We have come to help you."*

The only sign the phoenix gave that it could understand Edith was a single blink of its eye. Other than that, it remained motionless in the centre of its cage.

"You are in grave danger. You should flee." Its voice suddenly echoed in her head.

Edith felt the icy grip of fear clutch her and she swallowed it down, composing herself.

"We will help you escape."

"You cannot."

"You are at risk of a virus that will stop you being reborn. We came to free you and to give you a vaccine, to protect you."

"No."

The phoenix raised its leg off the ground, as if to emphasize the missing toes on its scaly foot.

"I wish to die."

"But you can't die…"

"I will eventually. As you can see – I am no longer whole. I have lived for several millennia. This man has mastered dark arts that should have been long forgotten. There is only one solution. He needs only take a little more and I will be gone. It will finish."

Edith's jaw dropped. The phoenix didn't want to be rescued. It was sick of living – and no wonder, Edith thought to herself, trapped in this metal cage at the top of his Tower.

"What has he done to you?" the Doctor muttered under his breath, staring at the dull-looking creature in front of him and oblivious to the exchange it had had with Edith.

The phoenix regarded the Doctor without any indication of alarm or surprise. It was almost as if the bird was indifferent to anyone or anything.

"Don't give up," Edith found herself thinking, half pleading with the bird.

The phoenix didn't react.

A sudden noise startled the Doctor and Edith. It was a key in the lock.

"Edie, it's the Count!" hissed the Doctor.

Edith scoured the room, seeing only cage after cage.

"Where can we hide?" Edith asked the phoenix.

"When he turns on the lights, he will see the whole room. The only hidden places are the cages," the phoenix replied.

"You mean we should hide in the cages?!" Edith thought, her heart racing.

The phoenix blinked.

The Count was trying to turn the key, not realizing the door was already unlocked. The confusion was buying them valuable seconds.

"Uncle, the phoenix suggests we hide in an empty cage." Edith cast her eyes frantically around the room. She could have sworn she could hear the door opening now. The Count was coming.

"Edie, this way!" The Doctor was moving quickly. He

dashed behind the phoenix, further back into the room, and with a flourish pulled a blanket off a cage.

Edith felt her heart lurch. Was some horrifying creature about to be exposed within?

To her immense relief, the cage was empty. The Doctor opened the door.

"You'll fit in here, Edie. Climb inside, I'll pull the blanket back over the cage."

Edith was halfway into the cage before she stopped.

"Uncle, what about you? Where will you hide?"

"Edie, there is no time for that; get into the cage quickly! I will find somewhere else. Hurry!"

Edith was plunged into total blackness as the Doctor pulled the blanket back over the cage. As she hunkered on the cage floor, she pushed her thoughts out to the phoenix.

"What is happening?"

The phoenix ignored her.

There was a click. Edith was suddenly aware of light creeping beneath the edges of the blanket over her cage. The Count had flicked the light switch.

There was no sound from outside. Edith strained her ears. Had the Count seen her uncle? She pushed down a growing sense of panic. She was in a cage, covered with a blanket, trapped in a room in the Count's Tower and unable to do anything about it. *At least he doesn't know I'm here*, she thought to herself.

"Impressive how you snuck in here. I thought it unlikely I forgot to lock the door, so I am quite prepared. I have my crossbow levelled at your head," a sharp voice trilled from what seemed like metres away.

Edith held her breath.

"I wondered when you would come back. You are not quite all that you seem, are you, Count? Not as shy, awkward and sweet as you'd have the world believe." It was her uncle's voice. Somehow, he sounded calm, rock steady. Unfazed to be confronted by the Count in his own home.

"How did you get through the door?" the Count demanded, ignoring the Doctor's jibe.

"I have a small selection of lock-picking tools. It was quite simple really to get into your old church and then up here – I was surprised how easy it was."

"You should have locked the door behind you. The very fact it was open prepared me. Give me your tools or I will shoot you in your leg."

There was the sound of rustling and then a thud as the small bundle of lock-picking instruments was thrown on to the floor.

"I only came into your Tower to get my dog back. You weren't in so I thought I'd come up and have a look for myself. Quite a collection of animals you have here. The phoenix we have been seeking, no less. Shall I take the other creatures with me when I go?"

The Count gave a dry chuckle. "I'm afraid they will all be staying with me."

"I beg to differ. I don't think they like it here. I plan to release them all."

"I fear it is very much the end of the road for planning

what you'd like to do, Doctor."

"What are you are doing," declared the Doctor, fire building in his voice, all pretence of civility suddenly lost, "is a disgrace. A horror. You are an abomination to mankind."

"An abomination? Far from it, Doctor. I am creating creatures you could only dream of. I am making life!"

"You create a few creatures by killing hundreds of others! And for what? So the Syndicate can sell these tortured creations to hunters? Where is the virtue in that?"

"I am making them perfect! I am helping evolution. I am creating the future inhabitants of the world. I am enhancing nature!"

The Count was almost screeching. The Doctor had clearly got under his skin. Was this his plan? Edith wondered. Would provoking the Count make him do something stupid, or would it just enrage him? The knot of worry hardened in the pit of her tummy as she listened, taking great care not to make any sound whatsoever.

"Arabella Spearstrike and her Syndicate want sport. People like her don't give a damn about evolution. They just want money and blood!" the Doctor shouted back.

"The Syndicate is a means to an end. I will play her

game for now, but my vision goes far beyond satisfying Arabella Spearstrike. Like all creators, there must be experiments. She can utilize them as she sees fit, but each time I am improving upon the last."

"And your goal? Your final wolpertinger? When will you stop?"

"When I have created the ultimate creature! A creature I will become a part of myself. A creature like no other on the planet, a creature that has all the powers nature can provide. Imagine being able to fly, gallop and swim. People and animals will worship me!"

The Count was pacing as he spoke. Edith could hear him walk right past her cage, the tone of his voice changing as he uttered the words.

"I will become a god!" he cried.

"You are deluded," the Doctor retorted.

The Count hissed and from the vehemence of the noise, Edith could tell he was furious.

"One bolt from my crossbow is all it will take, Doctor."

"Are you going to kill me? Is that your plan? People might not miss the animals you capture, but if I go missing there will be a search, you will be discovered. Your sick little laboratory will be taken away."

"No, Doctor. It is *you* who will be discovered, not me. Your body will be found, make no mistake. Well, at least most of it will be. A terrible hunting accident can leave a corpse quite mutilated. I need to progress to the next stage of my experiments … you see, I have evolved beyond just fusing animals. The thumbs I took from the couple I killed in the forest all those years ago, they were just the start."

"You killed that old couple and took their thumbs?"

"They knew too much, having helped me build the Tower. There was no choice. It was for the greater good. I used their thumbs for my first experiments. Human wolpertingers are complicated, as I discovered, but I have much more advanced skills now." The fervour in his voice made Edith shudder.

There was a sudden whistling sound. Without any further warning, the Count had pulled the trigger on his crossbow. Edith gasped. She tried to clamp her hand over her mouth to mask the noise, but it escaped before she managed to muffle it. The Doctor cried out, a hiss of pain and shock as the crossbow bolt struck him.

"The next bolt won't be so carefully aimed, Doctor. That is a mere flesh wound. Your shoulder is sliced but no bones are broken. That can change in a heartbeat. Now move. There is an empty cage at the far end of the room – pull back the blanket and climb into that."

Edith could feel her heart pounding in her chest.

Had the Count heard her? Did he mean the cage she was hiding in? Was she about to be discovered as well?

"And if I don't? You're going to kill me anyway," the Doctors voice sounded as though he was speaking through gritted teeth.

There was the sound of a cover from nearer the front of the room being pulled back.

"Arnold!" she heard her uncle exclaim.

"Your demise will be imminent, but you will witness that of your dog first."

"Arnold!" Edith thought.

"Don't make a noise, Edie, stay hidden!" Arnold's voice sounded strong in her head. *"The Doctor will find a way out of this, but he needs to know you are safe. The Count has no idea you are here as well. It must stay that way!"*

As Edith forced herself to remain immobile in her hiding place, she continued to listen. She could hear the Doctor shuffling backwards. He was moving away from her, not towards her cage after all.

"There's no need to hurt Arnold. Let him go. I'll be part of your experiment," the Doctor said, his voice tight with pain.

Edith could hear her uncle climb into his own empty cage and the Count sliding its bolts across, locking it shut.

"Indeed you will, and your love for him is

admirable – but you misunderstand. I won't hurt him unnecessarily, but he will not be released. You see, I too admire his magnificence – as I do all the animals I collect," the Count said. "His strength will be a foundation for what you will become. You and he are destined to be together for ever. You will become yet another fitting tribute to my genius."

"My compatibility with Arnold will not please Arabella." The Doctor managed to bark a soft laugh. "You have completely lost your mind. One individual's strength is another's imperfection. This is not evolution; it is nothing but dangerous science. What else will you fuse with us?"

Edith froze. Her uncle didn't need to say this; he was stalling. Was he trying to tell her something? But what? Edith thought desperately. There was nothing she could do.

It was the Count's turn to grin; Edith could hear it in his voice.

"You see! Even you are now intrigued, Doctor. You want to know what you will become! Indeed, it has been a most successful day. Not only do I now have you and your dog – I have also found an old creation I had discarded near to my tower. Oh, you have no idea how much I wanted to successfully fuse a bat. Months of searching, stalking, waiting outside that snake-infested cave to capture it and then, after all that, a failed attempt with a squirrel. I discarded the useless creature. But now I find I have another chance! The senses of that otherwise useless wolpertinger combined with the power of your dog, all fused with the heart of a man. Now that would be something. Arabella will be pleased."

For the second time in as many moments, Edith clamped her hand across her mouth. A bat wolpertinger? The Count had caught… No! There could only be one explanation. Blaze hadn't made it.

"Blaze? Is that you?" Edith thought.

"Edie! I'm sorry."

Edith's stomach lurched. Things couldn't get any worse.

"What happened?"

"The glue didn't hold. I should have waited. The Doctor was right, it needed more time to set. As I flew over the Tower, the wind caught me. I was too weak. I felt my wing go again."

Edith almost couldn't bring herself to ask, but she had to know.

"Did you see any of the bats? Did you manage to tell anyone—"

"I never made it, Edie. I came down on the bank by the river and that's where he caught me."

Edith forced herself to think. There had to be a way out; there had to be a way to save her uncle, save Arnold, save Blaze, save Francis and save the phoenix – but what?

"Don't despair."

Edith jumped at the sudden voice.

"You have more friends than you realize."

The phoenix spoke calmly, and Edith felt her pulse slow.

"What should I do?" Edith said.

"Wait."

"Wait!"

The phoenix didn't speak again, and Edith sat motionless as she listened to the Count pacing around the room.

"Now, Doctor," the Count's voice rasped. "I am just going to give you a little injection, something to help you relax. You'll need your strength tomorrow, after all."

"You're going to sedate me then. What with, I wonder? An animal drug? One ml of xylazine, perhaps?"

"It is refreshing to talk to a fellow scientist, Doctor – why yes, that's right. An animal sedative, I know, but I think it will work very nicely in your case."

"I hope you have an equal volume of antidote if I become too sedated? Atipamezole, perhaps. I could die otherwise. I'll be no good for your master creation if that happens."

The Count chuckled. "Don't fret, Doctor, I am quite an experienced anaesthetist."

Edith strained her ears. There was something in the Doctor's voice that made her wonder – was he trying to tell her something? Why had the Doctor talked about the drug dosages? It was almost as if he was encouraging the Count. Then she felt the vials in her pocket. Carefully she pulled one out. The label said *Atipamezole*.

Atipamezole – the antidote to the sedation. She peered at the label in the small amount of light that seeped below the edge of the blanket.

"Indicated for reversal of the sedative and analgesic effects of…"

This was it! The Doctor had even told her how much to use. To reverse the sedation the Count was giving him, she needed to give her uncle 1 ml of this.

The Doctor made an audible wincing sound and Edith guessed the Count had injected him through the bars of the cage.

"Sleep well, Doctor, I will see you shortly."

There was the sound of footsteps retreating. Edith heard the click of the glass door being released at the far end of the room and, shortly afterwards, the clang of the heavy door being pulled shut. She hadn't been discovered, the Count hadn't heard her. Edith waited a moment longer for the unmistakable sound of a key turning in the lock; then she pushed the door of her unlocked cage open.

The blanket slid to the floor and Edith crawled out, blinking in the light. She looked around at the cages, all of which were covered with blankets again.

"Uncle! Arnold! Blaze!" she whispered.

"Edith!" It was Arnold's voice. Edith turned, unsure which blankets to pull off, fearful to expose the creatures, thinking of the noise they would make and the danger they could bring.

"You have more friends than you think," the phoenix's voice echoed in her head again.

"What do you mean?"

"They are as trapped as you. They have no reason to hurt you."

Edith blinked in surprise. Was the phoenix saying she shouldn't worry about disturbing caged wolpertingers?

Racing forward, she began to pull blanket after blanket off the cages, peering inside, desperate to find those she loved.

To her surprise, despite their strange appearance, the creatures didn't look as terrifying as she expected. None of them hissed, barked or roared at her. A few opened one sleepy eye, but most sat quietly, looking frightened, confused and lost. Her heart went out to them. They weren't monsters; they were victims.

After the fifth cage she came to, Edith pulled back a blanket and Arnold looked up at her with a huge beat of his tail. Stooping, she quickly unbolted his cage. The big dog pushed out and gave her a huge slobbery lick with his tongue.

"*Quick, Arnold! Let's find the Doctor and Blaze. Help me pull off the blankets,*"

Arnold bounded forward and, using his teeth, slid blanket after blanket on to the floor.

The Doctor lay in a crumpled heap, his cap askew and his cape folded around himself. Blood seeped from the wound on his arm where the Count had shot him with his crossbow.

"Uncle!" Edith cried, unbolting his cage and half climbing in so that she could check his breathing.

"*He's been sedated, Edie,*" Arnold said. "*There is nothing you can do.*"

Edith's mind once again went to the vial the Doctor had given her. She pulled it out from her pocket.

"*The Doctor gave me this before we left. I think it's an antidote for the sedation.*"

Arnold gave a whine. "*But what if you're wrong, Edie?*"

"*I'm not,*" Edith thought. She was sure of it. Her uncle had trusted her enough to give her the vial and she wasn't going to let him down.

"*He must have suspected the Count would use his tranquillizers again, like he did on your sausages.*"

"*I can't resist a sausage,*" Arnold said.

Throwing a quick raised eyebrow in Arnold's direction, and before she had the chance to agonize a moment longer, Edith reached into her pocket and pulled out the needle and syringe. Drawing up 1 ml, just as the Doctor had instructed, she stuck it into the top of his uninjured arm and pushed the plunger.

Biting her lip, she stepped back, watching her uncle intently.

"Hey!" a voice called out. *"What about me?!"*

"And me!" shouted another almost next to it.

Edith turned her head in the direction of the voices just as there was a groan in front of her. It took about a minute before the Doctor's eyes flickered open and he gave her a weak smile.

"Ah, that was exciting, wasn't it? Well done, Edie. I can always depend on your quick wits and nimble mind. Have you freed Arnold and Blaze yet, my dear?"

A wave of relief washed through Edith. Running over to the last few cages, she pulled off the blankets. Sure enough, Blaze blinked up at her – and next to him, the small shape of Terry the fire-bellied toad looked up groggily.

"You forgot me!" Blaze said a little crossly.

"I didn't," Edith replied. *"I just had to help my uncle. But I've got you now."*

Edith quickly unbolted Blaze's cage door and he hopped over to Edith, casting a wary eye over the large form of Arnold, who gave his tail another wag.

"Nice to see you again, Edie," said Terry sleepily. *"Leave the door open, I'll just finish my nap first."*

Edith smiled at the creature. Then she turned to look at the phoenix.

"Time to get you out," Edith thought.

The phoenix regarded them all in silence, but Edith wasn't deterred; with two quick steps forward, she unlocked the door to the aviary and swung it open. The phoenix didn't move.

"OK," Edith began, looking around at them all. "Let's get out of here."

It was her uncle who quelled her excitement.

"We can't, Edie. There is no escape. The Count has locked the door and taken my lock-picking kit. We are still trapped, merely in a bigger cage."

Edith's face fell. Without thinking, she ran to the glass partition, pushed the button and then gave the huge heavy door the biggest tug she could. It didn't budge a fraction. Her uncle was right – they were locked in.

"I can get out," Blaze's voice piped up. *"There is one window that isn't blocked up. The one between the heavy door and the glass partition. I can get through it; I can try and make it to the colony. They will help us."*

Edith eyed the small window, thoughts racing

through her mind.

"What is it, Edie?" the Doctor said, watching Edith's face as she looked at Blaze and then at the window.

"Blaze thinks he can escape through the window at the entrance to the room. He can get help."

"But he can't fly; that's why he was captured," the Doctor said, shaking his head.

"I can walk or crawl, though! It'll take some time but I can do it!" Blaze protested.

"I could carry him," Edith said slowly to her uncle. "I could fit through that window as well – it would be a squeeze, but I could manage it. I can run with him. The river is right below that window, isn't it?"

The Doctor didn't comment immediately. Instead, he opened the glass door to the partition and strode over to the window to take a look. Pulling himself up on to the ledge, he peered through the narrow gap.

"It would require a jump quite far out to make sure you landed in the middle of the river where we know it is deep enough," he said, shaking his head. "It's incredibly fast flowing, Edie – remember how hard it was getting Francis out? The dangers of the jump, the current taking you, if the Count sees…"

"Zee-Zee will be there to help me get out of the river when the current slows downstream. I'll easily make the distance. All I have to do is keep my head above water and let it take me. Zee-Zee will be watching. He won't let us down."

The Doctor stared at her for a long moment.

"I don't like it, Edie," he said. "I think we could try to rush the Count when he comes in, force our way out. He won't be expecting us to be right behind the door."

"But he might have the crossbow and he might have that huge wolpertinger with him. And if we don't manage to overpower him, he'll have us all and Francis will die. But if I can get out with Blaze, we can get help."

"And if you don't make it?"

"Then you can still try to rush him and escape. I wouldn't be much use in fighting him anyway." Edith heard herself say the words much more bravely than she felt.

The Doctor shook his head. "Betty will have such words with me. Putting you in this situation."

"Edie, you can't go. It's too dangerous," Arnold whined, padding round to block Edith's way.

"I have to, Arnold. We need help."

"Where is Francis?" Arnold asked.

Suddenly Edith realized the big dog didn't know what had happened. He had no idea of the true extent of the predicament they were in.

She filled him in quickly, Arnold giving low, growling

whines of worry as he listened.

"We are in a mess. What if the colony bats don't come?"
Arnold thought miserably.

"I'll find someone, anyone. I'll get help," Edith replied
determinedly.

She looked at the Doctor.

"Uncle, Blaze can't do it alone. If I go with him, we can
get help, get everyone out of the Tower like we planned
and we can still free the phoenix. The Count will be
going for Francis next, and he is weakened and alone in
the guest house. If Blaze and I get help, we can protect
him as well."

The Doctor, realizing he had
little choice, gave her a grim
nod. "Remember to jump out
as far as you can, Edie; you
need to land in the middle
of the river."

Edith pulled herself
up to the ledge and,
pushing the window
open as wide as she
could, she leaned out.
A thought struck her.

"Uncle, should I

take the phoenix? If we can get the phoenix out of the Tower, then at least the Count can't make any more wolpertingers."

The Doctor shook his head. "The phoenix would light up the forest, Edie; there would be no hiding. Besides, I doubt it can swim given the state the poor bird is in."

"The Doctor is correct; I cannot escape. My destiny is clear." The phoenix spoke slowly and its voice startled Edith.

"No – we've come to rescue you. It's the reason we're here!" Edith blurted out.

"What is it, Edie?" the Doctor asked, concerned at Edith's expression.

"The phoenix has given up."

The Doctor shook his head wearily and looked over at the sorry state of the once-magnificent bird.

"I'm afraid that would be against everything we stand for, my friend," he said softly.

The phoenix blinked once in response. It didn't disagree, it didn't stir. It didn't seem to care.

"You can live free once we have stopped the Count," Edith said.

"There will always be another Count," the phoenix replied.

"We can save you," Edith pleaded, but the phoenix

said nothing. She turned to her uncle. "I should go now."

The Doctor, who had been watching Edith's silent communication with the phoenix, stepped close to the window and lifted Blaze up on Edith's lap.

"What will you do, Uncle?" Edith asked, trying not to look down.

"We'll go back to our cages and play the parts of captured specimens. If the Count comes in with his crossbow, a cursory glance may convince him all is well. We want to give you as much time as possible to arrive with reinforcements. But if it comes to it, we will be forced to make a break for it and fight him," the Doctor replied.

"I'll be as quick as I can, Uncle."

Blaze shuffled forward in Edith's lap.

"Let me go first, I should have enough wing drag to control my descent. I'll be a lot less noticeable than you jumping out of this window! As I go down, I'll check the coast is clear for you. Just try not to splash me too much when you land!" Blaze said, and before Edith had a chance to react, the little wolpertinger hopped off her lap and hurled himself out of the window.

The tear in his wing was obvious to Edith as she watched, but Blaze somehow managed to control his downward spiral to the river below. He landed with a small splash; then, just as the current started to pull him down the river, he rolled over on to his back, so that he bobbed to the surface.

"Can you hear me?" he shouted.

Edith raised her hand.

"No one seems to be about, no one looking out of these lower windows. Now is as good a time as any – jump!"

With a fleeting glance at the Doctor and Arnold, Edith sucked in a great big breath of air. Then, looking straight out towards the far bank of the river, she hurled herself off the window ledge.

With a soundless cry, her legs cycled in the air as she plummeted down towards the frothing river's bubbling waters.

CHAPTER THIRTEEN

*In which Edith and Zee-Zee try to recruit
help and win some warriors to the cause...*

Edith couldn't have screamed even if she'd wanted to –
the terrifying drop sucked all the air from her lungs.
Remembering to keep her arms down by her sides and
point her toes as she entered the water, she hit the river
like a torpedo.

Immediately, she plunged deep beneath the surface.

The coldness of the water engulfed her like an icy
blanket. Kicking hard, she tried to push herself back up
towards the surface, but her strength was fading fast with
the effort and she knew she was in serious trouble.

"Use your arms!" shouted Blaze's voice in her head.

"Pull yourself up as you kick!"

Edith did as she was told, and with one last effort her head broke the surface of the river. She drew in a huge lungful of air, gasping in relief, before she felt herself ducking back under the water again as she was swept downstream.

"Let the current take you, don't fight it!" Blaze's voice said.

As her head broke the surface a second time, she saw the bank racing by and she tried to angle towards it.

Blaze was floating on the surface of the water with his wings outstretched. Somehow managing to slow himself, Edith soon caught up with him and he hooked a claw on to her jumper so they swept downstream together.

"We're a good way from the Tower now; I can feel the drag is getting less. Let's see if we can get to the bank."

Edith didn't reply. She could hardly think – her head was full of the chilled water rushing around her – but she kicked her legs and tried again to edge them to the side of the river. It seemed to take an age – but then suddenly, her feet touched the bottom and, shivering with cold, she could wade towards the bank. Blaze was still firmly hooked on to her top.

A figure rushed down the bank towards them. Fearing that it might be a wolpertinger that the Count had released from the Tower, Edith instinctively reeled backwards.

"It's OK, Edie, it's me. That was quite some jump!"

"Zee-Zee," Edith managed through chattering teeth as Zee-Zee unzipped his coat and handed it to her.

"What happened?" Zee-Zee asked, his eyes wide with concern.

"L-l-long st-st-story," Edith stuttered, teeth chattering with the cold.

"Keep moving or you'll feel worse," Zee-Zee instructed her. "We need to get some warmth back into you."

"B-Bl-Blaze is…" Edith gestured down at the bedraggled creature now tangled up on her chest.

"OK – you walk around here and put on my coat. I'll unhook Blaze and warm him up."

By the time Zee-Zee had dried off Blaze, Edith felt slightly better. She'd managed to wring out some of her clothes, wrap herself in Zee-Zee's coat and tip all the water out of her boots.

"Nice jump!" Blaze said, and Edith flashed the little bat a smile.

"You too!" Edith said. The wolpertinger grinned back.

"Zee-Zee, we have to hurry. The Count – he captured the Doctor; he plans to make him part of a wolpertinger with Arnold. We've got to get help."

Zee-Zee's eyes widened in alarm. "I'll call the police," he said.

"There's no time; we need to help now, before the Syndicate return, before the Count can hurt my uncle and Arnold. Blaze is going to take us to the bat colony."

"Bats? How are bats going to help us?"

"Is he doubting bat power?" Blaze said indignantly.

"How far do we need to go, Blaze?"

"As it turns out, not far at all," Blaze replied.

"What do you mean? Surely we have to go into the forest and get to the cave?"

"Not exactly."

"But…" Edith began.

"They are watching us now," Blaze interrupted.

Edith spun her head round, craning her eyes up to the sky and expecting to see thousands of black specks approaching them.

"Edie," Zee-Zee said quietly. He was pointing behind Edith. "We have company."

Looking over to where Zee-Zee gestured, Edith could make out six small shapes coming towards them. As they neared, Edith determined they were the most bizarre group of bats she had ever seen in her life. The one in the centre was about the same size of Blaze, but the one immediately to its left was a huge bat, easily three times the size of its companions. The others came in very distinct shapes and sizes. One was whip thin, another had a huge grinning mouth, one seemed to have one leg slightly shorter than the other and walked towards them with a pronounced limp. The sixth bat hung back slightly and regarded them from a distance. It seemed smaller, slighter than the others. She noticed Blaze was fixing his eyes on the bat at the back.

Pirates, Edith thought to herself. If they were a group of people, they would look like pirates.

"Let me do all the talking," Blaze said quickly as the bats approached. *"The Sentinels can be a touchy lot and need careful handling,"*

"The Sentinels?" Edith asked but there was no time for Blaze to respond as another voice cut in.

"Is that ... it can't be ... what's happened to your face? And you've got a squirrel's tail?!" one bat cried incredulously.

"All right, Blaze," said the bat in the middle. *"How's things?"*

He or she must be the leader, Edith realized.

"All right, Beo."

"Beo?" Edith couldn't help herself.

"Short for Beowulf," Blaze replied quickly.

"Do all bat names start with B?" Edith giggled.

Blaze flicked her a glance that told her to be quiet.

"Can she talk bat?" Beo said, seemingly unfazed by the revelation.

"Yes, she helped me outside the cave..."

"We know, we saw," said the huge bat in a deep, sonorous voice.

"Hello, Bucky," said Blaze. He sounded shy but happy, Edith thought.

The big bat moved forward and the two embraced, Bucky effectively smothering Blaze with his bulk.

"What happened to you?" Bucky asked. "I've missed you. How come you're with the humans – and your body..."

"I've changed, but I'm still me!" said Blaze. "I was captured but I got out and now I need your help."

"We saw you crash-land by the Tower," said the bat with the huge grin.

"Couldn't believe it. Quite a jump by your girlfriend, by the way," said the whip-thin bat.

"She's not my girlfriend," Blaze blurted out.

"She's your friend and she's a girl, isn't she?" the bat with the limp said. "Then she's your girlfriend."

"Why do I have to be anyone's girlfriend? Besides, surely it's up to me who I choose to be my boyfriend?" Edith couldn't help herself interrupting. This was ridiculous; Arnold and the Doctor were stuck up in the Tower and all these bats could do was tease each other.

"Feisty girl you've got there, Blaze," one of the bats called out, and the rest of them all laughed.

Edith found herself not liking the Sentinel bats very much. Beo seemed to sense her disquiet. He held up a wing and the others fell silent.

"Let the girl who can speak bat talk," they said.

Edith hesitated, then said, "Who are you all?"

"We're the Sentinels," the one called Bucky said.

Blaze explained. "They are the bats who guard the colony, who live on the outside and carry warnings back to the colony if there's trouble."

Beo nodded. "To be a Sentinel you must be one of the toughest, most resourceful, most independent and..."

"Ugly," chipped in Blaze.

"You'd fit in well then, wouldn't you?" replied Bucky with a grin.

"... and have pledged yourself to the protection of the colony," finished Beo.

Blaze nodded wistfully. "It was always my ambition to become a Sentinel, you know."

"You'd fit in with us like a claw in a hole," said the whip-thin bat. "Tragic what happened to you, Blaze. First the snake bite, then being captured and all."

"You want to join this lot?" Edith interrupted, giving Blaze an incredulous look. "They're ridiculous. A claw in a hole – what does that even mean?"

Blaze cleared his throat, pointedly ignoring Edith's question.

"We've come to ask for your help," he said.

"I thought it was us who have come to you?" the whip-thin bat chipped in.

"OK, lads, enough is enough. Let him talk," Beo said, once again waving a wing in the air to calm things down.

As Blaze began to tell the story, Edith shared a look with Zee-Zee, who raised his eyebrows in an unspoken question.

"The Sentinels," Edith said quietly. "They're some sort of bat guard."

It took Edith a moment to realize Blaze had stopped talking and all the bats were looking at the sixth bat, the one at the back of the group.

"Hi, Blaze," said the bat softly, moving closer.

"Bree... I thought it might be you... I..." Blaze stuttered. Edith had never thought the little wolpertinger could be lost for words.

"I've missed you. We searched everywhere."

"I've changed, Bree, look what's happened to me."

"You're still Blaze, aren't you?" Bree said.

Blaze hung his head and Edith wanted to scoop him up and console her little friend, but Zee-Zee cleared his throat.

"But we can't rescue the Doctor and Arnold with just six bats helping us!" he said, raising his hands in the air helplessly and looking at Edith.

"Who said we were just six?" Beo replied. "There's the whole colony. The question is, why should they help you?"

"Because the Count is an evil man," Edith replied earnestly. "He's capturing all the forest creatures. He captured Blaze, so he has no love for bats. One of you could be next."

"We know he's evil. We want him gone for sure," the whip-thin bat replied boldly.

"Although dying doesn't sound hugely appealing," one of the others chortled.

"But you're right, the Count is an evil man. So we're with you to the end, but the colony will be harder to persuade," said Beo. "We need time."

"Time is something we don't have," said Edith. "We need to rescue my uncle, Arnold and free the phoenix along with all the other creatures he's got trapped up there."

The bats all gave a sharp intake of breath.

"Did you say free the phoenix?"

"Yes. He has a phoenix locked up in the Tower and he is using it to make all the wolpertingers."

There was a silence, then the Sentinel bats all huddled together in a little group. Edith shared looks with Zee-Zee and Blaze, wondering what the Sentinels were thinking. She tried to listen in, but no voices projected in her head.

"That's strange," Edith said to Blaze. *"I can't hear them."*

"They've gone super high frequency," Blaze explained. *"We do that when we want a private chat. The sound doesn't travel as far."*

Just then the group of bats broke apart and Beo took a few steps forward.

"We'll help," he said, *"but if things are as desperate as you say, we don't have time to go to the council and persuade the colony. So if you've got a plan, now would be the time to share it."*

"I've got a plan," Zee-Zee suddenly declared

The bats all crowded forward; one of them twitched slightly and Edith saw him dragging his leg.

"Don't mind Blaine – he's our best fighter," Beo said softly, noticing Edith's concerned expression.

"Are you sure we can do this?" said Edith, biting her lip. "There's only six of you."

"That's not true," said Bree with a smile.

"Isn't it?"

"We've got Blaze remember? We're not the fantastic six any more – we're the magnificent seven."

CHAPTER FOURTEEN

In which the rescue attempt begins,
but things don't quite go to plan…

In the end, it was agreed that Bucky would go to the colony and try to rally them to help. Which left five Sentinels and Blaze to lead the rescue.

Zee-Zee and Edith outlined the plan.

He would go to the Tower, pretending he had an urgent message for his mother. The Count should be unsuspicious because it was quite commonplace for Zee-Zee to go and see his mother, take messages or deliver parcels. Whilst speaking to her, Zee-Zee would ask his mother to check the side door and make sure it was still unlocked from where she had let the Doctor and Edith creep into the old church before. They would then ask her to distract the Count so they could creep inside and hide.

When the time was right, Edith and Zee-Zee would sneak up the stairs, get to the room and free their friends. It sounded possible. But as they walked towards the Tower, Edith's heart was fluttering in her chest. Could they pull this off?

Zee-Zee was also starting to worry. "You said there's a massive door to get into the room – remind me how we're going to get through that?"

Edith grinned.

"We'll hide in the chapel until the Count arrives, then we'll follow him up the stairs. When he unlocks the door and goes in, we'll follow – it'll be the last thing he expects. As we enter, Blaze, who will be with us, will call a hypersonic signal. That is when the Sentinels will surge through the window from which I jumped – which should still be open – and we can surprise him." She tried to inject as much confidence into her voice as possible.

"But if he has a crossbow, he'll just shoot us," whispered Zee-Zee.

"That's why we must be fast. Surprise will be everything. Remember, he'll be distracted by the bats. Both my uncle and Arnold will be in the room. Also, the Count still thinks my uncle is sedated and he won't be expecting the cages to be open. The animals and creatures there might help us."

Zee-Zee raised an eyebrow at Edith, who offered him a weak smile in return.

"I know it's a bit risky, but what other options do we have?" she said.

"Beo and the crew are ready, Edie," said Blaze. *"We should do this before your boyfriend has second thoughts."*

Edith blushed. *"He's not my…"*

"Well, he's a friend and he's a boy, isn't he?" Blaze chortled.

Edith glared at the little bat, who grinned back at her with a mischievous glint in his eyes.

"Bree seemed happy to see you," she thought.

Blaze gave a sigh. *"She was, but I'm not good enough for her now. I'm a bat with a squirrel's tail and a fluffy face. I'm a joke."*

"You're not a joke! You're brave and courageous."

"Right," said Zee-Zee, oblivious to their exchange, "we can't walk any further and not be seen by the Tower. You need to go down the bank and walk along by the river's edge. I'll go and see my mother. See you round the side in about ten minutes?"

"Good luck," Edith said.

"We're both going to need plenty of that," Zee-Zee replied as he padded off towards the main entrance to the old church.

"*This is it then! We're going back in!*" Blaze said.

"*The Sentinels won't let us down, will they?*" Edith asked.

"*Not a chance,*" Blaze replied confidently. "*A few of them might be a bit eccentric, but we can count on them.*"

"*As long as the Count doesn't just bat them away.*"

Blaze gave a little chuckle at his own joke before pointing with his wing.

"*Look, Zee-Zee's about to knock on the door!*"

Edith looked over to where the distant form of Zee-Zee was approaching the main entrance. Ducking down slightly, Edith began to run down the bank and skirt along its edge back towards the Tower. Below the line of the bank, she was out of sight of anyone who might be outside the Tower or looking out of the window. The rushing water of the river would also mask any sound of her approach.

Casting her eye further upstream, she could just make out six little specks of black all perched on a branch at the treeline to the forest. The Sentinels were ready.

"*Will they hear your hypersonic call from inside the Tower?*"

"I can call out at one hundred and forty decibels! That's as loud as a jet engine taking off! They'll hear me!"

Edith marvelled at how a tiny creature like Blaze could promise to make such a loud noise and was quite glad she wouldn't be able to hear it.

Time seemed to stretch inexorably onwards as Edith and Blaze waited, readying themselves for what was to come. Edith tried not to think about how much was at stake. What if they couldn't rescue the Doctor and Arnold? What if they got captured and turned into wolpertingers as well? What if Francis never recovered? It didn't bear thinking about – they simply had to succeed.

It was just as Blaze was starting to twitch with frustration and Edith was about to pop her head up to see what was going on, that Zee-Zee slid down over the top of the bank to land beside her, panting as he caught his breath.

"I think that went well," he said.

"Did you see the Count?"

"No, my mother answered the door – she didn't know the Doctor has been captured; she thought you might still be hiding in the room."

"Did you tell her I escaped?"

"Yes, and she's going to open the door when the Count isn't there so we can get back in unnoticed. She also said we should hurry because the Count seems to be getting things ready for something."

"Getting things ready?"

"I guess all the equipment he needs for his experiments."

"Making wolpertingers," Edith replied flatly.

"My mother doesn't want me to go," Zee-Zee said. "She wanted me to run back to the guest house and call the police."

"What did you say?" Edith asked quietly.

"I said it would take too long and I was helping my friends, that's all there is to it," Zee-Zee replied, giving Edith a smile.

"Thank you," Edith said.

"Thank me when we've done this. Come on, let's go."

The two of them crept up the slope of the bank and headed to the door. Crouching by the door, they waited. Blaze was motionless in Edith's hand as the three of them strained their ears, waiting for the door to be unlocked again.

"She will open the door, won't she?" Edith whispered.

Zee-Zee didn't reply for a moment. His expression seemed a little strange and Edith wondered if there had been more to his exchange with his mother than Zee-Zee had let on, but she didn't have time to press him for an answer because right then, the door clicked open.

Edith's heart gave a little jump and Blaze craned his head up towards her.

"I'll look after you. No way he's getting me a second time. Don't you worry, Edie, I've got your back."

Edith reached over and gave Blaze a little stroke with her free hand and, this time, the bat didn't complain but instead pushed his head upwards against her fingers. A nudge from Zee-Zee signalled her to move forward and, before she could think about what they were going to do, she found herself edging through the door into the darkness beyond.

The interior of the church was eerily silent and both Edith and Zee-Zee kept low as they moved along the wall, ears and eyes straining to hear and see.

Casting a furtive glance back at Zee-Zee, Edith led them nearer to the door behind the altar and the steps that would take them up into the Tower.

A tug made Edith stop, and she turned to see Zee-Zee frantically signal that she should move back. Without hesitating, Edith did as instructed, and no sooner had she done so than she heard the soft footsteps of someone padding down the central aisle of the old church.

Ducking low behind a pew on the side of the hall, Edith watched the shape of the Count advancing towards them. His head was slightly bowed, as if he was deep in contemplation, and Edith realized she was holding her breath.

The Count walked past painfully slowly, unaware of their presence, before unhurriedly gliding through the doorway behind the altar.

With a conscious effort, Edith forced herself to relax and slowly breathed out. "Now is our chance, we have to follow him," she whispered.

"We have to let him get a bit ahead of us, otherwise he'll hear us on the stairs," Zee-Zee cautioned.

Edith began a slow count to forty in her head. Then she quickly ran through the doorway after the Count and up the stairs, Zee-Zee on her heels.

Being careful not to make any noise on the stone steps, they began the climb upwards. When they reached the landing, they paused by the tapestry until they heard the metal clang of the key in the heavy door above, and then an audible grunt of effort as the Count began to heave it open.

"Let's go," hissed Edith. The two of them immediately began to power up the stairs.

Well done, Edie, we can do this! Keep going!" Blaze exclaimed as Edith climbed, her legs burning with the effort.

Zee-Zee wasn't far behind and, in moments, the

children were outside the huge, heavy metal door. The Count must now be inside, the door unlocked behind him.

"This is it," Edith said.

"I'm ready with the bat call," said Blaze.

"As soon as we go through the door, that's when you need to call the Sentinels. You must stay out of any fighting, you don't want to be a sitting target."

"No way," said Blaze. "I can't fly but I don't want to miss out on the fun. Chuck me straight at the Count. He won't expect that!"

"Er, well, let's see how it goes," said Edith diplomatically. She turned to Zee-Zee. "Ready?"

Zee-Zee nodded. He took hold of the door handle.

The sudden noise of a voice behind them made them all jump. Blaze almost fell from Edith's hand.

"Stop." The word was said quietly, but with an urgency that was both commanding and desperate. Edith spun round to see Ai Lam looking at them both, tears in her eyes.

"Mother!" Zee-Zee hissed. "What are you doing?"

"I can't let you do this," she said, wringing her hands. "He will shoot you."

"My friends need my help. Now we know what this man does, we have to stop him! He is dangerous!"

"I can't let you. I thought I could, but I can't. Don't do this," Ai Lam protested as a tear escaped and ran down her cheek.

"And what? Let Edie go in there by herself? I can't, Mother. I have to help her."

Ai Lam dropped her gaze, unable to meet her son's or Edith's eyes.

"It's OK, Zee-Zee," said Edith. "You should stay here with your mum. Blaze and I have got this."

Zee-Zee looked at Edith, his expression anguished.

Blaze shifted in her palm and Edith glanced down at the little bat.

"I can hear the Sentinels, they say the wind is picking up. We should make our move now or they might find it hard to get in through that window!"

Edith nodded. "I need to go in now, Zee-Zee."

"And I'm coming with you," Zee-Zee replied. He set his jaw and, before his mother could stop him, put his weight against the door.

The next few moments were a blur. Edith was vaguely aware of Ai Lam reaching out a hand to grab at Zee-Zee, but he was too quick and she clutched at empty air. As Blaze puffed himself up to give his call to arms to the Sentinels, Edith also leaned her weight against the opening door and they surged forward.

Zee-Zee barrelled through the opening and Edith followed, the bright light from the room beyond making them both blink.

"Blaze, make the call now!" Edith thought to the bat.

Blaze needed no encouragement and reared up in her hand, as if silently howling like a wolf, his hypersonic call signalling for the Sentinels to come to their aid.

The Count was there, Edith saw, walking towards the phoenix – he still hadn't heard them come in. Quickly, Zee-Zee ran over to the glass door, his hand reaching for the button that would let the bats into the inner chamber.

This is going to work, Edith thought.

Then a loud *thwack* by the window made her jump and she twisted around to see what had made the noise.

Thwack, thwack, thwack.

The noises came one after the other. At the same moment the glass door clicked open, Zee-Zee ran through and the Count spun round to see what the disturbance was.

It was only now that Edith realized their mistake.

"The Count must have shut the window! The Sentinels can't get inside!" Blaze shouted.

"Zee-Zee!" Edith called out, but it was too late. The Count had already raised his crossbow, a grin on his thin lips as he depressed the trigger.

A crossbow bolt shot forward. Zee-Zee gave a yelp of surprise and flung himself to the side. The bolt missed him by a millimetre and clanged heavily into the glass partition behind him.

Rather than shattering, a huge crack appeared down the centre of the glass pane. The Count cursed and reloaded, readying himself to shoot at Zee-Zee again.

"Zee-Zee!!!" It was Ai Lam's voice; she had followed them into the room and was standing there aghast.

"Mother, open the window!" cried Zee-Zee.

Edith, seeing Ai Lam was paralysed with shock, began to sprint towards it, just as Zee-Zee charged towards the armed Count.

The Count hesitated for only a moment, his eyes flicking over to look at Ai Lam and Edith who were still the other side of the now cracked partition, before sighting his aim at Zee-Zee.

"Brave but stupid," he hissed, and once again he depressed the trigger.

It was at this precise moment that Arnold made his move. With a deep growl, the huge dog burst from his cage and bounded towards the Count. Two great paws jumped up on his back and pushed him violently forward, forcing the crossbolt shot to go high. The bolt harmlessly struck the ceiling with a loud *zing*.

"Thank you, Arnold!" Zee-Zee called, still running towards the now prone man.

The Count was agile. Even as he fell, he managed to roll. Using lightning-speed reflexes, he was back up on one knee in the blink of an eye, and this time, instead of trying to reload his crossbow, a hand shot into his robe and pulled out a large red whistle. He put it to his lips and gave three loud blasts.

Movement from the back of the room made the dog half turn, just as the Doctor burst forward from his cage.

"Arnold! Stay close!" the Doctor shouted. "Zee-Zee, to me!"

Edith had made it to the window and scrambled up on to the ledge, fumbling with the catch. Then she froze, distracted by what was going on the other side of the partition. She heard herself gasp.

Two creatures had appeared from the recesses of the room. One was the same monster that had fought Francis, its colossal shape moving menacingly towards her friends. The other wolpertinger was smaller, spear-like stumps protruding from its head as it bounded around them, half roaring, half crowing.

The Count, still wearing that unpleasant grin, stood and calmly reloaded his crossbow. His head swivelled to regard Edith, who once again desperately tried to work the catch.

"It's jammed!" she cried in frustration.

"A valiant effort for one so young, Edie, and I see you recruited Ai Lam's son. I am grateful. An adult human body will be too big for some of the creations I have in mind. A child, though, will be perfect. Soon I will have two to practise with."

"No!" shouted Ai Lam, moving through the glass door, advancing on the Count.

The huge wolpertinger stepped towards her, baring its teeth, and she shrank back, horrified.

The Count gave a manic laugh. "I think it is time our visitors return to their cages."

"You are not alone."

A light suddenly blazed so brilliantly that all of them were forced to shut their eyes. The phoenix flared with a brightness of a fireball, dazzling everyone. When Edith opened her eyes again, she saw a small creature leap from the top of a cage and land on the Count. It darted under the collar to slip down the inside of the Count's robe.

The Count gave a screech.

"You want a toxic skin for your creations, try one first. See what it feels like!"

"Be careful, Terry!" thought Edith, remembering the little fire-bellied toad, as the Count started to beat at his

323

own body, trying to rid himself of the toxic amphibian that was burning his skin.

Edith turned to see the still glowing outline of the phoenix regarding her from the back of the room.

"*What should I do?*" Edith asked the bird.

"*Speak to them; they are not totally lost yet.*"

"Who?"

"*The wolpertingers,*" the phoenix replied calmly, its light now almost diminished.

It had never occurred to Edith to try to communicate with the wolpertingers under the Count's control, but now she realized it was likely their only chance. She slid down from the ledge and focused her mind on the largest of the two wolpertingers, forcing her thoughts out.

"*We are here to help you!*"

The large wolpertinger seemed disorientated, presumably still shocked by the blinding light. Now, for a fleeting moment, Edith thought it seemed free of something. As if the light had somehow broken a spell. A range of expressions flitted over its face, and it swivelled its huge head away from Ai Lam towards Edith.

"*We mean you no harm! We have come to put a stop to what he has done to you, what he is doing to you.*"

The Count, sensing something was amiss, raised his whistle and blew it again. Three short sharp bursts drilled out into the room. Arnold raised his hackles, ready to spring at the wolpertingers.

"Please," said Edith. *"We mean you no harm."*

Just then, there was an almighty crash, and Edith heard Blaze give a small whoop of joy.

A large black shape barrelled into the floor by Edith's feet, promptly followed by shards of glass from the window that had exploded inwards.

"Bucky! You broke through the window!" Blaze shouted.

Bucky righted himself, his body bleeding from the cut glass as he struggled to sit upright.

"I couldn't let you down, old friend!" Bucky replied, shaking his head after the collision with the window. *"I've brought some reinforcements."*

The noise that now filled the room was like rushing water, which quickly cascaded into a raging torrent of sound as black shapes began to flit through the shattered window. Initially, Edith could make out the shapes of the other Sentinels all flying through the door of the glass partition – but instead of only six, there was a stream of yet more and more bats which all poured in.

"It's the colony!" Edith shouted to Blaze.

Scooping Blaze up, Edith thrust him into her pocket before pressing herself to the ground as the stream thickened above her head. The bats, tens of thousands of them, started to fill the air and the room became a heaving mass of black wings and bodies.

"Arrrrghhhhhhhhhh!" The Count tried to blow his whistle, but to no avail. He was being buffeted by thousands of little creatures that threw him back against the wall, his crossbow falling as he raised his arms to cover his face.

The bats homed in and one after the other crashed into the Count's flailing body.

"It's magnificent, isn't it!" Blaze shouted over the tumult, his head poking out of her pocket and his voice somewhat muffled by the noise of the bats flying overhead. *"One bat can't do much – but a whole colony of bats – well, that's another story!"*

Edith found herself grinning, still pressed to the floor. She looked through the glass partition to see the Doctor, Arnold, Ai Lam and Zee-Zee all hunched together in a group as the bats flew around them.

The two wolpertingers, looking completely confused,

found themselves forced to the edge of the room.

"Pull open the main door as wide as you can, Edie!" Blaze cried.

Edith ran to the heavy metal door, which was still ajar from where she and Zee-Zee had crept through it moments before. With one huge effort, she pulled it as far open as she was able. Very slowly, it began to move, and as the gap widened, the bats started to stream through and down the stairs beyond.

A thick mass of bats burst through the tapestry and then surged down the next stairs and into the old church itself. It was impossible to distinguish individual animals, such was their number, and it was only after they had been streaming past her for what seemed like minutes that Edith realized something else utterly shocking.

"Where is the Count? Has he escaped?" she thought.

Blaze stared wistfully after the departing colony as if itching to be able to join them. *"No. They have taken him with them,"* he calmly replied.

"Taken him with them? You mean…"

"Yes, the colony have taken him with them to the cave."

Edith turned to regard the chaos in the room. The Doctor, Zee-Zee, Ai Lam and Arnold were still huddled together in the middle.

The two wolpertingers who the Count had summoned

to attack them seemed totally unthreatening. They made no move to go after their master. Instead, they shrank back, looking lost and bewildered.

"Edie!" the Doctor shouted.

"Uncle – are you OK?"

Edith ran over the glass and threw her arms around her uncle.

"That was very brave, my dear, and I see you recruited some help! Now I believe it is time to put your consummate powers to further use. Are you able to communicate with our new friends here?"

The Doctor gestured at the two wolpertingers, and Edith nodded, focusing her mind to reassure the confused creatures.

"Please, listen to me," she said.

The wolpertingers, free of the Count, slowly shuffled forward, under the watchful gaze of Arnold, who fixed each of them with a hard stare.

"Careful, Edie, they still look dangerous."

"Yeah, I wouldn't trust the little one!" Blaze piped up, his head still poking up from Edith's pocket and studying the smaller wolpertinger with its spiked head and razor-sharp claws.

Edith held her hands out, palms upwards, and approached the closer of the two, the huge wolpertinger, the one with the body of a bear, the head of a wolf and the fangs of a snake who had fought Francis. She remembered how the big man had told her that the creature hadn't bitten him on the head when it had the chance and, as she looked up into its amber wolf-like eyes, she saw that, if anything, the creature seemed more frightened of her than she was of it.

"It's OK, Uncle," she whispered. "I don't think they want to hurt us. They are just lost."

The Doctor nodded his understanding. "They are victims, Edie, not inherently evil – but trained to do the bidding of their creator. With him gone, his hold over them is diminished. For the first time, they can be ruled by their own thoughts and instincts. Treat them kindly. We will let them go free, my dear."

"Free, Uncle?"

"Yes, Edie, the forest is huge; they will find a home there. After all, they are made from creatures that lived there, they will find their way for the time they have left."

Edith looked at the two wolpertingers. *"You should go,"* she told them. *"Go back to the forest where you belong. You are free now."*

Slowly, looking bewildered and uncertain, the two wolpertingers moved past the group and made their way to door, before disappearing down the stairs beyond.

"Now, Edie, we shall free the rest. But first we must see to the phoenix."

"If we let all these creatures go, will they not hurt the villagers?" Zee-Zee asked suddenly.

"We should go downstairs and ensure they leave in the right direction," Ai Lam said quietly.

With that, she took Zee-Zee's hand, and they followed the wolpertingers down the stairs. Edith looked questioningly at the Doctor, who shook his head.

"Fear not, Edie, those wolpertingers only want to be left alone. They will not pose any risk to anyone, human or otherwise. Let Zee-Zee and Ai Lam go. Come, let us talk to the phoenix."

Edith followed her uncle to the dome of the heavy cage inside which the phoenix sat, watching them with a flat expression. She and the Doctor knelt before it.

Well done, the phoenix said, the jolt of its voice in her head making Edith jump a little.

"What is the phoenix saying, Edie?"

"It just said 'well done'."

The Doctor gave a wry chuckle. "High praise indeed from a species that has met people who have toppled empires."

A noise made them both turn. Arnold was snuffling a packet of something he had found on the floor. The

Doctor stood. "What have you found there, Arnold?"

He walked over, stooping to pick up the packet.

Meanwhile, Edith gazed at the extraordinary bird. *"Thank you for helping me, for telling me to try to talk to the wolpertingers."*

The phoenix gave a blink of its eye and briefly dipped its head.

"Will you come with us? Will you let us vaccinate you and try to help you?"

"You cannot help me; I am incomplete. He has taken too much of me. I can never be whole again."

"Will you not regenerate over time?"

The phoenix paused for a long moment before answering. *"I can easily be caught. I cannot fly. Now the Syndicate know the art of making wolpertingers, the danger to us phoenixes has never been greater. I would be used to create more horrors for their sport. At least my brethren are still complete. They will be strong enough to evade capture."*

"But you could live with my uncle at Forest Cottage. You would be safe there."

The phoenix didn't reply. It simply looked at Edith, its expression completely unreadable.

"Tell the phoenix we can look after it in the cave," Blaze piped up, squeezing himself from Edith's pocket

and dropping to the floor. *"The colony would be honoured to protect it. Who is going to come looking for it where we live? They'd never find it and the cave would be a perfect refuge."*

Edith relayed the message to the phoenix, who once again didn't say anything, but looked at them steadily. She opened the door and stepped back, wondering what the magnificent bird would decide to do.

The Doctor cleared his throat. In his hand he held the packet. It looked like a small plastic bag containing a pile of dust. He grinned over at Edith.

"Edie … you won't believe what Arnold has found."

The shout that echoed through the Tower cut the Doctor off, loud enough for the group to hear the anguish and pain that it carried. Edith turned to her uncle in alarm.

"Things are rarely as they seem," the phoenix said to Edith.

"The bats are calling hypersonically, Edie," Blaze said urgently. *"There is a calamity downstairs – quick, pick me up and take me down there!"*

The Doctor was already moving as another shout echoed up the stairs, this time even louder. It seemed to be a half sob, a half wail – and the group all bounded through the heavy door, following the flowing cape of the Doctor.

As Edith neared the ground floor and re-entered the church, she was not prepared in the slightest for the scene that confronted her.

The bats had lined the ceiling and walls of the church, carpeting every surface like a living wallpaper coating the cavernous expanse of the hall. A few, flying haphazardly over the long trestle tables, chattered away incessantly. The noise was all too high-pitched and frenetic for Edith to decode the words.

As they entered, the bats seemed to drop off from the ceiling and instantly the air was filled with a choking, heaving mass of black bodies that crowded around them. Zee-Zee appeared, fighting his way through the cloud to reach Edith.

"Can't you get them to calm down?" Edith cried to Blaze.

"But this is much more fun!" he squeaked. Edith could have sworn she heard a chuckle his voice. *"They'll settle in a minute, don't worry."*

As Edith listened, the noise, which had been like a wall of sound, slowly started to ebb slightly and she could pick out individual voices.

"Billy, you've flown into me four times in the last three seconds. What is wrong with you?"

"You're going the wrong way, that's what."

"The wrong way? You know we're all supposed to fly clockwise, it's the same every single time we swarm!"

"My right or your right?"

"It doesn't matter! We're facing the same way!"

Other voices cascaded down through the darkness.

"He doesn't look so mysterious now, does he?"

"No. Pretty pathetic, really."

Edith moved forward until she could see what the bats were referring to. Between the pews, in the middle of the church, lay the crumpled form of the Count.

Half draped over him was Ai Lam. His crossbow, having fallen from his grasp, had somehow been caught up in his clothes as he was carried out by the bats. It now lay discarded on the floor. Bats from the colony surrounded them, as well as those of the six Sentinels.

"What's going on here?" murmured the Doctor.

Edith turned to Blaze.

"Edie, the colony are not happy. They were removing the Count when Ai Lam jumped upon him and wrestled him to the floor. She is lucky to be alive. The swarm could easily have carried her off."

Blaze's voice sounded pained.

"They won't be satisfied until they can take him prisoner – not after all he has done."

Edith strained to hear what the other bats might be saying, but it was eerily quiet.

"What did he say, Edith?" the Doctor asked.

"Uncle, Ai Lam stopped the colony from taking the Count away. She protected him."

Her uncle stepped forward briskly, crouching beside Ai Lam and Zee-Zee, who was now kneeling beside his mother.

"I am sorry, I know he is evil, I know he must be stopped. But to kill him…" A soft sob came from Ai Lam and tears streamed down her face. Slowly she raised her face to look at the Doctor.

The Doctor nodded. Gently he leaned forward and checked the Count's pulse.

"Is he dead, Uncle?" Edith asked quietly.

"No, Edie, he is still breathing," the Doctor replied. "He is unconscious, but he'll come round soon."

"Why is Ai Lam protecting him?"

"Because she is a good person. He helped her when she had no one, when her husband was dying. Now she is returning the favour," the Doctor replied simply. "All life is sacred."

Zee-Zee swallowed, conflicting emotions battling on his face.

"Uncle, what do we do?" Edith said quietly.

"Tell her we are taking the Count with us," Beo cried. *"It is a great victory – this man cannot be allowed to continue to hunt and kill the forest creatures."*

"Beo speaks the truth. This man cannot be allowed to walk free." A small old bat shuffled forward, turning his wizened head to look at Edith as he did so. Edith noticed the other bats bowing respectfully.

"The leader of our colony has spoken. There will be justice for this man – but not from the laws of men. It is the law of bats which must abide here," Beo said. *"He will*

not be killed – but he will be kept prisoner for life."

There was a ripple in the room as the bats on the walls and ceilings all stirred with the proclamation.

As Edith repeated what the bats had said, the Doctor placed a hand very gently on Ai Lam's shoulder.

"I understand why you want to protect him, Ai Lam. He did help you, but only to further his own ends. The bats have promised to imprison him – he will not meet his death at their hands. It is the best justice he could hope for after all he has done."

Ai Lam gave a great sob and then nodded. The Doctor helped her to her feet.

An almost imperceptible noise rumbled from outside and the Doctor looked up. The bats, hearing it immediately, all seemed to tense.

"Vehicles approach," Blaze said.

The noise grew louder and, within moments, it was distinguishable as the sound of engines roaring towards the Tower.

"That engine noise sounds familiar," the Doctor hissed. "Arabella Spearstrike!"

"Uncle, what shall we do?" Edith called.

"Prepare to fight, Edie; it's the only option we have."

As the first truck pulled up outside, heavy car doors slammed, and the tramp of boots could be heard running towards the church. There was the sound of metallic clicking.

"Weapons," whispered the Doctor. "Warn the bats, Edith."

Quickly, Edith explained. *"It's the Syndicate, Blaze – the people who bought the wolpertingers off the Count. They have come back!"*

"We'll hold them off, Edie," Blaze replied. *"But don't let the Count escape!"*

At a silent hypersonic signal, the old church instantly filled with the noise of tens of thousands of bats all taking flight. In a frenzied cloud of black bodies, they began to stream out the door of the church, leaving nothing but the smooth stone where they had roosted just moments before. Then came the sound of gunfire. To Edith's horror, the last bat leaving the building was Blaze.

"Blaze! You can't fly! Stay with us!"

The little wolpertinger didn't answer but jumped on, determined to flutter his way outside.

With his arm still wrapped around Ai Lam, the Doctor looked at Edith.

"Edith and Zee-Zee, can you go upstairs and open all the cages. Let the creatures free. They might be able to help us. Arabella and her hunters will be through those doors in moments."

"I will go with them," Ai Lam said, casting one last look at the body of the Count.

Edith and Zee-Zee nodded, and the three of them ran back up the Tower to release the remaining wolpertingers.

CHAPTER FIFTEEN

*In which we have the final showdown, and
Arabella launches a full-scale attack…*

As bullets peppered the air and the bats wheeled, twisted and dived at the attackers, Arabella and Ivan ran through the swirling mass of black bodies, punching their way forward to gain entry to the church.

"It is hard to fight these blasted bats," Ivan snarled, slicing his knife through the air and missing as a bat wheeled out of the way.

"Hurry," Arabella hissed. "We must rescue the Count. I need his abilities to fuse creatures. Our automatic weapons will make short work of these vermin."

Ivan nodded grimly. He wasn't so convinced. The

bats whirled in the sky; they were impossibly fast-moving and fearlessly dived at the faces of the mercenary killers. He seethed with frustration as he and Arabella forced their way through to the main door of the old church.

The inside of the nave, free from the swarming mass of black bodies, possessed an eerie sense of calm as they stepped inside. Arabella and Ivan eyed the figure of the Doctor, who stooped over the prone body of the Count.

"Doctor. We do keep meeting in the most unlikely places," Arabella said, her voice smug as she glanced around the room.

The Doctor looked up sharply, his face creased in frustrated anger.

"The Count is finished, Arabella," he said, his voice hard and defiant. "Your twisted little sideline is ended."

"Oh, I must disagree, Doctor. I'd say it has only just begun. Are you by yourself this time? My, my, it's becoming easier and easier to corner you." She laughed.

The Count moved slightly on the floor, and the Doctor glanced down.

He was coming round.

"Step away from the Count. I won't kill you just yet, Doctor – you are my leverage to leave this godforsaken place."

"The bats will never let you leave," the Doctor replied firmly. His voice was laced with a suppressed fury that made both Arabella and Ivan grin.

"Are you saying I should simply kill you now?" Arabella replied. "Ivan would be delighted to oblige."

Ivan grinned, stepping forward in anticipation.

Arabella held up a hand.

"Do you have anything to say, Doctor? After all, we have quite a history now. I might almost miss you when this is over."

"I will miss you too, Arabella," replied the Doctor.

"A sweet sentiment but it won't help you."

"Like I'd miss a boil," the Doctor continued.

Arabella's face hardened with the insult.

"You are a plague on the world, Arabella. Even when I'm gone, others will step up to defeat you. We will always oppose you. The things you and the Count have created … it is a new level of depravity. Even for you."

"Wolpertingers are just the beginning, Doctor. The Count is a means to an end. I want dominion over the creatures I desire. Imagine being able to command a dragon to burn a forest of my choosing, to tell a kraken to bring me a whale to kill. To achieve that, I need to find someone whose power far exceeds that of the Count's. When I have found them, I will take their power for my own, the Count will fuse it to my being and I will control all the beasts of the world. Mythical or otherwise."

"What nonsense," the Doctor retorted. "There is no person with that kind of power."

"Are you sure, Doctor? How about the ability to speak to animals? Think what I could do with that. Someone with that power exists. I will track them down soon enough."

The Doctor opened his mouth to say something, to immediately protest it wasn't true, then clamped his jaw shut. He mustn't give anything away. No, he thought, Arabella didn't know about Edith. All she knew was that someone like Edith existed. Instead, he shook his head, as if incredulous at her words.

Arabella stared at the Doctor for a moment, then turned to Ivan.

"Has a cat got your tongue, Doctor? Perhaps we can find a cat and make that happen as well. It shouldn't be too complicated for our mutual friend." Arabella barked a laugh. "Enough chatter. It is fortunate indeed that we came back when we did. With the racket outside, I suspect we'll also have plenty of fresh bodies to use for our next orders. Ivan – kill the Doctor. I want to watch the light fade in his eyes."

Ivan took another step forward but, as he did so, something made him hesitate and glance to his left. Out of the shadows loomed a creature twice his size and unlike any he had ever seen before.

"No!" he shouted, but it was too late.

The giant wolpertinger had been quietly hiding at the side of the church and now it charged out into the centre of the nave. Huge, bear-like paws gripped at Ivan's chest as wolf-like jaws bit at his neck and the fangs of a snake lanced into his jugular. Ivan twisted to stab into the wolpertinger but, as he did so, a big brown shape crashed into his midriff.

Arnold locked his teeth on to the knife-wielding arm.

The Doctor, rolling to the side, dodged as Arabella threw a knife at him, which struck the stone floor where his head had been just moments before.

"Get them off me!" Ivan screamed, batting at the top of Arnold's head.

Arabella eyed her henchman and then cursed as she saw another wolpertinger hop threateningly towards her. It too had been hiding in the shadows. She reached for another knife in her belt, throwing it at the horned head of the small creature advancing towards her. The wolpertinger dodged the knife with ease and readied itself to pounce.

Just as the wolpertinger was about to strike, the noise of paws and claws coming down the stairs distracted it. Arabella, turning to look, drew a sharp breath as more monsters suddenly began to pour into the old church. Arnold and the huge wolpertinger stepped back out of their way, as Ivan crumpled to the floor with a groan.

"No!" Arabella hissed. "Count – get up, control them!"

The Count, recovering as every moment passed, pushed himself slowly up. His hood was back, his face ashen.

"Too many," he whispered. The wolpertingers were surging through the nave now, some making for the door, others darting into shadows. "But I can do this..."

The Count flashed Arabella a wicked-looking smile and reached out for his crossbow.

"Uncle!" Edith's voice cried out as she barrelled through the doorway at the bottom of the stairs, Zee-Zee at her heels. "Watch out!"

Everything seemed to happen at once. A huge *whoosh* of noise preceded a sudden blinding light that burst into the old church from outside the Tower. There were cries of alarm and the sound of automatic weapons ceased.

"The other phoenixes are here!" Zee-Zee exclaimed,

his face bathed in a golden glow as he squinted out of the window.

Edith felt herself grin and she rushed forward. At the same moment, she heard the click of a trigger being pulled, and something slammed into her hard, pushing her back into a pillar, all the air driven from her lungs. She slumped to the ground, winded.

"Edie!" shouted Zee-Zee.

The Doctor, forgetting Arabella or Ivan even existed, dashed towards his niece. Simultaneously, the main door to the old church was flung open even wider, and more light blazed into the nave from outside. A scream of anger and frustration pierced the air, and then the sound of an engine revving right outside reverberated around them. In moments, vehicles were tearing away from the Tower in a cloud of dust and noise. The blinding light faded almost as quickly as it had appeared and Edith drew in a long, gulping breath. Her eyes scanned the room around her.

The Northern Phoenix lay at her feet. A crossbow bolt protruding from its chest. Arabella, the Count and Ivan had gone.

"Edie, are you OK?" the Doctor said breathlessly, scanning his niece for injuries.

"I'm fine," she replied. "I was knocked backwards."

"The phoenix jumped in front of you. It shielded you from the crossbow bolt that the Count fired," Zee-Zee explained.

The Doctor stared at the punctured body of the phoenix. Slowly, as they watched, its feathers began to smoke.

With an exclamation, the Doctor reached into his pocket and pulled out a small bag. As Edith looked on, still winded from her fall, a glow lit up the interior of the church. She turned.

Five magnificent phoenixes stood in the nave, all eyes fixed on the body of the Northern Phoenix.

The Doctor held up the bag and, as the Northern Phoenix burst into flames, he took two quick steps forward and poured all the dust from the packet over the flaming body on the stone floor of the old church.

"Uncle! What are you doing?" Edith exclaimed, still wheezing slightly.

"Making our dear friend whole again, I hope," the Doctor replied. "This bag contained ashes – and I can only think of one creature whose ashes would have been collected by the Count." He smiled. "The ashes of a magnificent phoenix."

Francis stirred and opened his eyes as the bed gave an

audible creak.

"The bed is finally about to give up on you," the Doctor commented with a laugh.

"I've been in here long enough, it feels like part of me now," Francis mumbled back, his face cracking into a huge smile as he saw Edith, Zee-Zee and Arnold at the end of his bed.

"Who is that?" Francis asked, spotting a small black shape perched casually on Arnold's broad back.

"This is Blaze the bat," Edith replied.

"You mean Blaze the Sentinel," Blaze retorted. "The seventh and most heroic member."

"Alongside his girlfriend Bree," Edith smiled.

"I always knew she'd never be able to resist the squirrel tail really," Blaze thought as he gave Edith a sideways look and flexed his newly fixed wing.

This time, the glue had set properly and the seam where it had been fixed glistened in the light of the room.

Edith gave a little laugh.

"We have a lot to thank him for," she said to Francis, who looked perplexed.

"How do you feel?" Zee-Zee asked.

"Like a new man," Francis replied, flexing and unflexing his huge, ham-like fist.

"You now have phoenix, squirrel and bat blood

surging through your veins!" Edith declared with a grin.

"Bat blood? So am I related to our new friend then?"

"Oh yes, like a brother!" The Doctor beamed, bustling around to take a quick look under the bandage on Francis's shoulder and nodded to himself in satisfaction.

"And Arnold is safe!" Francis boomed.

The big dog gave a huge wag of his tail and slobbered his long pink tongue across Francis's outstretched hand.

"There is so much to tell you," Edith began, but her uncle held up his hand.

"There is indeed a long tale to be told, Edie, but we have a job to do to and it cannot wait. Francis, we have to complete our mission and it is only right that we all do it together."

The Doctor's eyes twinkled, and Edith smiled in understanding.

"To the Tower!" the Doctor declared, holding out his arm to help Francis haul himself out of bed.

Francis sat upright for a moment, then heaved himself upwards, steadying himself with the Doctor's help.

"Are you strong enough for a little stroll, my friend?" the Doctor asked.

"The phoenix?" Francis asked.

The Doctor nodded. "Yes. Or rather, all of them."

Francis's grin split even wider, and he took a few

tentative steps forward.

"Good as new," he declared.

"Who needs the Count to enhance things – look what my blood has done to Francis!" Blaze chipped in.

The group made its way out of the guest house and walked towards the old church.

The building seemed much less threatening without the presence of the Count and his wolpertingers living there. When they walked inside, they found Ai Lam sweeping away the detritus from the battle.

"Any sign of the Syndicate?" Edith asked Ai Lam.

Ai Lam shook her head.

"No. They have the Count and they know this place is lost to them."

"The Count didn't actually own the church, did he? He rented it off the Syndicate. What will they do with it now?" Edith asked, gazing at the walls.

"I suspect," the Doctor cut in, "our friend Arabella has the title deeds and, knowing the Syndicate, they will want to wash their hands of this whole business very quickly. Attention is the last thing they want. It will no doubt be back for sale soon. And, when it is, I may know someone who might invest."

His eyes glinted and Zee-Zee looked at him open-mouthed.

"You?"

"Why not, in partnership with someone who lives here, of course. I'd need people to manage it. I wondered if you and your mother might come in with me – look after the place and so on? An extension of the guest house, perhaps? Not for hunters, of course. Or ... an animal hospital, for the creatures of this forest?"

"Mother, did you hear that?" Zee-Zee exclaimed.

Ai Lam nodded. Her eyes were glistening with tears.

"Thank you," she managed to say, her voice breaking with emotion.

The pews had all been neatly pulled back into the centre of the church. It once again had a feeling of sanctuary and safety that had been absent from the building for so long.

At the far end of the room, where the altar would have been, the seven phoenixes waited for them. Calm and serene. As they saw Edith, each bowed their head in greeting.

"Uncle, shall we ask the Northern Phoenix if it wants its vaccine?" Edith asked.

"I think it is time. Please do the honours, Edie," the Doctor replied.

Edith moved towards the line of phoenixes who all faced her. The seventh phoenix was a tiny chick. Much

to Edith's delight it had all its toes, and its glow was restored.

"*You're complete again,*" she said.

"*Thanks to the Doctor's quick thinking,*" the phoenix replied. "*And to you, Edith.*"

"*Thank you for saving me.*"

"*My thanks are with you, for eternity,*" the phoenix replied.

"*Now there is hope and you can fly, may I give you the vaccine?*" she asked almost reverentially.

The baby phoenix fluttered forward. "*You may,*" it said, and Edith carefully administered the injection.

After it was done, the Northern Phoenix hopped back.

"*It is a millennium since any human has seen all the phoenixes together. Thank you for what you have done for our species. Thank you to the Doctor and all who have assisted.*"

Edith translated and the Doctor swept his cap off his head, then gave a deep bow. As he stood, he wiped a fat tear from his eye with a handkerchief he had pulled from his breast pocket.

"*Where will you go?*" Edith asked.

"*The world is a darker place than it has been for thousands of years. We must hide away. Should the*

Syndicate capture any of us again, the consequences would be severe. With the Count alive, they have the capability to create more creatures."

"And to destroy the natural order of things," another of the phoenixes added.

"If you need us, ask the owls," the Northern Phoenix said.

Each phoenix dipped its head and then, one by one, they flew off into the sky, the little chick soaring easily into the air.

The light in the church faded.

Awestruck by what they had witnessed, the group stared after the departing birds, now small bright specks in the sky, each seeming to spread out and fly off in a different direction.

"Excuse me?" said a little voice. *"Can you give me a lift home? I think I've had enough adventuring now."*

Edith laughed with joy as the little shape of Terry hopped towards her.

"Can I borrow your handkerchief, please, Uncle?" she said. "Terry needs a lift home."

"Of course, Edie. The bravest fire-bellied toad I ever had the pleasure of meeting. Without his intervention, I doubt we would have survived upstairs." The Doctor once again tugged his handkerchief from his pocket and would be very different!!!

Tremendous thanks to the über publishing team at Scholastic. Sophie had so many good ideas and pragmatic steer. She transformed the first draft with a combination of great suggestions and infinite patience. Sarah, Gen, Jessica and Susila in editorial, Jane the illustrator and Aimee the Scholastic wizard designer who came up with the concept of how to bring the book to life with such a brilliant cover, all played huge parts. Hannah and the marketing team are also a phenomenal force for good and a massive thanks to them for all the encouragement and eternal support in getting the Secret Animal Society books out there.

My friends and agents, the author Rob Dinsdale, awesome Elly and Queen Heather at the HHB Agency (my agents for The Vet books), once again supported and helped me with a great edit and solid ideas, aka Team Fantastic!!!

Thank you to my niece and nephew, Robyn (14) and Damon (12), for reading the final edit and giving me lots of encouragement and plenty of last-minute brilliant thoughts and suggestions. You rock.

The charity teams at Worldwide Veterinary Service and Mission Rabies also deserve a big thanks as they gave me the kickstart challenge to start these books – if you are interested in working with animals, please check out the Youngvetsclub.com and join the Secret Animal Society for real!!!

Finally, a massive thanks to you!!! Thank you for reading this book and I hope you enjoyed it!!! The feedback after the first one was totally inspiring. I love hearing your ideas as to what Edie and the Doctor could get up to next! Thank you as well to those of you that have listened to me talk at your school or at an event. Those opportunities give me huge fire to power on. I am always bursting to get on to the next story and that's just as well, because the Doctor and Edie have a long way to go yet...

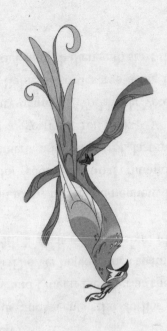